Trained togethe… e
six women vow…
need. Now one o… ,
and it is up t… killer—
before they become the next victims....

Alex Forsythe:
This forensic scientist can uncover clues others fail to see.
PROOF, by Justine Davis—July 2004

Darcy Allen Steele:
A master of disguise, Darcy can sneak into
any crime scene.
ALIAS, by Amy Fetzer—August 2004

Tory Patton:
Used to uncovering scandals, this investigative reporter
will get to the bottom of any story—especially murder.
EXPOSED, by Katherine Garbera—September 2004

Samantha St. John:
Though she's the youngest, this lightning-fast secret agent
can take down men twice her size.
DOUBLE-CROSS, by Meredith Fletcher—October 2004

Josie Lockworth:
A little danger won't stop this daredevil air force pilot
from uncovering the truth.
PURSUED, by Catherine Mann—November 2004

Kayla Ryan:
The police lieutenant won't rest until the real killer is
brought to justice, even if it makes her the next target!
JUSTICE, by Debra Webb—December 2004

ATHENA FORCE:
They were the best, the brightest, the strongest—
women who shared a bond like no other....

Dear Reader,

Like the fast-paced holiday season, Silhouette Bombshell is charged with energy, and we're thrilled to bring you an unforgettable December reading experience. Our strong, sexy, savvy women will have you cheering, gasping and turning pages to see what happens next!

Let *USA TODAY* bestselling author Lindsay McKenna sweep you away to Peru in *Sister of Fortune,* part of the SISTERS OF THE ARK miniseries. This military heroine must retrieve a sacred artifact from dangerous hands. The last thing she needs is a sexy man she can't trust—too bad she has to work with one!

Check out Debra Webb's *Justice,* the latest in the ATHENA FORCE continuity series. Police lieutenant Kayla Ryan will risk everything to find her murdered friend's long-lost child and bring down an enemy who is closer than she ever suspected....

In *Night Life,* by Katherine Garbera, a former spy turned mother and wife finds herself drawn back into clandestine games when her former agency calls her in to catch a rogue agent—her estranged husband.

And don't miss Patricia Rosemoor's *Hot Case,* the story of a detective who enters her twin sister's dark world of wannabe vampires—and maybe the real thing—to find out why dead bodies are disappearing almost before her eyes.

As an editor, I am often asked what I'm looking for in a Bombshell novel. Well, *I* want to know what *you're* looking for as a reader. Please send your comments to me, c/o Silhouette Books, 233 Broadway Suite 1001, New York, NY 10279.

Best wishes,

Natashya Wilson
Associate Senior Editor, Silhouette Bombshell

Please address questions and book requests to:
Silhouette Reader Service
U.S.: 3010 Walden Ave., P.O. Box 1325, Buffalo, NY 14269
Canadian: P.O. Box 609, Fort Erie, Ont. L2A 5X3

JUSTICE
DEBRA WEBB

Silhouette®

BOMBSHELL™

Published by Silhouette Books

America's Publisher of Contemporary Romance

Special thanks and acknowledgment are given to Debra Webb for her contribution to the ATHENA FORCE series.

 SILHOUETTE BOOKS

ISBN 0-373-51336-4

JUSTICE

Visit Silhouette Books at www.eHarlequin.com

Printed in U.S.A.

DEBRA WEBB

was born in Scottsboro, Alabama, to parents who taught her that anything is possible if you want it bad enough. She began writing at age nine. Eventually, she met and married the man of her dreams, and tried some other occupations, including selling vacuum cleaners, working in a factory, a day-care center, a hospital and a department store. When her husband joined the military, they moved to Berlin, Germany, and Debra became a secretary in the commanding general's office. By 1985, they were back in the States, and finally moved to Tennessee, to a small town where everyone knows everyone else. With the support of her husband and two beautiful daughters, Debra took up writing again, looking to mystery and movies for inspiration. In 1998, her dream of writing for Harlequin came true. You can write to Debra with your comments at P.O. Box 64, Huntland, Tennessee 37345 or visit her Web site at http://www.debrawebb.com to find out exciting news about her next book.

This book is dedicated to all the Athena Ladies and a terrific editor, Natashya Wilson—a true bombshell!

Chapter 1

Kayla Ryan eased her Jeep Cherokee into the alley between two long rows of U-Store-It buildings. She lowered the driver's side window and cut the engine.

For a full thirty seconds she sat very still, utilized all her senses to estimate the threat level.

The cool December air felt thick with tension in spite of the utter silence enveloping the deserted storage facility. Nothing moved.

They waited. Listening. Anticipating her move… her risk level. At least two men. Maybe three.

Now or never.

Ten seconds more and she'd be made.

No way backup would arrive in time.

Her partner would be pissed.

It wouldn't be the first time. She doubted it would be the last.

Her heart rate ramming into overdrive, Kayla opened her door and got out. She strode straight over to the nearest storage unit, number forty-two, and reached for the lock. Though she had no key, only a couple quick flicks with the lock pick she carried were required before the mechanism disengaged, falling open in her palm.

She removed the lock and raised the four-foot-wide overhead door. The grind of metal on metal screeched, shattering the silence and sending a clear message to the men about ten units down and on the next row who would be listening.

Nothing to worry about. Just someone adding to or taking from her storage unit.

Her gaze roving left and right, Kayla slipped into the shadows of the ten-by-twelve cinder-block unit. Whatever the boxes stacked nearly to the ceiling contained was of no significance. This wasn't about unit forty-two or its contents.

Keeping her attention fixed on the vacant alley-way, she relayed a text message to Jim Harkey, her partner, from her cellular phone. The message was simple. SOS...UStoreIt.

She'd sent it once already. He hadn't responded. Today was his day off. Hers too. But some things couldn't wait.

With the phone clipped back on her utility belt, she wrapped her fingers around the butt of her weapon. The hiss of cool steel sliding from her leather holster prompted a sense of calm that instantly neutralized the negative effects of the adrenaline pumping through her veins.

She might be off duty but she never went anywhere, not even to bed, without her weapon. To a cop, being unarmed was the equivalent of being naked on stage in front of a jam-packed stadium. Not a good thing—unless you're a part of a living art exhibit.

The muted sound of voices reached her position. She'd been right. Three. All male. All comfortable with continuing business since her presence had obviously been assessed as insignificant.

That kind of carelessness told her something else about her targets. They had grown complacent. Risky business for criminals.

Adopting a battle-ready stance, she eased out into the light of day. Her rubber-soled shoes made no sound on the concrete that formed the drive through the alley between the rows of storage units.

Four more units…three…she moved toward the end of the long row…two more. When she reached the final one she halted, held absolutely still and listened.

The voices were clear now.

"Twenty of the best," one man bragged. "I can get you as many as you require."

Kayla didn't have to see the product to know what the man was hawking. High-end bikes. Valued at upwards of hundreds, even thousands, of dollars each.

The goods were stolen from tourists who preferred to bicycle their way around Arizona's trails and from university students who considered the designer bikes to be "all that" and more. The more expensive the product, the better the students from wealthy families liked it. Titanium frames, leather seats…top-end bikes came just about any way a customer wanted them.

Though the consumer might have to work hours, days or even weeks to earn the cost, it only took the average thief about eight seconds to cut a lock and scarcely a few moments more to ride off. Especially on campus, where the thieves easily blended into the student population, likely wearing backpacks filled with the tools of their trade.

The risk proved minimal in most cases, the reward more than sufficient. At one time a thief could only hope to turn a twenty-five or thirty-dollar profit on a three-hundred-dollar bike, but now was a different story. The better ones went for hundreds or even thousands a pop. Considering the risk and the slap on the wrist thieves got if caught, it was a far more desirable business than running drugs.

No middleman required. No recipes to concoct. No dangerous chemicals to dispose of. Just simple bolt cutters or lock picks and a backpack. Well, and the physical endurance to ride the stolen bike to wherever your pickup contact waited.

This particular group of thieves had been eluding law enforcement for months now. No one could determine where and how they disposed of the stolen bikes. Serial numbers were apparently changed, since the few registered ones stolen never surfaced. These guys would get more than a mere slap on the wrist. Petty larceny was one thing, but this was considerably bigger. Estimates put these guys at a six-figure business annually.

Athens was the perfect location. Situated close to Phoenix, a big college town, Athens offered a quick, neutral place for storage and distribution. Far enough away from the scene of the crime for comfort and yet close enough to facilitate the job.

But this was her town.

Criminals were not going to be allowed to operate under her jurisdiction as long as she could help it.

With one final deep breath, she braced herself for moving around the end of the building. If she waited for backup, chances were the deal would be done. She wanted the buyers as well as the seller.

When she would have swung around the corner, the sound of a car braking to a stop thirty or forty yards behind her drew her up short.

She swore softly. All she needed was the owner of storage unit number forty-two showing up and throwing a fit. Distraction was not a good thing, nor was being made by the bad guys because of an unfortunate twist of fate.

Her gaze narrowed on the dark sedan that parked behind her Jeep. She frowned. The vehicle looked familiar.

When a tall guy wearing jeans, a sweatshirt and a baseball cap strode up to one of the units and proceeded to tinker with the lock she let go the breath she'd been holding. Nobody.

Now, if he would just stay put and not come nosing around the corner in the event the next few moments got out of hand....

As the new arrival pushed the door of his unit upward Kayla turned her attention back to the voices on the other side of the narrow block buildings.

The deal had been made.

She had to move in now.

Hesitation stalled her. Something still didn't feel right. She didn't like having company show up at the last minute like this. She glanced toward the man in the ball cap one last time. He'd disappeared into the unit he'd opened. Just like she had when she first arrived. Too coincidental for comfort.

The voices around the corner snagged her attention once more.

She couldn't wait any longer.

As she prepared to advance around the end of the building, a vague sort of recognition clicked in the back of her mind and she hesitated once more. She couldn't shake the feeling that there was something important about the guy in the baseball cap that she'd missed here.

Then she knew.

She whipped around just in time to come face-to-face with the man in question.

"You still going after the bad guys all alone," he commented quietly, for her ears only.

She glared up at Detective Peter Hadden. "What

the hell are you doing here?" Her demand came out a whisper but there was no mistaking the ferocity. Ire roared through her, boosting the adrenaline already searing through her veins.

Hadden was with Homicide and Robbery in Tucson. This damn sure wasn't his jurisdiction. Not to mention she was still irritated with him after their last chance meeting, which she realized now hadn't been any more inadvertent than this one.

He was following her. She'd experienced that sensation far too often lately.

The shift in the tone of the exchange on the other side of the building drew her attention back in that direction and alerted Kayla to her new status.

She'd been made…at the very least deemed a possible threat.

The perps would scatter.

She had to act *now*.

Another curse hissed past her lips as she swung around the end of the building and lunged forward. She paused at the final corner that stood between her and the perps doing their dirty business.

A gunshot whizzed past as she stole a look around that corner.

She jerked back. Gritted her teeth and readied to swing around and return fire.

In a blur of unexpected motion Hadden charged past her.

What the hell was he doing now?

Gunfire erupted. Hadden's as well as the enemies'.

She dived for the ground, rolled into the open and

fired. One man was down, writhing and howling in pain. Hadden and another were entangled in a savage, rolling-on-the-ground hand-to-hand battle.

She fired once more. Her target stumbled when the shot tore through his thigh. But he didn't stop. He headed straight for one of two vehicles waiting nearby.

She scrambled up and burst into a dead run. "Stop! Police! Drop your weapon!"

He glanced back, fired twice. Sent her ducking behind one of the vehicles.

So much for negotiations.

If he got away…

Her feet were moving even before the decision fully penetrated her brain. She dashed from her cover and made a dive for the passenger side door of the second vehicle at the same time her perp went for the driver's side.

Weapons drawn, barrels leveled, they slid into the front seat simultaneously.

"You got a death wish, bitch?" he growled.

Pain glittered in his eyes. Kayla didn't have to look to know that blood pulsed from the wound like a mini-geyser. It was possible he hadn't noticed or that he just wasn't ready to give up.

"Maybe," she said, her voice dead calm. "But I'm not the one bleeding to death."

He flinched. Didn't look down. Damn, she mused. A real tough guy.

"I don't want to have to shoot a cop," he warned, his face already growing paler.

She wondered at that. Why would a bike thief, even a well-connected one making six figures, risk this level of jeopardy? It didn't make sense.

No time to worry about that now. The black, somber barrel of his weapon remained aimed directly at her.

"Do you know how long it takes the average human to bleed out?" She cocked her head, peered around the lethal barrel and deliberately assessed him for a second or two. "Not very long when an artery is involved. After you lose that first liter it all goes downhill from there. It takes only minutes to reach a point where no amount of medical care will make a difference."

He swallowed hard, the difficulty clear in the workings of his throat muscles.

"Do you really want to die over a bunch of over-priced bikes?" A line of sweat had already formed on his brow and upper lip. She took a risk, glanced at the leg. "Damn, it's pumping out pretty fast. You feel dizzy yet? Cold?"

His hand shook—once, twice—before he lowered his weapon. "Call me an ambulance," he choked out.

Kayla confiscated his weapon, called for the paramedics then made a makeshift tourniquet with his shirt when she couldn't stop the flow of blood any other way.

Hadden had the guy he'd been tangoing with cuffed and was attending to the one he'd been forced to shoot. A shoulder wound involving mostly soft tissue, but the guy was crying like a baby. The buyer, Kayla surmised. He looked a little pudgy and had that fluorescent-lighting pallor of the skin—definitely not the type to be out pirating bikes.

"Ouch," Hadden said as he looked over her handiwork on the guy with the femoral artery injury. "That'll leave a mark."

"He'll live." As long as the ambulance gets here in a hurry, she added silently. She'd have to keep a close watch on the jerk until then. Inflicting a lethal wound hadn't been her intent, but she'd done what she had to in order to stop the perp from fleeing the scene and to protect herself…which might not have been necessary at all had she not been interrupted. She scrubbed her bloody palms over her jeans and eyed her uninvited backup. "What the hell are you doing here, Hadden?"

He lifted one broad shoulder in a negligent shrug. "Just driving by, thought you might need some help."

"Bullshit," she tossed right back. If he thought she was that naive he'd better get a grip.

Before she could pursue the point, two Pinal County cruisers arrived along with the ambulance.

"Hell, Ryan," one of the deputies said as he surveyed the aftermath. "Why didn't you just kill 'em all and save the taxpayers the cost of a trial?"

"Funny," she muttered as she started walking toward the vehicles. She glanced over her shoulder at Hadden. "Don't you go disappearing on me, we're not finished yet."

Two hours later, with two of the perps in the OR for surgery and the other in county lockup, Kayla had finished going over the scene with Steve Devon, the best county investigator in the Sheriff's Department.

"I'll need your report on my desk first thing in the morning," Devon told her before letting her go. He flicked a sour look at Hadden. "Yours too, *Detective*."

Devon didn't have to spell out what that meant. A report was SOP, standard operating procedure. The urgency, however, was related to two wounded perps. Anytime shots were fired, the department flinched.

The investigator's stern questions only added to Kayla's building annoyance at Hadden. She glared at him as they walked toward their abandoned vehicles.

"This should have gone down without any shots fired." If his arrival hadn't set her targets on alert, a good portion of what transpired could have been prevented. She prided herself on doing her job with the least excessive force possible.

"You just keep telling yourself that if it makes you feel better, Ryan," he snorted. "But those guys had no intention of being rounded up today, otherwise they wouldn't have been armed. Or willing to shoot at a cop," he added.

That part was true. She'd been surprised briefly by the unexpected exchange. But she still didn't like him horning in on her bust.

She went around to the back of her Jeep and opened the hatch. After pawing through a dozen items that she didn't know why she hauled around, she finally found the antibacterial wipes. For the good they would do. She had that scumbag's blood all over her.

Hadden, playing it smart, kept his mouth shut as she cleaned herself up. By the time she'd gone through half the container of thin wipes her hands felt reasonably clean. There was nothing to be done about her clothes. The jeans and sweater were ruined.

She closed the hatch and settled her renewed fury on Hadden. "Now tell me what you were really doing here. This is my jurisdiction," she added. "You have no business nosing around here without giving someone at the Sheriff's Department a courtesy call."

He grinned. A spear of warmth went through her. She looked away. She hated that he so easily turned the tide of her emotions. That was one reason she'd avoided him the past couple of months. Getting involved with another cop wouldn't be smart. And she could see that coming a mile off. She knew Hadden's type—nice guy, the kind who made lonely women fall in love all too easily.

"Now we're even," he said jokingly, but she knew that whatever his motivation, it was no joking matter.

"Don't even go there," she cautioned. Tucson was his jurisdiction, but her friend Rainy Carrington's murder was her jurisdiction, no matter what the invisible boundary lines said. She would not give up on finding the whole truth. Not now…not ever. Hadden might as well get used to it. This had been a bad year for Kayla. First she'd lost her grandmother. Then, a few months later, one of her best friends had been murdered.

"I've been watching you the past couple of days," he admitted, surprising her all over again.

She schooled her expression and planted her hands on her hips. "What for?" Every instinct told her she wasn't going to like his answer. He'd been hiding things from her all along. But, so far, she'd had no reason to complain. God knew she was hiding plenty from him. That was another reason she'd steered clear of him the past couple of months.

"Why don't we go someplace where we can talk?" The suggestion was accompanied by a long, searching look from those piercing blue eyes.

A shiver chased over her skin. Kayla gritted her teeth and would have liked nothing better than to chalk the reaction up to the weather, but, unfortunately, in southern Arizona that wasn't likely. Even with only two weeks left before Christmas the temperature hung around fifty to fifty-five degrees Fahrenheit. Not cold enough to bring on the shivers.

It was him. There was no denying that reality. She'd been pretending for months now. Keeping him at a distance for more than one reason.

Though instinct warned her yet again that letting him too close would be a mistake, she just couldn't help herself. For Rainy, she reasoned. If Detective Peter Hadden had discovered something related to Rainy's murder, Kayla needed to know. The Cipher, the assassin who'd killed Kayla's best friend, was dead. Samantha St. John, another friend and schoolmate, had taken care of him. But whoever had sent him was still out there, the motivation a puzzle of bits of information that didn't yet connect.

If it was the last thing she did, Kayla intended to solve that mystery. She wouldn't rest until those responsible for Rainy's death were brought to justice…or were six feet under. And she had to keep searching for Rainy's child—or children—until she found them or proved none existed. That was the part that hurt the most. Rainy had wanted children so badly and all along she might have had at least one. The bastards who had mined her eggs when she was young herself had robbed her of her ability to conceive and also deprived her of knowing whatever offspring had resulted. And when Rainy had discovered what they'd done and tried to find them, they'd had her killed. Kayla would find the truth.

The Promise.

She and her closest friends had made that promise to each other all those years ago while students at Athena Academy. Each year the class was divided into small groups of students who worked together all year long to become the best they could be in all aspects of their academic lives. Kayla's group had been called the Cassandras. Headed by Rainy, their senior mentor, the seven of them, including Sam St. John, had become extremely close and had ultimately promised to come if any of them needed help—no questions asked.

Rainy had called them together. Now she was dead. Murdered. Kayla and the rest of the Cassandras had a new promise to keep—solving the enigma of Rainy's death and ensuring that all involved paid dearly.

For that single reason she would do whatever it took. Like risk getting close to a man who reached her on a level beyond the professional.

She realized Hadden was waiting for her to answer his question. Should they talk? Kayla glanced at her watch. "I don't know, Hadden." She shrugged indifferently. "It's my day off and I actually have plans." It was a lie but he didn't know that. Well, there was one little thing she had to do—smooth things over with her partner. As she'd suspected, Jim had called during the middle of the wrap-up with the county investigator. He wasn't happy. "I should probably get a move on."

Hadden angled his head skeptically, clearly struggling to keep another grin off those nice lips. God. She resisted the urge to shake her head. Why did she have to notice his every damned asset?

"You expect me to believe that you just happened to be driving by this morning?" He gestured to the rows of storage units. "And discovered a deal going down involving a group of felons you, among others, have been tracking for months?" He was the one shaking his head now. "Give me a break here, Lieutenant Ryan."

"I got a tip, all right?" It was true. She'd received an anonymous call just after she'd dropped Jazz off at school and headed for the gym—her plans for the morning. For a single mom with a career in law enforcement, free time was at a premium. Most of what little she had was either spent as quality time with her eleven-year-old daughter or in physical training.

Just another thing she'd already lived to regret—never taking the time she should for friends and family. Rainy was dead. And Kayla barely remembered the last time they'd gotten together before that tragedy.

"So, are we having coffee or what?" Hadden pressed.

Kayla looked straight at him, assessed what she saw in those intense blue eyes. He needed to share something with her. Anticipation and an underlying urgency radiated from his every feature.

"Sure, why not." She shrugged again, as if whatever he had to say didn't matter. "As long as you're buying."

Kayla climbed into her Jeep without looking back. When she heard Hadden pull out onto the road she backed up her vehicle, pulled forward and followed him. Attempting to guess what was on his mind would be a supreme waste of time so she didn't bother.

He drove to a coffee shop on Olympus Road, the main drag in Athens, and parked in the lot. Kayla's little community wasn't that large, a few shops, a bank, a post office, and a supermarket. The only reason the tiny spot in the road had actually developed into a town was because the Athena Academy, the all-girls school Kayla had attended from seventh through twelfth grades, was nearby. Luke Air Force base was also close by, but there wasn't much else around. Most folks around Athens went to Phoenix for major shopping and medical care.

Still, the town had amassed a population of about five thousand, and the powers that be had managed to wrangle a satellite station for the town from the Sheriff's Department. The small law enforcement office was manned by two sheriff's deputies at all times. With its continued growth Athens would no doubt be incorporating and forming its own city government in the next couple of years. So far members of the community had been in no hurry to take the formal steps. But that would soon change.

Nothing stayed the same.

Hadn't she learned that the hard way?

Hadden emerged from his car and strode toward Kayla's Jeep. She took her time getting out, turning her attention once more to consideration of his motivation for keeping her under surveillance. Professionally speaking, the only thing they had in common was the murder of Lorraine Carrington. Kayla flinched at the memory of that Saturday night back in late August. More unpleasant thoughts tumbled in on the heels of that memory.

Somehow Athena Academy was involved in Rainy's death. Kayla didn't want to believe it. She'd reasoned that the involvement only went as deep as certain personnel, but she couldn't be sure.

That suspicion was just one of the secrets she couldn't share with Peter Hadden. Was the primary reason she'd backed off from her original plan to work fairly closely with him. This was Cassandra business, to be shared on a need-to-know basis only.

His gaze locked with hers at precisely that moment, as if he'd read her mind and somehow summoned her full attention.

Keep this on the surface, in neutral territory, Kayla. You don't know all the facts and Athena Academy certainly doesn't need the bad publicity.

Shannon Conner, a TV news reporter and the only person ever to be expelled from Athena, had already done enough damage in that department. In the early months after Rainy's death, the vengeful woman had done all within her power to make the school look bad. She'd showed up at Rainy's funeral and implied that Athena Academy used its students for scientific experiments. More recently she'd tried to compromise Kayla's fellow Cassandra Josie Lockworth, a captain in the Air Force. She'd reported on Josie's fast rise in the force; but had tried to win her career by implying Josie was involved with a fellow officer. It hadn't worked.

Victoria Patton, better known as Tory, another of the Cassandras and a top TV news reporter, had worked overtime to put the right spin on Conner's negative reporting. But there were others out there who would like nothing better than to bring down the unusual preparatory school. Just another factor to consider in all this. Perhaps someone wanted Kayla to believe that the school was responsible for what had happened to Rainy. But the evidence continued to mount…there was no denying that.

When she and Hadden had settled at a small table in the farthest corner of the shop, away from the few other customers, he didn't waste any time.

"There's a new development in the Carrington case."

Anticipation raced through Kayla. She'd been right. "What kind of development?"

Before he could respond the waitress arrived and took their order. Two black coffees. Kayla considered having a pastry but this wasn't a social meeting. Even though there were times when she would kill for a chocolate-filled croissant, this wasn't the time. She needed to focus.

"What kind of development?" The question was out of her mouth the instant the waitress moved away.

"As you well know, we've exhausted all avenues in an attempt to determine exactly what happened to Lorraine Carrington."

The one thing she did know well was that she and the other Cassandras were the real ones who made up the *we* he spoke of. As far as Hadden and his department were concerned, there was no overwhelming evidence to prove Rainy's death was anything more than an accident. Another reason Kayla couldn't help being suspicious of Hadden's continued interest in the case. A seat belt malfunction and a driver dozing off and running off the road was hardly the stuff murder investigations hinged on.

But Kayla knew the real facts. Rainy hadn't simply fallen asleep at the wheel. Her sudden collapse into slumber had been brought on by the Cipher and a gadget he'd used on Alex—Alexandra Forsythe, another of Kayla's Cassandra sisters—as well as on Kayla herself. On separate occasions in totally different locations, both she and Alex had fainted for no apparent reason during the weeks after Rainy's death. Like Rainy, Alex's incident had occurred while she was driving. It was a miracle she hadn't been badly injured…or worse.

The Cipher had paid for his part in Rainy's death.

CIA agent Sam had tracked him down and had been forced to kill him in a standoff. But they were still no closer to finding whoever had sent the assassin than they had been weeks ago.

"In pursuing this investigation," Hadden went on, "we've uncovered a number of details that don't add up where Marshall Carrington is concerned."

Kayla's hackles rose instantly. "Look, Hadden, I know it's SOP to suspect the spouse first and foremost when someone dies, but I can vouch for Marshall Carrington. There is no way he would have killed his wife. He loved Rainy." Kayla blinked back the emotion that stung her eyes. "I know Marshall. He would never have hurt her. Never." She couldn't tell Hadden about the Cipher or anything else she and her Cassandra sisters had discovered. Not yet anyway.

The waitress set two cups of steaming dark brew on the table. "Anything else?"

Hadden lifted his hand in a negative signal and the young woman scurried off to help another customer who'd just arrived.

"I don't doubt Carrington's character as a husband," Hadden said, some indefinable emotion filtering into his tone. "This is about his business dealings."

Confusion lined Kayla's brow. Hadden's tone as well as his statement bewildered her. "Marshall is an archaeology professor. Outside his occasional jaunt to search for some ancient relic, what on earth could you find questionable about his profession?"

Hadden's expression closed then, like a bank vault

door slamming shut to fend off trespassers. The abrupt change set Kayla on edge. Whatever he intended to share with her, there was a great deal more he planned to keep to himself. Somehow it related to Marshall. And she knew before he spoke that it was not good.

"We have reason to suspect your friend Marshall is eyeball deep in a smuggling ring."

Chapter 2

Noon had come and gone by the time Kayla showered twice—once just wasn't enough, with her feeling as if that perp's blood had penetrated deep into her pores. She'd scrubbed until her skin felt raw.

She laid the hair dryer aside and stared at her reflection. But was the blood really what bothered her just now? Peter Hadden's words kept echoing in her brain. *We have reason to suspect your friend Marshall is eyeball deep in a smuggling ring.*

Not possible.

Rainy's husband would never be involved with any sort of criminal activity. Not knowingly anyway.

Rainy's husband.

Kayla looked away from the telling emotion in her

eyes. She'd gotten a little too attached to Marshall these past few months. It wasn't intentional…she hadn't meant to allow her feelings to stray into dangerous territory. But it had been like trying to stop an avalanche. Impossible.

She'd always genuinely adored Marshall. Who wouldn't? He was handsome, well-built, immensely charming and he had treated Rainy as if she were the absolute center of his universe. Who wouldn't want a man like that?

No. Kayla shook off that line of thinking and retreated to her bedroom to pull on some clean clothes. It wasn't about Marshall either. It was about Rainy.

Kayla sighed as she looked at her unmade bed. There was just never enough time. She dug through a pile of freshly laundered clothes that she hadn't put away yet and selected her favorite jeans.

Rainy had always teased Kayla about her ability to make a place look lived-in without any real effort. That was the way Kayla preferred things—no fuss.

She tugged on her jeans. She missed Rainy so much. The hurt and tension stemming from her murder had drawn Kayla and Marshall together, that's all. She knew better than most that stress did that sort of thing. It happened when you felt lost or detached from the rest of the world. You reached out to the closest human who might understand.

Her thoughts drifted to her final year at Athena Academy. Rainy had graduated long before and gone off to Harvard. Alex had graduated as well, one year previously. Though Kayla had loved her other Cassandra sisters, she'd missed Rainy and Alex to the point of distraction. Her Navajo heritage had tugged at her more strongly that year than any other. She'd just felt out of sorts, torn between what she'd been taught as a child and all that she'd learned at Athena.

Not that anything she'd experienced at Athena could be called bad in any way, but it had been different than the usual academic curriculum. Martial arts, weaponry, survival courses, multiple foreign languages. Too many other available studies to recall at the moment. The overall goal was the advancement and empowerment of women. All good. But somehow, in her senior year, Kayla had gotten off track, had lost some vital part of herself. In the search to regain completeness, she'd met and fallen for a cocky young officer from the Air Force base.

The image of the man she'd allowed to break her heart all those years ago flashed briefly through Kayla's mind. Her automatic instinct was to banish any thought of him. But Josie's call a couple weeks ago had Kayla hesitating. Josie Lockworth was a dear friend and a Cassandra, as well as a rising star in the Air Force. The same branch of the military in which Jazz's father still served.

Mike Bridges wanted to know his daughter. Jasmine Michelle Ryan. The daughter Kayla had raised all alone. Admittedly, he had sent child support since the day Jazz was born, twelve years ago next month. And Kayla had been blessed with the full support of her family, so to say she'd done this alone wasn't exactly accurate.

But so many times she had felt alone.

She shouldered into a sweatshirt, pulled her hair loose and began to braid it. Maybe that was part of the reason she'd been drawn to Marshall so strongly.

It had been so very long since she'd allowed herself to need a man on a personal level, much less an intimate one. Peter Hadden slipped into her troubled thoughts next. Her heart reacted instantly, picking up a few extra, foolish beats.

She couldn't help smiling when she thought of the way he always looked a little rumpled. Sexy as hell. Totally the opposite of meticulously groomed Marshall. Peter Hadden was one of those men who made the just-dragged-out-of-bed look so appealing.

Damn him.

How many times had she longed to run her fingers through his tousled hair? To yank his rumpled suit clean off his body. To ensure that it was properly laundered and pressed, of course, she'd assured herself.

Yeah, right.

And those eyes. Amazing, she admitted, allowing the momentary lapse in sanity while no one was around to notice. But it was that damned smile that got to her the fastest. Sexy, flirty, and so warm. No, not warm. Hot.

And even more than that, she found his dogged persistence dangerously tempting. No matter how often she pushed him away, he kept coming back. You had to love a guy who didn't give up.

Why couldn't she simply enjoy him? Her fingers faltered in their work as she secured the end of her waist-long braid. Good question. She was twenty-nine. She'd scarcely even dated since Jazz became a part of her life. What prevented her from having a no-strings physical relationship with a man?

Warmth spread down her limbs at the concept.

Mike popped back into her head. Because her life was complicated enough.

She'd fallen for a sexy smile and amazing eyes once before. Though Mike's were hazel, the same combination of green and blue that Jazz had inherited, the effect was the same. He'd turned Kayla inside out with just a look.

Maybe it was past time she'd allowed a man back into her life. Didn't her own mother and sister broach that very subject now and again? Like clockwork.

Still, now was not the time. Until those behind Rainy's murder and the fate of her offspring were solved, getting involved with anyone was out of the question. Especially considering this latest turn of events where Hadden was concerned. Kayla owed it to Marshall to protect him.

No. She owed it to Rainy.

Rainy had loved Marshall. Kayla would protect him for that very reason if for no other.

She walked over to her bedside table and picked up the framed photograph of her precious daughter. Jazz had the same long dark hair as Kayla, the same features. Only the color of her eyes had made it from her father's side of the gene pool. No fancy Ivy League college or high-powered career could have made Kayla's life more complete. Like all Athena graduates she had received a scholarship offer from a prestigious school, Princeton, in fact. But Jazz was far more important to Kayla than anything else.

The idea that Rainy might have at least one child out there—a child she hadn't even known about—squeezed at Kayla's heart. What had become of that child or children—if it even existed—was just another piece of the puzzle surrounding Rainy's death.

During Rainy's autopsy, Alex had discovered that Rainy still had her appendix. Yet, all those years ago in school, Rainy had supposedly had an appendectomy during seventh grade.

In the autopsy, Alex had also discovered scars—old scars—on Rainy's ovaries. Now the remaining Cassandra's were certain that someone had actually faked the appendectomy to mine her ovaries, stealing her precious eggs.

Marshall had explained that when he and Rainy hadn't conceived, they'd sought help from a specialist to no avail. That must have been when Rainy had begun to suspect the truth. And she'd never had a chance to tell her friends those suspicions.

Kayla desperately needed to talk to that specialist. But Dr. Deborah Halburg had been out of the country for months now. No one knew when she was expected to return to her practice in Tucson.

Darcy Steele, a Cassandra as well as a private investigator, had managed to find one woman, a Las Vegas showgirl known as Cleo Patra, who had gotten paid to be a surrogate mother around the same time as Rainy's supposed appendectomy. Cleo had given birth to a baby, but had no idea what had happened to the child.

Alex had connected with Justin Cohen, whose sister had died giving birth to a surrogate baby about nine months after that time. Justin was certain Athena Academy had something to do with his sister's death, and the Cassandras had come to believe him.

Tory, using her reporter's instincts and connections, had discovered that a fertility clinic had been burglarized all those years ago and that one of the missing sperm specimens belonged to Navy SEAL and hero Thomas King. And when Tory had been sent to interview King on a completely unrelated story, someone had tried to kill them both.

Sam had taken down the Cipher, the man who'd killed Rainy.

Josie, who had connections in Army Intelligence, had looked for more information on the Cipher and had learned of an obscure lab, numbered 33, connected to some kind of an experiment called "cipher." So far, they had found no connection between Lab 33 and Athena Academy. In fact, they'd found no further information about the mysterious lab at all. But the investigation was far from over.

Using the skills Athena Academy as well as life had taught them, the Cassandras would work together to solve the rest of this mystery. Rainy might never have had the opportunity to know her child. But, if that child existed, it would know about its biological mother.

The telephone rang and Kayla jerked out of her agonizing thoughts.

She'd already heard that the two injured perps were out of surgery and stable. Maybe the investigator had more questions. She hoped not. Even the idea of a shooting being questioned by superiors gave most cops the willies. Kayla was no exception. Though she knew she hadn't done anything wrong, that fact didn't keep her from experiencing a moment's trepidation.

"Ryan."

"Kayla, it's Alex."

A new kind of anticipation erupted inside Kayla. "You have news?" She could scarcely breathe as she waited for Alex to respond. Alexandra Forsythe had once been Kayla's best friend. That relationship had been strained this past decade or so. But she and Alex were working on that. It was a damned shame it had taken Rainy's death to make them both realize they couldn't let their old disagreement fester forever.

Alex was still working with Justin Cohen, who was now an FBI agent, to find the truth about Justin's sister and how her death might be connected to Rainy's, so many years later.

"Not the news you'd like to hear," Alex told her, her tone far too somber.

"What's up?" Kayla sat down on the edge of the bed and tried not to jump to any conclusions or fear the worst. Even if all their leads ran into dead ends they had to keep searching. Couldn't stop until they knew the whole truth.

"This may be nothing, but I've got a feeling we shouldn't let it pass without finding out." Alex hesitated a moment as if she wasn't one hundred percent certain of how to proceed. "Allison called me this morning."

Allison Gracelyn had attended Athena. She'd been in Rainy's grade and was older than the Cassandras. Allison and Rainy had been good friends. Since Allison's mother had founded Athena, Allison now served as a consultant on the school's board. Like Kayla and the other Cassandras, Allison grieved Rainy's loss.

Alex continued, "I got the distinct impression that she was fishing. She'd tried to call Tory but couldn't get her. She's off on some story. Anyway, Allison wanted to know if we anticipated any further damage from Shannon Conner. I told her we thought Tory had that situation under control. But during the course of the conversation, Allison mentioned that there was an Athena Academy meeting of the board at one-thirty this afternoon."

"You think I should be there," Kayla offered. Though she hadn't been invited. That little detail wouldn't stop her. Kayla glanced at the clock. 1:15 p.m. She might make it if she left right away.

"I do, Kayla." Alex sighed. "It's difficult for me to bring myself to speak this way about the school, but something somewhere isn't right. One or more members of the staff are hiding something. We have to know what that is."

Betsy Stone immediately came to mind. The Cassandras had learned that Ms. Stone, Athena's school nurse, had also worked part-time for a Dr. Henry

Reagan, at the time of Rainy's "appendectomy." They were convinced that Reagan had something to do with the surrogate mothers and Rainy's eggs. Dr. Reagan had been Justin Cohen's sister's doctor during her pregnancy, as well as Cleo Patra's.

Nurse Stone admitted having worked with Dr. Reagan two days a week in his office years before his death, but knew nothing of any unethical practices.

Then there was Christine Evans, Athena's principal since the day the doors opened. Alex felt certain Christine was hiding something. Kayla got the same impression.

But hunches and gut instincts alone didn't solve cases.

"I'm on my way," Kayla assured Alex. It felt so good to talk to her again without all those years of tension in the way. Mike Bridges had done more than break Kayla's heart. Getting involved with him had caused a twelve-year rift between Alex and Kayla. Alex had tried to talk Kayla out of getting too serious with Mike all those years ago. They'd argued bitterly. But that gap was slowly closing now. "I'll let you know how it goes."

At 1:25 p.m. Kayla turned off Olympus Road and headed down Script Pass. She might make it on time. Showing up uninvited was tactless enough. Walking in once the meeting had officially begun went against the grain of even the most liberal etiquette.

She stopped at the new guard shack that graced the entryway to the school and shuddered as she was re-

minded of just why the guard was now necessary.
Christine Evans had decided, after Rainy's death and
subsequent suspicious events at the school, to post a
guard twenty-four hours a day, even on holidays, to
monitor visitors.

She flashed her ID and continued on to the school
buildings.

She parked in the circle drive in front of the main
building and jumped out of the Jeep before it stopped
rocking at the curb.

Kayla hurried up the walk that cut across the well-
manicured lawn. Usually when she arrived at the
academy she took a moment to admire the lawn and
beautiful fountain surrounded by the current season's gorgeous flowers. But that was the furthest
thing from her mind today. The fact of the matter
was, most things had taken a back seat to Rainy's
murder since that muggy August night.

Whatever her distractions, Kayla always experienced an overwhelming sense of déjà vu when she
entered those massive front entry doors. Boundless
halls. Quiet rooms filled with memories. Voices and
images from the past spent within these walls filtered
through her mind, reminding her of those wondrous
formative years shared with the Cassandras.

If there was a long-buried secret hidden within
these walls—walls that had always felt safe—Kayla
had to find it. Not only for Rainy, but for all who
would pass through these halls in the years to come.
This school was a very special place. Whatever
wrongs had been committed here would be righted.

Kayla bypassed Christine's office and headed straight for the conference room. Thankfully, the board members were just settling down around the long table as she entered the room.

Christine Evans was the first to notice Kayla's arrival. A former military woman, Christine still had that authoritative bearing, squared shoulders and head held high. Her short gray hair added to her distinguished air. "Kayla." She met her halfway across the room. Gave her a quick hug. "What brings you here today?" Worry lines marred her brow as she surveyed Kayla's face. Long ago, a military training accident had left Christine blind in her left eye, but she missed nothing. "Nothing's happened, I hope."

After what they'd all been through since Rainy's death, the worst was the first thing that came to mind for anyone involved. Christine's expression—and the question—were sincere.

"Kayla." Allison Gracelyn came up next to Christine before Kayla could respond. Her shoulder-length brown hair was pulled back in a large barrette. "I haven't seen you since…" Her words drifted off. She didn't have to say the rest…since the funeral. Allison's brown eyes reflected the same ache that Kayla felt.

Kayla managed a smile, pressed her cheek to Allison's in a brief gesture of affection. "It's good to see you, Allison."

One by one the members of the board who were present greeted Kayla, made her feel welcome despite the unexpectedness of her appearance. No matter how cordial each was, Kayla could feel the underlying tension simmering in the room.

"I heard about today's meeting from a friend," Kayla said, prompted by Vice Principal Rebecca Claussen's question as to what brought her to the school today. "As a member of law enforcement in Athens," she took a moment to meet each board member's gaze, "and a graduate of Athena, I feel a close bond with this school and recent events have raised a number of concerns."

Now she had everyone's attention.

Christine paled. Her vice principal, Rebecca, looked every bit as stricken. Her bright hazel eyes stood out in stark contrast to her fair skin and dark, gray-streaked hair.

"Explain what you mean by concerns," Adam Gracelyn demanded in the judicial tone he'd honed over a lifetime on the Arizona Supreme Court as vice chief justice. His brown eyes bored into Kayla's, ensuring she understood that he possessed a great deal of power and influence. He would not be intimidated.

Which was not her intent, she argued mentally.

Or was it?

There were secrets here and she knew it. Some she had already learned. Like the fact that a Dr. Carl Bradford had been dismissed around the time Rainy's eggs were probably mined. Christine had insisted that his dismissal was a result of inappropriate behavior toward Nurse Betsy Stone. Somehow that just didn't sit right with Kayla.

Kayla doubted she would have any better luck interrogating this group than she'd had with Betsy Stone. Whatever secrets they shared, if any, they intended to keep quiet as long as possible.

But not all were involved in this conspiracy. She hoped.

Could she allow what one or more persons had done to influence her judgment of everyone affiliated with the school? That didn't seem fair…but what choice did she have? There simply was no way to know who had participated in the evil scheme that had prevented Rainy from bearing her own children.

No one suggested they sit down, so Kayla pushed aside her troubling thoughts and forged onward. "There are still a number of unanswered questions regarding Rainy," she said bluntly. "And the leads seem to dead-end at the school."

Christine flared her hands. "We've cooperated with your every request. What more would you have us do?"

"This has something to do with that awful Conner woman's exposé," Allison countered, her brown eyes every bit as stern as her father, the judge's. Allison wasn't actually a board member, just a consultant who flew in from D.C. for certain meetings, but she had every intention of seeing that the school was run as her mother, Marion, the school's founder, would have wanted. Her motives were good. But how far would she go to protect the school's reputation?

"In part," Kayla allowed. "Although I think Tory has the situation under control with her insider stories on the academy. Viewers believe Tory. When she exposed Shannon Conner's lies for what they were, I'm confident she undid most of the damage." Tory had also recently gotten the better of Shannon when Shannon had tried to hurt Air Force captain Josie Lockworth's career with yet another tasteless exposé on Athena students.

"But how can we be sure," the elder Gracelyn argued. "We have to take a long, hard look at how this kind of negative publicity could affect funding."

Nods and sounds of agreement went around the room.

"Especially considering that we're moving into an election year," Christine added sagely.

"You're aware," the judge said to Kayla, "that our funding from the government is at the President's leisure. Should a new commander-in-chief decide that our work here has outgrown its worth, that funding will vanish in a puff of bureaucratic smoke."

Kayla knew how much the school depended upon funding. The truth was that the government's paltry contribution was not nearly enough. Wealthy private donors were the school's livelihood. Bad publicity could do far-reaching damage. That was one reason the school had always maintained such a low profile. No publicity equated to good publicity was the motto. Don't draw attention. For weeks Shannon Conner and her twisted accusations had drawn the scorching scrutiny of most of the free world.

Uncertainty lanced Kayla. She hadn't wanted to believe that Shannon's stories carried any merit, but when she thought of what had been done to Rainy, doubt crept in.

Had this revered school experimented on its students?

Was there anyone else who'd fallen victim as Rainy had?

Kayla swallowed back the doubt. She wouldn't believe that. Couldn't believe it. This situation had to be isolated, involving one or two members of the staff at most. To believe anything else would shake the entire foundation of all she held dear.

"I know you're all very concerned about the publicity over the past few months, but its novelty has almost worn off," she said. "Once the fall session started and Tory worked her magic with some positive stories, Athena was scarcely mentioned in the media anymore. I think that's behind us." She braced herself for a maelstrom. Her next words would wreak a havoc of their own. "What I don't think we've cleared up is this school's involvement in what happened to Rainy."

Rebecca Claussen threw up her hands. "I can't believe you're bringing that up again." She shook her head. "What do we have to say to convince you that whatever happened didn't happen here?"

"Kayla," Christine put in, "you know we wouldn't allow anything like that. How could you even think such a thing?"

The Gracelyns glared at her. No one wanted to discuss the issue. No one wanted to believe. The truth was, no one even wanted to know. They wanted this over and forgotten. Buried.

Hell, Kayla didn't want to consider the idea either. But it was necessary. As a cop, she could put aside her personal feelings and see that need. But these people weren't cops. And she was talking about their baby. Everyone in this room had given their all for Athena Academy. Allison's own mother, the founder, had paid the ultimate sacrifice. She had died here.

That last thought stuck in Kayla's brain and reverberated for a moment. Marion Gracelyn had been murdered on school grounds a few years back. She was thought to have been a victim of an interrupted burglary. But was that what really happened?

Before any more new conspiracy theories could formulate, Kayla clarified her position on the matter of Rainy's medical mix-up. "I know it didn't happen here. Both you and Nurse Stone," she said to Christine, "have explained that Rainy was rushed to the hospital in Phoenix when she got sick. And the mistake in her medical chart must have happened there. I know. But we're missing something. And I can't let this matter rest until I find the whole truth." She looked straight at Christine as she said the last.

Christine averted her gaze.

The judge broke his simmering silence. "You do what you have to do, Lieutenant Ryan." That he used her title and last name told Kayla the position he'd taken. She was now considered an enemy to some degree. "This school is beyond reproach," he continued. "As an Athena graduate you should be ashamed of yourself for even suggesting that this fine institution would be involved in any such evil deeds." He leveled a gaze on Kayla that unsettled her to her very core. "Do what you must, but remember we have nothing to hide."

Judge Gracelyn's words were still echoing in Kayla's ears as she reached her daughter's school later that afternoon. She pushed the unsettling subject aside and focused on the here and now. Pinal County Elementary. Next year Jazz would attend middle school. That idea made Kayla feel old.

She pulled alongside the schoolyard curb behind the dozens of other vehicles waiting for the final bell to ring. It felt impossible that Jazz was almost twelve. How could that much time have passed so quickly?

Kayla thought of those first few months after graduating from Athena, when her pregnancy could no longer be kept secret. It hadn't been so easy then. Though her parents had accepted her situation more readily than Kayla would have guessed, there had been some amount of strain. And yet, each and every member of her generous family had pitched in, gone above and beyond to help. When Jazz had turned one, Kayla had known she couldn't wait any longer to get on with her life. She'd gone to the police academy and had acquired a college degree in night school. And when she'd finished, Collin Masters had just been elected county sheriff and had invited her to join his department. It hadn't hurt that he was a longtime friend of Kayla's father.

She loved her job and hadn't looked back.

Until now.

She couldn't help wondering how life might have been different if things hadn't happened as they had. What if she'd never met Mike Bridges? Never fallen for the cocky jerk?

She wouldn't have Jazz.

Just then, Jasmine Ryan came bursting through the school doors.

A grin split across Kayla's face as she watched Jazz hurry toward her through the sea of students. It didn't matter what might have been. All that mattered was that she and Jazz had each other. No way would Kayla's life have been complete without this little girl. No way.

"I hate boys!"

This announcement was made scarcely before Jazz plopped into the passenger seat.

Kayla smothered a laugh. "Really? Now, why is that?"

Her brow furrowed with concentration, Jazz buckled her seat belt. "Because they're stupid." Her task complete, she leaned back and folded her arms over her chest. "Why would I like a stupid boy?"

Kayla resisted the urge to encourage her daughter to keep that attitude. She pulled away from the curb and pointed the Jeep in the direction of home.

At age eleven, boys could seem awfully silly. By twelve or thirteen a girl's outlook on the subject always changed. She glanced at her daughter. Nature had a way of working its magic. Poor kid. She had no idea. There wasn't much parents could say to prepare their children for adolescence.

During the drive home the conversation shifted to Christmas. Friday was the last day of school, Jazz reminded her. Like Kayla could forget. That meant she had to get the last of her shopping done this week.

She parked in the short drive in front of their small bungalow.

"I'll get the mail!" Jazz unbuckled herself and bounded out the door. She slowed only long enough to tug her backpack onto her shoulders. Since she'd gotten that pen pal from Croatia she couldn't wait to check the mail every day.

Kayla eased out of the vehicle a bit more slowly. The aches and pains from this morning's bust had settled into her muscles and joints. She'd hit the ground hard after Hadden made that lunge into the open. He'd left her no choice. Mentally swearing, mostly at him, she pushed his image aside. She wasn't going to let him creep back into her thoughts any more than she would the ongoing investigation into Athena Academy. Her time with her daughter was far too precious. There would be plenty of time to mull over the day's events after Jazz was tucked in for the night.

Kayla had just unlocked the front door and pushed it inward when her daughter raced up beside her.

"Yours." Jazz thrust a handful of mail at her. "Mine." Her face beaming, she held up one envelope for her mother to see the overseas address. "I gotta go do my homework." She sprinted through the door like a gazelle.

Inside, Kayla flipped through the envelopes, tossing a couple in the trash and a couple more onto the stack where next month's bills waited. The last one brought her up short. She scrutinized the elegantly embossed return address, her heart pounding.

Athena Academy.

Her fingers cold and shaking, she tore open the envelope. By the time she unfolded the enclosed letter her knees had given way, forcing her to seek a place to sit down.

It is with great pleasure that we extend this very special invitation....

Jasmine Michelle Ryan...

...seventh-grade class commencing in September of the upcoming year...

Attendance at Athena Academy was by invitation only. No amount of money...no amount of power and influence got a girl through those doors. Only the best...only the ones considered special were invited.

Kayla knew her daughter was exceptionally bright. Extremely athletic. Those qualities combined with her age made her the perfect candidate.

But...God...Kayla wasn't ready for this. Not *now*.

Athena wanted Jazz.

Chapter 3

For a long moment Kayla watched her daughter sleep. It was 6:15 a.m. Fifteen minutes past the time she usually woke Jazz for school. Somehow she couldn't seem to bring herself to move forward into this morning.

It wasn't even light outside, wouldn't be for another hour or so. Mornings like this Kayla wanted nothing more than to crawl back under the covers and snuggle with her sweet child. But there was life to contend with. Work for Kayla, school for Jazz. Even at the ripe old age of eleven there was still the occasional morning during summer vacation or winter break that the two of them enjoyed a few extra minutes together, giggling and cuddling.

How much longer would her little girl indulge her mother's sentimental need to cherish those swiftly vanishing moments of childhood as the child became a woman?

Jazz was growing up so damned fast. Kayla's heart squeezed painfully in her chest. Where had the time gone? It seemed just yesterday she was in diapers and squealing in delight the moment Kayla walked through the door to pick her up after work. Now they talked about boys and argued over what clothes were appropriate for a girl who had outgrown corduroy overalls and pigtails but who hadn't quite made it to high heels and highlights just yet.

"I'm not a baby," Jazz would argue. She wanted to dress like her favorite pop diva. A pretty scary idea to Kayla's way of thinking.

But not nearly as scary as some things.

Kayla crossed the room and stared out the window, watched the dark split apart as the sun reached ever upward, sending forth fingers of light, banishing the final remnants of night. She'd spent that night, most of it anyway, tossing and turning, mulling over the past as well as the future.

She'd loved her time at Athena Academy. No question there. She'd formed bonds that would never be broken this side of the grave. Had learned and experienced far more than a student could hope to in public school. For years Kayla had secretly wondered if her daughter would receive an invitation as she had. She was one of the only two Cassandras who'd done the motherhood thing, and Darcy, the other mother, had a four-year-old son. Were the others wondering if Jazz would be invited to attend Athena? Had it even crossed anyone else's mind?

Kayla would have to ponder the concept awhile herself before she went to her parents for input. They had once been faced with this same decision.

She needed to get used to the idea. To talk it over with Jazz, see how she felt. She'd shared stories about her time at the academy with her daughter. Especially the survival courses at Yuma. Jazz loved to hear about those. Kayla considered that as a student at Athena her daughter would have access to the kind of math and science classes most high school students didn't even know fell into the categories, like astronomy and cryptology, forensics and genetics. The field trips and other courses, such as weaponry, martial arts and foreign languages, were just a few of the perks. The expectations and level of higher thinking were far broader and deeper than even the best private schools in the country.

And it wouldn't cost Kayla a penny. Her child would receive all these wondrous benefits simply because she'd been invited.

But what if Kayla learned that Athena was deeply involved in what had happened to Rainy? Could she assume her child would be safe there? *She* had been safe. Outside her own imprudence, no harm had come to her at Athena. Only good.

Kayla moved back to the bed and smiled down at her child. And even her foolish behavior during her senior year had resulted in a very good end.

This wasn't a decision she could make right now. There were far too many considerations. Would Jazz even want to leave her friends? Kayla had struggled with that aspect of Athena life, as most of the students surely had. Admittedly, new, strong bonds had been formed by all. But did that make it the right thing?

A heavy sigh pushed past her lips. Being a parent was a tough job. She leaned down and kissed Jazz's cheek. "Wake up, sleepyhead," she murmured. "Time to get up." Her daughter roused slowly, reluctantly, giving Kayla a fleeting glimpse of the child who still lingered on the edge of Jazz's grown-up attitude and maturing body.

While Jazz had her breakfast, Kayla strapped on her weapon and pulled on her jacket. Her uniform consisted of khaki pants and shirt with a black jacket. The black utility belt and rubber-soled shoes were her only accessories other than the khaki-colored baseball cap that sported the county sheriff's emblem. There had been a time when all sheriff's deputies had worn round-billed headgear that looked a little like a Smoky the Bear hat, but not anymore. Thank goodness.

Eventually Kayla intended to work her way up to county investigator, but she was in no hurry. She liked staying around Athens, being close in the event Jazz needed her. Moving up to the position of investigator would require that she work all over the county. For now she wasn't interested in working cases that far away from home. Later, maybe. She'd reached the rank of lieutenant a year ago and that was about as high as she could hope to go if she wanted to stay local.

Her partner, Jim Harkey, had never bothered with anything beyond the sergeant's exam. He liked being a sergeant and wanted no part of the political crap, as he called it, of obtaining a higher rank than his current one. He had no interest whatsoever in becoming a part of the brass. No offense to her, he would always tack on to the statement. Kayla took no offense. To each his own, she told him.

This morning after she dropped Jazz off at school she had follow-up work on yesterday's larceny bust. On her lunch break she intended to drop by the Academy to talk to Betsy Stone once more. Kayla had no idea how much good it would do since she'd already talked to the nurse on two occasions and gotten zip, but she had to try again. *Try* being the operative word, since the nurse almost always managed to be gone when Kayla popped in. Every instinct told her Betsy knew a hell of a lot more than she was telling. And Christine was hiding something as well. Maybe nothing significant…but something.

Dr. Reagan was the key to this. She knew it with every fiber of her being. Reagan had overseen the surrogates.

Too bad he was dead.

Kayla's gut told her that there was something mighty suspicious about his sudden death four years ago. No one seemed to know where he was buried. Hopefully, his files would hold some answers. All she had to do was find them. The storage facility that housed retired files from numerous physicians in the Tucson and Phoenix area and that had Reagan's files listed in their inventory could not explain the missing files. They were simply gone. Another dead end.

"I'm taking your backpack to the car," Kayla called to Jazz. That was her official ten-minute warning. Once the backpack was in the Jeep the clock was ticking down. 7:15. Kayla liked being on her way no later than 7:30. That gave her time to drop off her daughter and get to the office before eight.

"I'm brushing my teeth!" Jazz shouted from down the hall.

It was the same routine every morning. Jazz took her time with breakfast, which was okay with Kayla, then finally decided upon one of the three outfits they'd gone round and round about the night before. Narrowing it down to three without an all-out war was the best the two headstrong ladies could do before bedtime.

Just something else Jazz had inherited from Kayla's side of the family, a stubborn streak a mile wide.

By ten-minute warning time her daughter was generally ready to roll with the exception of brushing her teeth and one final check to see that she had everything she would need for the day.

Outside, the sun had peeked over the hills and chased away the lingering dusk. A few shadows still hung around, mostly from the neighbor's two-story house and the scattering of trees between the two homes. Kayla breathed in the crisp morning air. She loved it here. Felt safe in a way big-city living could never offer. Alex and Tory might like the faster pace of the city. Rainy's career and marriage had taken her to Tucson. Josie lived wherever the Air Force assigned her. Darcy had moved to a small town to escape her abusive husband but Kayla suspected she would move to a bigger city and expand her P.I. business now that he'd been arrested. Kayla would take her small-town home over anything else.

She tossed the backpack into the front passenger seat but hesitated before closing the door. Chill bumps whispered over her skin. She frowned. Shook herself. What the hell?

Kayla couldn't say what it was for sure, but she had the almost overwhelming sensation that someone was watching her. She resisted the urge to whip around and survey the neighbors' yard.

She shook herself again. Had to be her imagination running away with her. But then, this wasn't the first time she'd felt someone watching her. Each time she'd rationalized the episode away. Now she wondered if Hadden was lurking out here in her yard somewhere. If so, she might just have to kick his fine-looking backside.

Slowly she closed the door and turned back toward the house. Nothing moved. As she headed in that direction she covertly scanned the yard, hers as well as the neighbors'. Nothing.

Still, that insistent internal alarm wouldn't let go.

The front door slammed.

Kayla jerked at the sound, her eyes instantly going to the small covered porch.

"I locked the door!" Jazz flew down the steps. "Don't forget I have choir practice after school."

Kayla let go the breath she'd been holding. "Got it."

Forcing the disturbing feeling from her mind, she dropped her daughter off at school and drove to the office.

The satellite station that served Athens wasn't very large. Just a couple of small rooms that shared an even smaller lobby and bathroom and a sort of conference room designated so merely by virtue of the long table and mismatched chairs sitting about. A coffeepot and soft drink machine occupied one corner of the lobby. Shirley, who served as a receptionist and a liaison to the community, kept a tidy desk in the center of the lobby. Five upholstered chairs and a couple of large plants took up the rest of the space.

Kayla shared one of the offices with her partner while a second office served as a workroom for files.

"Good morning, Shirley." Kayla offered her usual smile and saluted the middle-age lady with her take-out coffee cup. It wasn't that Shirley didn't make good coffee, it was just that Jim usually beat Shirley into the office and his coffee made paint thinner smell good. Kayla'd never worked up the nerve to try it.

"Morning, L.T." Shirley said this with nothing more than a cursory glance over her morning newspaper. "Heard about the excitement yesterday. Thought you had the day off."

"L.T." was Shirley's way of showing off that she'd spent twenty-plus years as a military wife. She re-

ferred to Kayla as her husband had the lieutenants in
the Army. Her remarks about yesterday's little bust
were nothing more than roundabout inquiries as to
what Kayla had been doing working on her day off
without her partner. Which also meant that Jim and
Shirley had talked. The two considered her their er-
rant cub that needed guidance as well as protection.

"You know how it goes," Kayla offered noncha-
lantly, but there was nothing casual about the way she
braced herself for facing her partner. He'd already
said plenty on the phone. He'd no doubt saved his
best disciplinary remarks for this morning when they
would be face-to-face.

In reality Kayla outranked Jim, but he'd been in
this business twenty years longer than her so to his
way of thinking, he was senior.

Couldn't argue that. Most of the time, anyway.

"Good morning, Jim," she said, all smiles and as
chipper as hell as she strode into their office. If he
wanted a fight he'd have to start it.

He growled something that resembled "morning",
then folded his newspaper into a wadlike mass and
tossed it aside.

"So tell me again how you got this anonymous tip."

Kayla sat down at the desk that faced her partner's.
She propped her feet on the edge and crossed them
at the ankles, then took a long swallow from her coffee. Might as well let him stew another few seconds.
She swallowed and made a contented sound in her
throat. Jim's left eyebrow arched, indicating his patience had reached an end.

Eventually she shrugged. "I was at home minding my own business and the phone rang. End of story." The statement sounded like a truly bad lie but it was the God's truth. She understood that it was unusual. But a good cop took tips anywhere she could get them. They didn't always pan out but this one had.

His elbows propped on the arms of his chair, Jim steepled his fingers. "It didn't cross your mind that the whole scenario went down a little too smoothly?"

"Sure it did." She sipped her designer coffee blend. "I figure the snitch was someone the perp had pissed off. Somebody who wanted revenge."

"Or maybe someone who wanted to throw the cops off his own scent."

That had entered her mind as well. "It's possible."

"Investigator Devon says one of the guys is trying to cop a plea. He wants immunity for what he knows."

Kayla sat up, her county-issue shoes slapping against the tile floor. "Does he have anything that important?"

Jim kept his expression closed but Kayla didn't miss the flicker of a smile around one corner of his mouth. "He says he can give us the number one player, who deals not only in bikes but cars."

Now that would be a major coup. "We should go down and see what he has to say." Anticipation bubbled like an uncorked bottle of champagne.

Jim shook his head and held up one hand. "Can't do that. Devon doesn't want us anywhere near this guy. Apparently the perp's still a little ticked off that you shot him. Even threatened to sue for excessive force."

Kayla swore. "It wasn't like I was aiming for his artery. I was just trying to keep him from running. If I'd wanted him dead I would have aimed a few feet higher."

"He could walk," Jim said, his tone as well as his expression solemn. "If he rolls over on a player that big, he could walk." His gaze leveled on hers. "There's always the possibility that he'll want to get even."

Kayla absorbed the implications of that statement. In this line of work there was always that possibility. But it didn't make the prospect any easier to deal with, especially not with a young daughter at home. "Is Devon going to keep us informed?" Investigator Steve Devon was generally very good about keeping the cops who made the collars up to speed, but this time could prove different.

"I'm sure he will." Jim leaned forward, braced his arms on his desk. "Tell me how your friend Detective Hadden got involved."

She'd known that one was coming. Even an old dog like Harkey could get jealous when someone invaded his territory. Kayla would need to tread carefully here. Yesterday she'd done what she had to do, and today she had to smooth her partner's ruffled feathers. Jim would have done the same thing if the situation had been reversed. For that she felt no guilt.

The big difference between the two of them was that Jim would have found her yesterday. He wouldn't have given up until he did. Maybe she hadn't tried as hard as she should have to locate him. She'd wanted those guys. Wanted them bad. Had the fire burning in her belly to finally bring them down adversely affected her judgment?

Maybe she had stayed in this job too long. Gotten too cocky. Too self-assured. It happened to the best.

Just something else she'd have to consider. Her years at Athena Academy had planted the yearning for growth, for advancement, deep inside her. Maybe she was fooling herself by thinking she could be happy staying at this level any longer. When she considered the high-profile careers of her fellow Cassandras she had to admit that even Darcy's self-made private investigations business and covert support of abused women took a big leap out of the box.

Was complacency Kayla's real problem? Professionally as well as personally? She didn't want to believe there was any truth to that theory, but could she risk being wrong? One glance at Jim's expectant expression and she knew she'd better get him placated first.

The infirmary at Athena Academy looked deserted. Giving Nurse Betsy Stone grace, it was lunchtime. Still, Kayla had called and left a message. It seemed that Betsy Stone either never got her messages or chose to ignore them.

The latter fit more conveniently into Kayla's profile of the woman. She was avoiding further questioning.

Kayla shuffled around the room and considered

reviewing more of the files, but it felt like a monumental waste of time. For three months she had been using every opportunity to look into the files.

It wasn't always easy. Not that Christine or the school hadn't cooperated. To the contrary, Christine had pretty much given Kayla carte blanche. But it took time to go through decades of files. Thousands of young women had passed through these walls. There were only so many chances within a given week. Kayla did have a job and a daughter, both of which had to come first.

Still, she had spent several hours each week during the past three months reviewing and analyzing data. And what had she learned? Not much.

Rainy had been an outstanding student. Physically, she had been an excellent candidate, if one were looking for a good specimen on which to experiment. But why here? Who was responsible for allowing it to happen?

The first question was a no-brainer. Here, because attendees of Athena Academy were the cream of the cream of the crop. The second question needed answering.

The invitation Jazz had received in the mail flashed through her mind. Definitely she would not rest until she had solved this puzzle.

According to Cleo Patra, the one surrogate they had located alive in the investigation, she had been under Dr. Reagan's care in Phoenix. According to what Kayla had learned so far, Reagan was indeed dead. His files were who knows where. Kayla desperately wanted to find those files. She had a feeling that answers lay within those medical notes.

And what of this Lab 33? Did Josie or her sister, Diana, who was in Army Intelligence, dare look more deeply into that aspect? That kind of digging could get them killed. There were elements, government-sponsored ones, that were never supposed to be exposed. Shadow and black-bag operations.

Kayla huffed out a breath and admitted defeat. She had no alternative except to go to the files room and take up where she'd left off. It was all she had at this point. Somewhere in those files there had to be something. All she needed was one little lead and maybe it would take her the distance. Rainy couldn't have been the only one taken advantage of.

The hour she'd given herself to devote to the case had flown by when a sound jerked Kayla's attention from the mound of manila folders. Someone had entered the infirmary.

She hoped Nurse Stone had returned from lunch or some errand. She could let Jim know she needed a few more minutes if she got the chance to grill Stone again. The idea that Betsy Stone could have left for vacation since Athena was closed for December pinged her thoughts.

"Kayla, here you are."

Christine Evans. Principal and friend. A friend with secrets, however.

Kayla relaxed from her alert status. "Looking through a few more files."

Christine nodded but didn't meet Kayla's gaze. "Have you spoken with Betsy?"

It was more the way she asked the question than the question itself. Like Betsy Stone, Christine was hiding something. Kayla narrowed her gaze and scrutinized the woman. She had known Christine for many years. No one could ask for a better school principal. As headmistress of Athena Academy since its inception more than twenty years ago, Christine had devoted herself completely to the school and its students.

What could she possibly be hiding?

"No," Kayla said in answer to her question. "She always seems to be out of pocket when I come looking for her."

Christine's gaze did meet hers then. "Kayla, you must know how busy Nurse Stone is when the students are on campus. One nurse with two hundred adolescent girls. Surely you remember."

Kayla nodded, acknowledging the point. "But what about now?" The girls were gone for winter break. "Why is it I can never nail her down now?"

Christine shrugged, her gaze scooting away once more. "There's a lot of catching up to do at the end of a session. Just ask any of the teachers or other staff members."

"She hasn't left town as far as you know?"

"Not that I'm aware of. Why don't I make it a point to have her call you?" The smile that made an appearance didn't reach the principal's eyes.

"Sure, why not?" Kayla started to leave the issue

at that but the need to learn the truth wouldn't let her. "Christine, do you think what happened to Rainy had anything to do with Dr. Bradford?"

Christine paled as she usually did whenever the subject of Rainy came up.

"I don't see how it could."

Kayla drew in a deep breath and released it as she settled onto the edge of Nurse Stone's cluttered desk. "You told me that the two of you had parted ways on a sour note." Kayla's brow furrowed as if she'd lapsed into deep concentration. "I believe you said that he was harassing Nurse Stone and that you recommended he not be called back as a guest lecturer." Athena Academy searched far and wide for ways to broaden the student learning experience. Guest lecturers from around the world were a regular feature of the curriculum.

"That's correct," Christine allowed, her tone, her entire demeanor closed, guarded. "When Nurse Stone reported to me that Dr. Bradford had behaved inappropriately toward her, I immediately sought action to see that he never returned."

"If he behaved inappropriately toward a staff member, how can you be certain he didn't do the same with students?" The notion made Kayla shiver with revulsion.

"Of course he didn't harass any of the students!"

There was the reaction. Christine was incensed. Offended even.

"But his behavior wasn't above reproach," Kayla cut in. "Why else would you have asked that he not be allowed to return?"

For several seconds they stared at each other. Silent. Kayla was certain there was more. Then Christine broke. Vulnerability flashed in her good eye.

"All right."

Christine turned away, clearly unable to look at Kayla as she uttered whatever confession she was about to make. "I wasn't completely honest with you before, Kayla." She spread her hands in defeat. "I didn't want to tell you."

Kayla pushed off the desk and went to her. Whatever she had to say it wasn't going to be easy. She needed to know that Kayla was only trying to help.

"Just tell me the truth, Christine," she said gently as she placed one hand on her arm. "I know you. Whatever it is it couldn't have been your fault."

Christine's head came up, her suspiciously bright gaze collided with Kayla's. "Well…yes it was. What happened to Rainy may have been entirely due to my foolishness."

The earth shifted slightly beneath Kayla but she held herself steady, kept her touch light. "Tell me what happened." It was all she could do to keep the shock out of her voice.

"Carl Bradford and I had an affair." She closed her eyes and visibly fought to control her emotions. "I didn't mean for it to happen. But I felt so alone. Changing careers, in charge of this whole, new school…I needed someone. He was a handsome man." Her eyes opened, sought Kayla's. "He knew all the right things to say and do to make me feel like a woman."

Kayla nodded, genuinely understanding. Though she'd been much younger than Christine and her motives had clearly been different, she did understand. Hadn't she sought solace in the arms of the man who'd fathered her child?

"Bradford never harassed Betsy. That was the story I told the board to save face. I caught them together one night." She shook her head, her features going hard. "I'd been so stupid. We argued. I told him he could never come back."

So Betsy Stone had been involved with Bradford. Yet she'd gone along with Christine's story, saying he'd made a sexual move on her and she'd reported it to the principal to ensure he was sent away.

"I was jealous," Christine admitted. "At that moment the only interest I had on my mind was my own."

Kayla squeezed her arm reassuringly. "You made a mistake. We all do." She, of all people, knew.

Christine was shaking her head again. "You don't understand. Before I found them together, I had caught him going through the files. He said he was pulling together some information on the brightest students to use in a statistical paper about private schools." She pressed her hands to her face, looking nothing like the tough former Army officer and strict taskmaster Kayla knew her to be. "I should have known better. I should have told someone." She lifted her tear-filled gaze to Kayla's. "What if I let this happen to Rainy? What if that's what Bradford was looking for? An egg-mining candidate? Dear God!"

Kayla turned this new angle over in her mind. As

much as Kayla didn't want Christine to shoulder this burden alone, she suspected that Christine was right on at least one score. Bradford had been looking for something. Was he connected to Dr. Reagan? Like Reagan, Bradford had once run his own private practice in Phoenix, but it had closed years ago. And no one knew where Bradford had gone. But she damn sure intended to nail down Betsy Stone. She was the only link they had to Reagan and Bradford, whether she admitted knowing about any unethical dealings or not.

"Christine." Kayla drew back, held the woman firmly by the shoulders. "I have to talk to Betsy. She may very well know what Bradford was doing and who he was working with."

Christine nodded. "I understand." She let go a shaky breath. "The way I see it, we're going to have to trap her into a meeting." Christine's watery gaze leveled on Kayla's. "I'll help you. I'll do anything you need me to do."

Christine told Kayla what she could about Betsy Stone's schedule. Betsy might not know anything that would help, but one way or another Kayla intended to find out.

When she would have left, Christine stopped her. "Kayla, I know you must have gotten Jazz's invitation by now."

Kayla turned back to her, unprepared to discuss the matter just now. "I did."

Christine's hands knotted together in front of her. "Whatever my past sins," she urged, "please don't hold them against this school. Jazz deserves this opportunity the same way you did. You know what attendance at this school could mean for her future."

Kayla managed a smile. "We're going to talk about it."

As Kayla left the Athena campus she wouldn't allow herself to consider that Jazz's invitation might be a prod for her to leave this investigation alone. No way. This school was too important to too many powerful people. They would never invite a student for any reason other than a legitimate one. Athena Academy wanted Jazz. There was no second-guessing that conclusion.

The only question that remained was if Kayla was ready for her daughter to take that kind of step.

Kayla called Shirley to let her know she'd decided to stop at home for a sandwich before heading back to the office. The morning had been long and emotionally draining. Kayla wanted to recharge before dealing with the afternoon.

But that wasn't going to happen.

The red SUV sitting against the curb between her house and the next didn't give her much of a pause on first glance. But when she parked in her driveway she saw that someone waited for her on her front steps.

It only took one look for her to recognize her unexpected visitor.

Mike Bridges.

Jazz's father.

Chapter 4

Kayla couldn't move. She sat in her Jeep, staring at the man who'd broken her young, foolish heart more than a decade before. She hadn't seen him since.

Why was he here?

Her heart started to pound like a drum.

Jazz.

He was here to see his daughter.

Josie had warned her that he was asking about Jazz. She had worked under Mike's supervision recently, and when they'd figured out their mutual connection—after some very rocky circumstances that still incensed Kayla—Mike had asked Josie about Jazz. Somehow Kayla had thought he'd just go away, the same as he had all those years ago.

Clearly she'd been wrong.

He was here.

In the flesh.

Her hand shaking, she opened the door and stepped out of the vehicle. Her legs felt suddenly rubbery.

Kayla swallowed hard and summoned her courage. Why was she letting him do this? He hadn't even spoken yet, and already she felt afraid. Afraid of what he might say…what he might do.

No way.

Fury, mostly at herself, blasted like a furnace deep inside her. There was nothing for her to be afraid of. Jazz was her daughter. Mike had merely been the sperm donor. The few dollars he sent each month was a pittance, a pathetic attempt to assuage his conscience. He had no right to make her feel this way. No right at all. Especially after what he'd almost done to Josie.

"What do you want?" The words came out every bit as cold as she'd intended. He flinched. A rush of glee went through her. She couldn't help it. She wanted him to suffer. Wanted him to feel just a smidgen of the uncertainty and fear she'd felt twelve years ago when she'd been young and pregnant and unmarried. And so afraid.

He pushed to his feet. Managed a smile, though it in no way resembled the high-wattage charmers she remembered. "I apologize for showing up unannounced, Kayla." He shrugged those broad shoulders. "I thought if I called to let you know I was coming you wouldn't be home. I didn't know what shift you worked, so I decided to wait around until you showed."

She planted her hands on her hips and told him the truth. "You figured right. Look at it from my side, Bridges. Why would I want to see you?"

He nodded once, the move was jerky but humble all the same. It just didn't mesh with his personality, but then time changed people. Had Mike Bridges really changed? Josie had told her about the trouble she'd had with him. That he would make a pass at one of his female subordinates like that—almost getting her kicked out of the Air Force in the process—indicated to Kayla that he hadn't changed at all.

"I guess Lockworth told you about our run-in," he suggested, evidently recognizing the disgusted look in Kayla's eyes.

"She did." Kayla felt absolutely no sympathy for his having lost his command. According to Josie he'd been transferred from Palmdale, California, to Nellis Air Force Base over in Nevada. Chances of him being promoted beyond major after that fiasco were about nil. Could he have finally learned his lesson?

Kayla wasn't about to wager Jazz's feelings on the probability. Not with his record.

Mike looked away.

As much as she didn't want to, Kayla couldn't help studying his features. He hadn't changed that much. Had a bit of a leaner edge about his profile. More manly, less boyish. His hair was still thick and dark, his eyes that mischievous hazel she saw in her child's every single day. He looked comfortable in his civilian attire, jeans and a simple gray T-shirt with the Air Force logo emblazoned across his chest. The bomber jacket was well-worn leather and suited his *Top Gun* image. There was no denying that Mike Bridges was a handsome man. He just didn't understand the meaning of responsibility and commitment.

The sole commitment he'd made was to the military. To being a pilot. Until his recent run-in with Josie, he'd apparently been on the upwardly mobile trek. A revered Air Force pilot. Too bad he'd screwed it up doing what he did best, attempting to take advantage of a woman. Not that those kinds of maneuvers were anything new, but this time he'd gotten caught.

Kayla couldn't pretend complete innocence in what had happened between her and Mike, but she had been painfully young. He should have recognized that fact. Instead he'd taken her word that she was eighteen. The rest, as they say, was history. He'd left, she'd borne his child.

"Look." His gaze settled on hers once more. Incredibly, the depth of regret she saw there surprised her. "I know I haven't always done the right thing." He lifted one shoulder in a weary attempt at another gesture of uncertainty. "I can't promise I will in the future. But I can't let my daughter grow up without getting to know her. Being a part of her life." He shook his head, stared at the ground. "I just can't do it."

She knew the deal. His career had stalled and he was scrambling for some kind of emotional purchase.

Kayla tamped down the hint of empathy that welled in her chest. *Stupid, Ryan,* she scolded. "She'll be twelve next month, Mike. I don't know that I want to throw this at her right now. Adolescence is a tough time." *You're too late,* she didn't add. Couldn't he see that? He should have had this epiphany years ago.

But would she have liked it any better then than she did now? Probably not.

"I only have a few days before I have to head back to Nevada," he went on. "Think it over. I want to know her. I have the right to know her."

He said the last with a kind of conviction that sent fear trickling down Kayla's spine.

"Is that a threat?" She searched his eyes, his face, looking for signs of just how far he intended to take this.

He blew out a big breath and scrubbed one hand through his hair. "I don't want to do it this way." That hazel gaze turned dead serious and bored straight into hers. "But I will if I have to. I want to see her, Kayla. I want to get to know her. I'm her father. You can't keep me shut out."

A new charge of fury scorched through her. "Shut you out?" She stabbed an accusing finger at him. "You were the one who couldn't get away from here fast enough. You were the one who didn't look back."

"But I kept up the child support payments," he countered. "I did my duty."

Oh, yeah, there was that. His *duty.* "Being a parent is about a hell of a lot more than doing your patriotic duty, Major Bridges," she railed. "Who sat up with her at night when she was sick? Helped with homework? Took her for dance lessons?" She hitched a thumb at her own chest. "Me. I've been here for her every moment of her life. Where were you?"

"Helping to keep this country safe and free," he snapped. "Someone has to do it."

"Do all the other Air Force dads abandon their kids? Their responsibilities?" The very idea that he would use that excuse infuriated her all the more.

His gaze narrowed accusingly. "You didn't want me involved, Kayla. Not really. And you know it. You had your family. You didn't need me."

The moment of silence stretched. Maybe he was right. He'd admitted he didn't want to get married. She'd been devastated. Hadn't wanted anything else to do with him after that. Kayla had turned to her family and...never looked back.

"I still don't need you," she couldn't resist informing him.

Mike surveyed her uniform. "I can see that." He moistened his lips, whether from necessity or design, she didn't know. Didn't matter. She wasn't taking the bait. "You've done real well, Kayla. But I knew you would. Jazz is lucky to have you for a mother."

"Flattery will get you nowhere," she retorted before she could stop herself. She didn't want to hear his compliments. Didn't trust him to mean what he said. She'd believed in him once and he'd let her down. Or maybe she'd let herself down. Either way, she wasn't going to travel that road again.

They'd been bad for each other all those years

ago, and there was no reason to believe things had changed since. And yet, this was not about her or Mike, this was about Jazz. She had a right to know her father. As much as Kayla would like to pretend the need could be ignored she knew it couldn't. She'd read plenty of stories about children growing up and going out in search of a biological parent they'd never known. Why put her daughter through that? Surely she and Mike could work out something.

It wasn't as if Kayla had kept him a secret. She and Jazz talked about him. Jazz had started asking questions when she was five. Kayla had told as much of the truth as she felt comfortable with, saying Jazz's father was a dedicated soldier who had chosen duty over family. Her daughter seemed to accept that explanation.

"Kayla, don't do this," he urged, his voice soft and cajoling. He evidently took her silence for an outright refusal.

As much as she didn't want to be swayed by his needs, and certainly not by his charm, how could she say no? Jazz deserved this opportunity.

"All right. But we do this my way."

He nodded, albeit reluctantly. "Does she know about me?"

Kayla rolled her eyes. "Of course. How do you think I explained where she came from?"

He smiled, the expression visibly relieved. "I'm grateful for that."

She shrugged, almost too prideful to admit the next. "I have that picture we had made together at the spring carnival. She knows who you are."

He blinked, but not quickly enough to conceal the surprise that glittered briefly in his eyes. "That little thing?"

"I had it enlarged to a five-by-seven. It's not that bad." The picture had actually been an accurate depiction of their time together. Mike had been standing behind her with his arms wrapped around her and the huge teddy bear he'd just won. In the photo they were both smiling, unabashedly happy smiles. The image of him captured on the film had been precisely the way she'd seen him during that short affair. A single moment of happiness trapped in a mere photograph. Two young people too crazy in lust to think clearly.

She had been just as much at fault in the whole mess as Mike, hadn't she? Kayla felt uncomfortable making that admission. And even so, could she trust him with her daughter's heart? God help her, maybe this wasn't such a good idea.

"When can I see her?"

Fear attacked Kayla all over again. "Let's not be hasty," she countered. She rubbed her damp palms on her hips and tried not to look as nervous as she suddenly felt. "We have to go slowly with this. Let me talk to her first."

Irritation sparked in his eyes once more. "I don't want you putting me off. I want—"

She held up her hands to ward off whatever he would have said next. "I'm not putting you off. But this is pretty sudden, you have to admit."

He didn't agree, but he didn't disagree.

"Let me talk to her. I'll call you tonight and set something up. That's fair, isn't it?"

When he was slow in responding, she added, "After all, her feelings are primary here, right?"

Kayla held her breath until she saw the signs of capitulation in his posture. Thank God.

"Let me give you my cell number."

She withdrew the notepad she kept in her jacket pocket for jotting down info at crime scenes and from perp interviews and took his cell phone number as well as the name of the hotel in Phoenix where he would be staying for a few days.

"I'll call you tonight."

He took an abrupt step in her direction. Kayla's breath caught in her throat.

"Don't forget, Kayla," he reminded her. "If I don't hear from you tonight, I'll be back tomorrow."

She didn't have to ask this time. She knew the statement was a threat.

Before she could pull together a proper comeback a sedan pulled up behind Mike's SUV. Recognition flared instantly.

Hadden.

Perfect.

Peter Hadden emerged from his vehicle looking as he always did, rumpled and sexy as hell. Colombo meets James Bond. He strolled right up to where Kayla and Mike stood on the sidewalk in front of her house as if he lived there.

Despite her worries where Mike was concerned, Kayla suddenly wondered if Hadden brought news

regarding their joint investigation. Something besides his insistence that Marshall Carrington was
some sort of smuggler.

"Kayla," Hadden said with a dip of his head.

She blinked, startled. She couldn't recall once his
having called her by her first name. "Hadden," she
returned. "What's up?"

Just when she felt certain things couldn't get any
stranger, his gaze shifted from her to the man standing nearby. "I don't believe we've met." He thrust out
his hand. "I'm Peter Hadden, homicide, Tucson."

"Major Mike Bridges." Mike gave Hadden's hand
a brisk shake, his demeanor stiff, noticeably tense.
"Jasmine's father," he pitched in with a distinct edge
in his voice.

If the last surprised Hadden he showed no sign of
it, but then he was a good detective, well versed in
the proper methods of negotiations. *Never let the
enemy see you sweat.*

"I hope I'm not interrupting anything," Hadden said
with a smile. He looked from Kayla to Mike and back.

"Actually, Mike was just leaving." Her gaze was
direct when she addressed the man who wanted to invade her daughter's life. "I'll call you tonight."

The familiar glitter that ignited in Mike's eyes
shocked her just a little. She knew that look. Had seen
it before. Anytime she and Mike had gone out all
those years ago he had been fiercely possessive. A
single glance from another man would set him off.

Jealousy?

How could he be jealous?

Then the answer dawned on her. If he believed she and Hadden were a couple, Mike would see Hadden as competition where his daughter was concerned. His jealousy had nothing to do with Kayla. The very idea was ludicrous.

Mike acknowledged her promise with a nod. "If I miss you tonight," he warned, "I'll see you tomorrow."

And then he was gone.

She watched him drive away, the *1Pilot* vanity license plate reinforcing what she knew deep in her heart. He might be feeling humble just now due to recent events in his personal as well as professional life, but Mike Bridges would never, ever change.

When his sporty red SUV had disappeared down the street, Kayla turned her attention back to Hadden.

"What're you doing here?"

"I called your office. Shirley said you were here." His gaze still lingered in the direction the SUV had taken. "I didn't know he was still around."

The comment on top of his sidestep around her question ticked off Kayla. "Why would you?" It wasn't like they had gotten to know each other on that level. They'd locked horns more often than not on Rainy's case. Other than her ridiculous physical attraction to the man, she wasn't even sure she liked him.

He shrugged. Was it her imagination or was that gesture suddenly rampant among the men in her life?

"I thought you were raising Jasmine alone." His gaze settled on hers now and there was no way to miss the sincerity there. He really wanted to know the situation.

Kayla wasn't sure she could take any more surprises today. "This is the first time I've seen Jazz's father in more than twelve years," she admitted.

Hadden's brow furrowed as if the thoughts whirling around in his head disturbed him. "He's not giving you any trouble, is he?"

She sighed. Just more proof of her suspicions that Hadden was a threat to her solitary state. He was always looking out for others. "The jury's still out on that one," she admitted. Again, she didn't know why she confessed anything to Hadden. Maybe it was simply the idea of us against him...an ally in this battle with Mike. Would she need an ally? Could it really get dirty?

The possibility was there. She was all too aware of that glaring fact. *If I miss you tonight, I'll see you tomorrow.* His warning rang in her ears like Sunday morning church bells, but with a distinctly more menacing message.

The idea that he might take legal steps if she didn't cooperate was a risk she couldn't afford to take. If she worked something out with him, on her terms, maybe it wouldn't come to that. She could hope. Even the remote notion of her daughter being forced to go spend time with her father, a man she didn't even know, in a place she'd never been before, ripped Kayla's heart right out of her chest. But it could happen. As a cop she was well aware of that fact. She'd seen it happen.

She had to talk to her family, to Jazz. And somehow she had to work up the courage to call Mike back this very night. She couldn't let anything get in the way of resolving this issue. Allowing him to take the ball and run with it would be a mistake of mammoth proportions.

"Well, here's something that might cheer you up," Hadden offered.

Kayla stared up at him, doubtful that anything he could say just now would lift the dark cloud of utter depression from her head.

"Dr. Deborah Halburg is back in town."

Kayla's heart kicked into a faster rhythm. "When? Where has she been all this time?"

Deborah Halburg had served as Rainy's gynecologist for more than two years. When Rainy had died, Dr. Halburg had been out of town, unreachable. Kayla desperately needed any and all information on Rainy that the doctor might have.

"Apparently her father was some kind of missionary serving somewhere in the far East. He fell ill and she's been there with him for the past four months. He died two weeks ago. She's back now and playing catch-up."

Dr. Halburg's receptionist and nurse had not been able to provide any helpful insights into Rainy's case. Rainy's files were missing—had probably been stolen—and only Dr. Halburg herself could provide the necessary details Kayla sought. Kayla had been waiting for the doctor's return.

Anticipation burned through Kayla now. Any new evidence could be helpful.

"When can we see her?" She used the term "we"

since she felt confident Hadden wasn't about to miss out on whatever Halburg had to say. No point pretending he wasn't involved. Trying to rationalize his motivation for continuing to investigate the case was futile as well. Early on he'd made his conclusions clear—he thought Rainy's death was an accident. Kayla knew better, but she could not discuss with him the things she and the Cassandras had learned.

Not yet anyway.

"We can see her today." He glanced at his watch. "She told me to come by before her clinic closed for the day. I thought you'd want to come along. I cleared it with your boss."

Kayla swore silently.

He'd driven all the way from Tucson to dangle this carrot in front of her, knowing she couldn't refuse. Hadden was up to something. Part of her wanted his showing up in person to be about their attraction—but she suspected it related more closely to his personal agenda for the case against Marshall. Still, she did want to see Dr. Halburg ASAP. And talking to Halburg over the phone might cause her to miss something crucial that the doctor's expression would reveal. She'd have to get her sister to pick up Jazz. Dammit. She hated doing that too often. Not that Mary minded. She didn't. Her boys, eight and ten, looked up to Jazz like a big sister. They all loved Jazz and Jazz loved staying over. But Kayla preferred all the quality time she could rake and scrape with her daughter. Not to mention she had to talk to Jazz about her father. There was no getting out of that one.

Then there was the invitation to Athena.

"I have to check with my sister to see if she can pick up my daughter." If Jazz got her homework done by the time Kayla returned they might still have time to talk. It would be late after a trip to Tucson and back, but as long as she called Mike tonight that's all that mattered. He hadn't specified a time. God, she hated that she had to jump at his command. Renewed ire twisted in her belly.

Hadden gestured to his sedan. "I'll drive."

Kayla didn't like the way he studied her. Could he see how vulnerable she felt right now? She hoped not. But she had a feeling he suspected a great deal more than he would dream of saying. Great. All she needed was him prying into her life. It was bad enough he'd insisted on participating in this investigation.

She made the call to her sister, locked up her house and settled into the front passenger seat of his utilitarian sedan. Maybe *bad* wasn't the right word, she mused as she analyzed Hadden's profile. *Bad* applied to the bike thieves she'd collared yesterday. *Bad* was what happened to Rainy. This thing between Kayla and Hadden wasn't really bad, it was simply unfortunate.

Unfortunate because she felt certain she would never be able to open herself up to the possibly of hurt once more. How could she ever hope to have a satisfying relationship with a man if fear kept her from opening up?

Hadden braked at a light and glanced in her direction. Too late to look away. He'd caught her staring at him. Her cheeks scalded. He simply smiled, showing off those appealing dimples.

"I'm not that complicated," he said bluntly.

"What's that supposed to mean?" She hadn't intended to sound so pissed off, but then she was…at herself mostly.

He reached over and smoothed her brow with the tips of his fingers. The crackle of electricity his touch generated heated her skin, sent her tummy into an acrobatic act.

"You look as if you're having a difficult time figuring me out." He smiled patiently at her and turned his attention back to the task of driving. "All you have to do is ask when you want to know something."

Her humiliation dissipated instantly in light of the surprise that claimed her. Confident, wasn't he? She'd just see how deep that confidence went. "Why do you keep coming back?" she asked with all the bluntness he'd used before. "I know you think Rainy's death was an accident, why trouble yourself with my personal investigation?" Why drive two and a half hours to pick me up? she didn't add.

He considered her question for a bit and yet his relaxed posture didn't change. He remained calm, collected. Irritatingly so. Her own rising tension had her pulse skipping, had her muscles flexing with tension.

"I've checked up on you, Lieutenant Ryan," he began.

She restrained the need to demand an explanation of his simple, however complex, announcement. She'd checked him out, too. He lived in Tucson, in a comfortable neighborhood. He dressed well, had an excellent reputation. Not a single mark against him professionally, or personally. Perfect credit record. No mistakes in his past, unlike hers. He was straight as an arrow, dependable…all the things she'd failed to consider when she fell for Mike all those years ago. Somehow, Hadden's stellar record made her uneasy. *He's too good to be true.*

Because not for a second did Hadden seem boring. Not at all. There was a mystique about him that his records couldn't reveal, something simmering beneath all that composure. A composure she kept wanting to ruffle.

Hadden glanced at her, perhaps surprised that she hadn't responded. He continued, "You're a good cop. Your superiors have recommended you for the position of investigator twice already and yet you've chosen to remain in your current position."

"I have my reasons."

He cast a knowing glance in her direction. "Your daughter."

It wasn't as if the conclusion required a degree in rocket science. "That's right."

"You pride yourself in your work, go the extra mile without hesitation or question." He flicked another analyzing but brief stare her way. "Like following up on that tip about those bike thieves."

She'd thought about Jim's hypothesis that the tip had been a distraction of some sort and was now certain it had been. Either someone on the team got scared or pissed off or someone wanted this particular ring of pirates off their beat. Whatever, the case belonged to the county investigator now. But she hadn't forgotten, nor would she pretend it didn't matter to her anymore. Athens was her community, and anything that affected those under her jurisdiction kept her attention.

"So you think I'm onto something in Rainy's case?" she ventured, veering back to the original question.

"If you weren't you wouldn't be wasting your time." His smile broadened into a grin. "She was your friend, you miss her. But you're too smart and savvy to let your personal feelings invade your professional reason."

"Then you believe she was murdered as well."

Another of those sidelong assessments sent heat rolling through her limbs. "I believe *you* believe she was murdered. And that's good enough for me."

But was that his real motivation for staying on top of her, so to speak?

"It's about Marshall, isn't it?" However careful he thought he'd been, Kayla understood, at least to some degree, where his motivation originated. If Rainy had been murdered, and Marshall was guilty of smuggling, chances were there was a connection. If you didn't know what Kayla knew. Fury mounted inside her. She didn't like being used.

"In part," he allowed.

Kayla nodded. She'd thought as much. "Let me clarify this for you," she went on. "Marshall Carrington is a good man. There is no way he's capable of what you're proposing. His wife, my friend," she re-iterated, "was murdered. I'm one hundred percent on that. And I'm not going to let this go until I know who is responsible for her death." She snapped her mouth shut on the *and* that almost popped out. The part about Rainy's possible child or children was off-limits. There were too many unanswered questions.

Hadden nodded perceptively. "That would mean you've already established motive."

Kayla's tension ratcheted up a notch or two. "I have a theory or two."

The detective chuckled. "Don't tease me, Ryan. You have the why, it's only the who that's driving you nuts."

There were things she couldn't share with him no matter how perceptive the good detective proved. Her suspicions about Athena Academy were still that, suspicions. She needed cold hard facts before she marred the school's reputation more than Shannon Conner already had.

"I tell you what," Hadden cut into her musings, "you tell me why you think your friend was murdered and I'll tell you why I believe her husband is a smuggler."

Far too intrigued to ignore the offer, Kayla chose her words carefully. "Rainy's autopsy showed her appendix was intact and her ovaries were badly scarred."

"Is that why she was seeing Halburg?"

"Probably. About the scarred ovaries, I mean."

"What's the big deal about her appendix being intact?"

Kayla wet her lips and forged ahead. "When she

was a girl, she got appendicitis. At least, that's what she was told when she got sick and had to have an operation. Her medical records showed as much. But it was a mistake—or a lie."

Hadden considered that information a little too long for Kayla's comfort. "And?"

"I believe her illness and surgery were staged so that someone could mine her eggs. I found evidence that she was researching egg mining. We—" she glanced at him "—Rainy's other friends and I, believe that she'd learned the truth and was going to tell us about it the night she died. Someone wanted to keep her quiet."

That was about as revealing as she could be.

"This mysterious operation happened while she was a student at Athena Academy didn't it?"

Apparently she hadn't been quite vague enough.

Kayla knew without asking that he was drawing conclusions based on Shannon Conner's exposé that had cited hideous experiments having been conducted on Athena students.

"This is about Rainy, not about Athena," she insisted. She prayed the conviction she didn't quite feel came across a little more strongly in her voice.

He nodded. "I see."

Time for a change of subject.

"Your turn," she countered. "What makes you think that Marshall would do anything even remotely illegal?"

"Maybe it's the false reports he files each time he returns from some trip related to his teaching."

"False in what way?" The demand wasn't subtle but she didn't like hearing her friends accused of wrongdoing. Marshall Carrington was a good man.

"He lies about where he goes and to whom he speaks. All of it."

Kayla couldn't bring herself to believe Marshall would lie, much less steal anything. "I'll need to see the proof for myself." No way was she taking anyone's word on a matter this important.

"That's all I can give you right now," Hadden said flatly. "I guess you'll just have to trust me a while longer."

She choked out a laugh. The sound echoed in the cramped space of the vehicle as his gaze collided with hers.

"Who said I trusted you, Detective Hadden?"

Lucky for her—or him—his cell rang just then and the conversation was shelved.

But Kayla knew she wouldn't rest until she'd talked to Marshall. Whatever he'd done he would have a reasonable explanation for it. Of that she was certain.

Rainy would never have married a liar or a thief. Never.

Chapter 5

Dr. Deborah Halburg's office was located in downtown Tucson, in an upscale, fashionable building with its own underground parking garage. Even this close to the traditional closing hour the lot was still about half-full as Hadden parked his sedan a row or so back from the bank of elevators.

They emerged simultaneously, the closing doors echoing ominously in the expansive, dimly lit cavern of parking slots. Neither spoke as they crossed to the elevators then waited for a car to arrive. The doors slid open to reveal an elegant marbled and mirrored cubicle that glided upward as smoothly as any luxury automobile. Upon reaching the lobby, they stepped into yet another expansive space, only this one was brightly lit by towering glass walls and shiny marble floors. The art alone would likely have paid Kayla's salary for a couple years. Maybe Hadden's as well.

Another bank of elevators waited across the seemingly boundless space of the ground-level lobby. Inside a waiting car Hadden selected the floor and another stretch of silence broken only by the chime announcing each floor accompanied their upward journey. Kayla studied the veined marble, mainly to keep her mind off just how great her companion smelled. The fragrance he wore was subtle, intensely masculine and wholly unsettling. Spending more than two hours closed up in the car with him had worn down some of her defenses.

Kayla emerged from the elevator grateful to be in the open once more. Somehow she had to get her perspective back where Hadden was concerned.

The seventh-floor reception area proved just as lavish as the one on the ground floor. A huge floral bouquet filled the air with pungently sweet scents, overwhelming the sensual aroma that still haunted her. Forcing herself back on task, she noted the suite numbers on the doors as she took the lead along the corridor. Her anticipation kicked into high gear. She hoped something Dr. Halburg remembered would somehow help her to put all the pieces together. For Marshall's sake…for the sakes of all those who had loved Rainy.

For Rainy.

"How much do you know about Dr. Halburg?"

Hadden asked as she hesitated outside the door of the suite belonging to the doctor she'd waited so long to interview.

Kayla considered the question a second, not really wanting to delay here. "She's the best in her field."

"The priciest as well, I'd wager," Hadden suggested.

The fabulous surroundings left no doubts there. "Probably. You get what you pay for, I guess."

Hadden hesitated before opening the door that would take them into Halburg's private clinic. "There's one more thing," he said ominously.

Kayla arched an eyebrow in question.

"The doctor's father was said to have been in excellent health. Whatever got him came on suddenly, then took its time eating away at his existence."

"Cancer?" Kayla suggested.

He flared his hands in a your-guess-is-as-good-as-mine gesture. "That's just it. They don't know. She had his body flown back here for an autopsy but found nothing. Things just slowed down and eventually ceased to function."

Kayla didn't respond. But her gut was tied in a thousand knots. All along she had felt as if someone were one step ahead of her in this investigation. How far were the powers that be in this ugly business willing to go to stop her—to stop all the Cassandras—from learning the truth? It seemed impossible that the cover-up could be so damned big.

And yet, on some level, she knew it was.

Deborah Halburg looked to be about forty. Tall, slim, hair more gray than blond, she had a pleasant face. One that spoke of deep concern for others…maybe too much. The lines etching the corners of her mouth and eyes proclaimed a weariness that likely had more to do with her father's death than with her profession.

"I was so sorry to hear of Rainy's death," she said as they settled around the massive cherry desk in her office. The office was large, each wall lined with either book-filled shelves or sprawling windows. "Such a waste. She was quite healthy and determined to have children." She shook her head. "I'm sure she is missed in numerous circles."

Hadden took the lead in the conversation, seeming to sense Kayla's struggle to balance her emotions at the moment. "You've been seeing Ms. Carrington for some time?" He took out a pen and small notepad similar to the one Kayla carried for interviews.

"Almost two years." Deborah Halburg frowned. "I can't believe someone broke in here and took her records." Her gaze shifted from Hadden to Kayla and back. "Nothing like this has ever happened before." Her gaze narrowed. "Is there something about Rainy's accident that you're leaving out?"

"We don't know all the answers yet," Kayla said, picking up on the doctor's developing uneasiness. "That's why we're here. We need to know all we can about those last few weeks of Rainy's life."

Halburg nodded. "I see. Well, I can tell you that Rainy Carrington was as fit as any woman her age can hope to be. A few months before her death I discovered some scarring on her ovaries that appeared to be the cause of her inability to conceive."

Kayla held her breath, hoping against hope that something would click here. She desperately needed answers.

"Was this scarring recent?" Hadden asked.

Kayla didn't look at him but she knew he was attempting to tie the problem to Rainy's time at Athena. Apparently he wasn't willing to let go on the doubts Shannon Conner had cast over the school. She couldn't let him make that connection just yet. Not until she had proof of what really happened.

The doctor shook her head. "It looked like it developed over time, from when Rainy hit puberty. Ovaries are smooth until the onset of puberty. After that, they become atretic, or scarred and distorted from repeated ovulations. Sometimes the scarring is serious enough to cause fertility problems. It's not too common, but does happen in a certain percentage of women. At first I thought that Rainy was one of them. We did some ultrasounds, though, and I noticed that her scars looked as if they could have been caused by fertility treatments. But Rainy said she'd never had any."

Halburg looked at them consideringly. "Given the circumstances of her accident, I will tell you that the ultrasound also revealed something that was very upsetting to Rainy. She seemed shocked to learn that her appendix was still in place. I questioned her about it, but she didn't want to discuss the issue further."

"Did you feel she was depressed or angry?"

Kayla had to grit her teeth to hold back the words she wanted to hurl at Hadden. He hadn't known Rainy. How could he even hint that her mental state might be a factor in the accident?

Her anger deflated when she considered that his not knowing Rainy was the very reason he asked. She was the one who needed to pull her objectivity back together here. Losing her focus wouldn't help Rainy.

Dr. Halburg clasped her hands in her lap as she continued, "I believe she was stunned and angry. Who wouldn't be? She wanted children. With the severity of the scarring, that most likely wasn't going to happen. At least, not naturally."

"What can you tell us about the scarring? Your theories?" Hadden pressed.

"Clearly she'd had a surgical procedure as a teenager. She had a scar on the abdomen that looked like a typical appendix scar. With the appendix intact I can only assume that it was an exploratory surgery of some sort. My first thought when I discovered the scarring was chronic infection. That happens with some women, but considering Rainy's insistence that she'd never had any such infection, I would have to say that some sort of surgical procedure caused the damage."

"Like egg mining," Kayla suggested, seeing no point in avoiding the subject.

Halburg didn't look startled by the suggestion. "The usual term is harvesting. That's possible. However, the harvesting procedure is generally reserved for in vitro fertilization and the like. There just wouldn't be much reason to perform it on a teen. And in my opinion, no skilled surgeon would do the kind of damage I noted on Rainy's ovaries." She heaved a sigh. "But to be quite frank, I can't think of any other procedure that would have caused this particular damage."

"You and Rainy discussed this possibility." Kayla felt reasonably certain that the doctor's conclusions had led Rainy to research the egg mining. Harvesting.

"Of course. Two, possibly three months before her death. In fact I referred Rainy to a specialist who I hoped might be able to salvage any remaining eggs."

"Do you know if she contacted that specialist?" This from Hadden.

Halburg shook her head. "She didn't. I touched base with him after I returned and found out about her accident. It was a courtesy call since I'd contacted him previously regarding her case and my referral. He said he'd never heard from her."

Kayla stood. She'd heard enough. She extended her hand. "Thank you, Dr. Halburg. I hope you'll let us know if you think of anything else that might be useful."

Deborah Halburg reached for Kayla's hand and shook it, her movements slowed by uncertainty or distraction.

Hadden pushed to his feet and offered his hand next since Kayla had left him no choice. "I'll be in contact if we have additional questions."

* * *

Halburg's words haunted Kayla all the way back to Athens. Hadden had made up some lame excuse for their investigation but Kayla had a feeling Halburg wasn't buying it.

Everything the doctor had said reinforced what Kayla, Alex, and the others already believed. Rainy had figured out what had been done to her all those years ago and she'd delved into her own past to determine how and why. Her search for the truth had exposed her knowledge to the wrong person, setting off a chain reaction that resulted in her murder.

Kayla's heart wrenched painfully.

To her way of thinking that could mean only one thing—this was way, way bigger than mere egg mining. Someone had something enormous to hide. As much as she prayed it had nothing to do with Athena Academy, it looked more and more as if at least one member of the school's personnel was involved.

Christine's admission about catching Dr. Carl Bradford looking through the files came immediately to mind. Bradford seemed likely to have been involved in some kind of wrongdoing. Betsy Stone might know for certain. After all, she'd probably given him access. With Christine's confession, Kayla had the right kind of ammunition to go after the nurse the way she wanted to. Betsy Stone had better get her story straight damned fast because Kayla wasn't going to let her off the hook so easily anymore. Stone was about to find out just how dogged Kayla could be.

"Your friend knew what had been done to her,"

Hadden said, his voice sounding loud after nearly two hours of silence.

He was digging.

"Apparently." Kayla wasn't going to give him anything more than what she already had. Not yet.

"I suppose that's why she called her friends together for that promise you told me about."

She shifted in the seat, wishing they would get to her house so she could say good-night and be rid of him.

Kayla told herself over and over that she simply didn't want to answer his questions. But it was a lie. She wanted away from him, period. He made her tense. Made her uncomfortable. At this point he didn't even have to flash her that awesome smile. His mere presence prompted a reaction from her. That sexy male scent.

Bad, bad, bad.

"That would be my guess," she relinquished, knowing that to ignore him would only raise his suspicions.

She resisted the urge to power the window down or to hold her breath. When had her senses latched onto his scent and become so sensitive? That natural male essence combined with something subtle and vaguely citrusy nagged at her.

Her gaze kept wandering back to the steering wheel and his hands. She'd never really been a hands kind of girl. Sure, she noticed them. Big ones, small ones, dirty and well manicured. It was part of her job to notice things about suspects. But this was different. She wanted to study Hadden's. In the dim light from the dashboard she could see that his hands were big and square, but not too much so. Long fingers, not the delicate, artistic sort. Nope, those fingers were strong and capable-looking, blunt-tipped. She could imagine how they would feel skimming her body. A shiver of heat slid through her.

She looked away in hopes of distracting herself but it didn't work. He'd touched her once or twice and she'd noted that his skin felt nice. Though his hands were hard and male, the texture wasn't rough. Pleasant and smooth, warm.

Her eyes rolled so far back in her head at her ridiculous thoughts that she would surely have seen her brain had it not been missing in action.

Okay, he was a good-looking guy. Get over it. He was also the detective who thought Marshall was a criminal! She had to remember that. Thinking badly of her friends definitely lowered his standing. Or it should, for Christ's sake.

Kayla shook off the bizarre lapses in her mental processes and focused on the dark night outside the passenger side window. It was past seven already. She hated missing out on that time with Jazz. But it couldn't be helped.

She'd have to do something special with her this weekend to make up for her recent extra-long hours. The curse of motherhood. One always felt intensely guilty even about the little things.

But time was precious. She'd learned that the hard way with Rainy's death as well as her grandmother's. No one was promised tomorrow. Better to make the best of today.

Hadden parked in her drive behind her Jeep. He sat there for a moment in the darkness not saying anything. The tension vibrating between them was palpable. She should speak up and get the parting comments over with before he had a chance to spill what was on his mind. He probably had more questions about Rainy.

He might as well forget it. She wasn't telling him any more than she already had.

"We have to talk about this."

Too late. Dammit. What was it about him that made her hesitate that single instant too long?

Kayla turned to him. His profile was just visible in the straining glow of her porch light. "What's to talk about? I've told you all I can." It wasn't an outright lie, but close.

He laughed softly. "I know this is seriously out of line, but I wasn't referring to the case."

Confusion snapped her mouth shut, the smart-ass remark she'd intended to toss at him evaporating.

Hadden turned to her, his new position combined with the sparse illumination displaying his best features in an even sexier way. God, he looked good in the dark. Her heart thumped anxiously. How long had it been since she'd sat this close, looked this deeply at a man in the near darkness? Stakeouts with her partner didn't count.

"Maybe I'm alone in this." He trailed a finger down her cheek. "But I have to get it out in the open."

Her pulse leapt. Between the heat and the shiver his touch elicited, she was losing ground fast here.

But she couldn't do this. Not now. Maybe not ever. There were too many obstacles to overcome. Jazz had to be her first priority. And there was Jazz's father. Not to mention Kayla's career and determination not to get involved with the wrong man ever again.

"I like you, Kayla," he said when she remained mute. "I can't keep pretending it's only mutual respect. I've been fighting the desire to get to know you better since the day we first met." He chuckled. "I drove all the way from Tucson to have time alone with you in the car."

She almost laughed at that. She remembered quite well the day they met. Marshall Carrington and David Gracelyn, Allison's brother, were at each other's throats. Rainy had just died. Things had been so confusing and emotional. But she had to admit that she'd noticed a number of Hadden's assets that very day herself. At least she hadn't been alone in her momentary insanity.

But, she had to get real here. Mike expected a call from her tonight and she hadn't even talked to Jazz yet. Wasn't even sure what she would say. And then there was the invitation to Athena for her daughter. Too much to deal with already. And there was that little detail that she couldn't be completely honest with Hadden. That was no way to start off a relationship.

No matter how badly she wanted to have at least a physical relationship with him. Incredibly, for the first time in a very long time she felt ready to dive in. Her body quivered then tensed at just the thought of making love with Hadden. He would be good.

Thorough, focused. She could very well imagine that his careful attention to detail on the job would carry through to his personal ventures. Need welled inside her. But it would be a mistake.

"O…kay," he said slowly, drawing out the syllables. "Clearly I've overstepped my bounds here."

Kayla managed a smile. She didn't know how. "It's okay. I…" What did she say? *Hey, I'd love to have sex with you but I have real issues. Big-time baggage. Maybe you'd better rethink your position.*

He faced forward, drawing back emotionally. "I'm glad we finally caught up with Dr. Halburg."

So…that was that.

"Yeah, me too." She reached for the door. "Thanks for the ride, Hadden. I'll see you around."

"Definitely."

Kayla got out of the car and watched him drive away. She tried to analyze the feelings that lingered. A mixture of regret and trampled hope. Why did relationships have to be so complicated?

Who knew?

Yet another mystery she doubted she would ever solve.

She trudged up to her door, unlocked it and went inside. She'd call Mary and give her a heads-up that she was on her way. Maybe then she'd call Alex with an update.

Her sister Mary insisted that Kayla either come over and have dinner with them or give Jazz another forty-five minutes to do so. Kayla agreed to the latter since she could use the time to touch base with

Alex. The real point was to avoid almost an hour in her sister's presence. Mary would pick up on her worries immediately. Kayla just wasn't ready to talk about any of it.

Alex answered on the second ring. Kayla had worried that she might be away on assignment or out with Justin. Those two were definitely getting closer. Good for Alex. At least one of them was headed for a decent relationship with a great guy.

It felt good to hear Alex's voice. How had they gone the past twelve years without this connection? It was still a little shaky but it was there.

"Is everything okay?"

Like Mary, Alex had noted the slightest change in the nuances of Kayla's voice. Damn. Could she not hide anything?

"I've just had an emotional day. That's all," she admitted in hopes of defusing the unwanted attention. "I finally caught up with Dr. Halburg."

"Did you learn anything new? Does she keep a backup for her files?"

"No backup files." Kayla answered the simplest question first. She held the phone between her ear and shoulder as she put on a pot of coffee to brew. This was going to be a long night. "She did say that Rainy had suspected her eggs had been harvested and that she was doing some research on the subject."

"Were her conclusions the same as mine and the medical examiner's?"

"Close enough." Kayla pressed the start button on the coffeemaker and took the phone back in hand.

"She recommended Rainy see a specialist for further testing to see if any eggs could be salvaged from the damaged ovaries, but Rainy never contacted the guy."

Alex made a speculative sound.

"That tells me," Kayla offered, "that she was too focused on finding out how and why this happened to her. We both know how badly she wanted children. That she would put her investigation ahead of that desire says a lot."

"I agree."

The silence dragged on a couple dozen seconds as the scent of strong coffee filled Kayla's kitchen. Apparently her attempts at alleviating her friend's concern hadn't worked.

"Has something else happened, Kayla?" Alex sighed. "I wish you'd tell me. I know we let the past get in the way for a while, but I want to put that behind us now. Talk to me."

Kayla sagged against the counter as her eyes closed with brimming emotion. She and Alex had been slowly inching toward this point since Rainy's death. But it wasn't until this moment that she felt like it was real.

"Mike Bridges showed up at my door this afternoon," she admitted, hoping like hell that the mention of his name wouldn't set back their forward momentum.

"He finally wants to be involved," Alex guessed, her tone leaving no question as to how she still felt about Mike Bridges. Most likely she'd heard about Josie's experience with him as well.

"Yeah." Kayla rubbed at her aching temple. This was definitely the kind of day to prompt a headache. "I don't trust him, Alex."

"I'd say you'd be smart not to. However…" She hesitated as if she either didn't know what to say next or resented the words to come to some degree. "He is her father. I know you'll do the right thing."

There was no holding back the tears that flowed down Kayla's cheeks then. To hear Alex say that meant the world to her.

"Christine called me," Alex went on before Kayla could find her voice. "She wanted me to hear from her what she'd told you."

Kayla scrubbed a hand over her damp face. "Betsy Stone must know a lot more than she's telling." Thank God her voice didn't sound as shaky as she felt.

"Be careful, Kayla. I don't trust Betsy. Justin's certain she was involved with his sister's death. And we have no way of knowing how close she is to those who want to stop us."

Kayla couldn't have agreed more. If only she could determine if Rainy had made contact with Betsy Stone with her suspicions.

Fury roared through Kayla. If she learned that Betsy Stone had somehow been involved in Rainy's murder, there would be no place on the planet the woman could hide. Kayla would hunt her down and tear her apart with her bare hands.

"Christine also mentioned that Jazz has been invited to attend Athena."

"I got the letter yesterday." Kayla fought hard to

pull herself together. Looking at her various quandaries from a rational standpoint was essential. She couldn't let Mary or Jazz see that she'd been crying. The next few hours had to be about reason and good, solid judgment.

"I don't have to tell you what an amazing opportunity this is," Alex commented. "Jazz is your daughter and I know you love her immensely. I'm certain you wouldn't want her to miss out on all Athena has to offer."

"No," Kayla agreed. "It's a once-in-a-lifetime kind of thing. I know. It's just that…" She moistened her lips and dredged up the bitter words that burned in the deepest recesses of her soul. "What if we learn that Athena Academy was somehow involved in all this, beyond just a staff member or two going rogue?"

"If," Alex said pointedly, "we learn such a thing then we'll see that it's taken care of. We won't let it happen again. Athena Academy is too important to let anyone use it for evil."

Alex was right. Even if Athena was involved more deeply than Kayla wanted to admit out loud, the wrong would be righted. The academy was still the finest school in the country. One that offered a chosen few young women an unequalled education. She would be a fool not to let Jazz take advantage of the invitation.

Kayla wasn't a fool. She had to do what was best for her daughter.

One way or another she would get to the bottom of this case first.

There was one more call she needed to make before picking up Jazz. She dreaded this one almost as much as she did the next one she'd have to make.

His voice sounded weary when he answered and Kayla's heart squeezed instantly. "Marshall, it's Kayla."

"Is everything all right?"

She hadn't called him in a while. It made sense that he would be surprised to hear from her. "I'm good," she assured him. "I finally caught up with Dr. Halburg today."

Marshall listened quietly as she relayed what she had learned, but Kayla could feel the hurt and anxiety building in his silence.

"This confirms what we thought," he suggested gruffly.

"It does."

Another long beat of silence. Kayla knew how hard this was for him. Marshall had worshipped Rainy. He was the most caring man Kayla had ever known outside her own father. The idea that someone had purposely hurt Rainy was killing Marshall.

"Find whoever did this, Kayla," he said, his voice breaking. "Find them and kill them. They don't deserve to live."

The pain in his voice, in his words tugged at her heart. "I will find them, Marshall. They won't get away with it. I promise you that."

"I'm counting on you," he urged, desperation keen in his voice. "I'm counting on you more than you know."

Chapter 6

Kayla paced the floor of her cluttered living room as Jazz dried her hair and got ready for bed. She told herself again that she couldn't put off this talk any longer.

But it was so damned hard. And the conversation with Marshall kept echoing in her head. He was counting on her.

She let go a weary breath and spun around to retrace her steps. The "dad" talk had to come first. Kayla just wasn't prepared to discuss Jazz going to Athena Academy at this point. There were too many things that had to be cleared up prior to that decision. For her peace of mind.

It was quarter of ten already, past her daughter's

usual bedtime. But Mary had insisted that Kayla eat when she arrived to pick up Jazz. A covered dish waited for her on the kitchen counter. What could she say? She had to eat. And snubbing her sister's hospitality would only earn her one of those you-need-to-slow-down talks, which would become a whole family discussion within the week.

Kayla's family held dear many Navajo traditions, although those traditions were blended well with modern society. Despite the family's contemporary outward appearance, the idea that wisdom comes from the stars and that one should find wonder and splendor on each path was deeply engrained.

Women were expected to use at least some of their time together to share cultural and family traditions. Like the fry bread her sister had painstakingly made that very day. To disregard such a gift from a family member would be the equivalent of a cardinal sin. Mary had likely included Jazz in the shaping, stretching and clapping of the dough that resulted in the round, golden delicious fry bread.

To this day Kayla wasn't so hot in the kitchen. But she had other assets, her mother would boast. Even her unexpected pregnancy at seventeen had been treated as a blessing. *Sometimes accidents are better than planning,* her mother had said.

That's how Kayla had survived her error in judgment where Mike Bridges was concerned. With her family's full support. And that's how she and Jazz would carry on. Whatever life threw in their path, family would always be there to back them up.

Mike would be waiting for her call. And if she didn't follow through he would be back tomorrow just as he'd promised. She remembered that he hated being ignored. His ego just wouldn't permit that sort of slight.

God, the idea had only just crossed her mind that as Jazz's father he might want to have some input as to whether she attended Athena Academy or not.

Kayla chewed her lower lip. Just what she needed. Him interfering with her plans for Jazz. Perfect.

She plopped down on the sofa. Her fingers automatically fiddled with the colorful throw her mother had woven. Kayla should take more time for that sort of thing. She gazed around at the paintings, all desert scenes, on the walls and thought of all the other cozy touches her family had helped her add to this home when she'd first bought it. Even the sturdy oak table and chairs of the dining room had been refinished by her father.

Kayla didn't seem to have inherited any basic artistic talent. She never felt as if she'd done enough at home.

At work decision-making felt so easy, came naturally. Tracking and taking down bad guys…protecting the community and its citizens. Piece of cake. Why did everything feel so hard at home? She worried over every little step with Jazz. But then, didn't every mother? Parenthood was tough.

A smile slid across her lips. But the rewards were incredible. She wouldn't trade the relationship she shared with her daughter for anything in the world. Maybe it was so wonderful because it was hard.

Hadn't her grandmother always sworn that anything worth having was worth working for? In other words, all good things came with a unique burden.

Just like the friendships she had forged with the Cassandras. If Jazz attended Athena, would she meet girls her age whose influence would follow her for the rest of her days?

Laughter bubbled into Kayla's throat when she thought of how they'd first met, she and her sisters in crime. Things hadn't gone so smoothly in the beginning. Talk about adolescent egos. Child genius Samantha, smart-mouthed Tory, eagle-eyed Josie, eager-to-please Darcy and cool-as-a-cucumber Alex. Kayla had been the overly serious one, the girl who took everything and anything too close to heart. Come to think of it, being Jazz's age hadn't been easy, either. How had she forgotten how difficult being a kid could be?

But Rainy had pulled the ragtag group together.

At first, Sam had walked around with a chip on her shoulder the size of Mt. Everest. Part of the problem had been the fact that she was about two years younger than everyone else and nobody really tried to relate to her. Kayla and the others had felt far too old for fraternizing with a "kid." Tory had never, ever shut up. The girl had to be the center of attention. Oh, yeah, and Josie was nothing but a tattletale. Kayla grinned. How had she forgotten those quirky little details?

Admittedly, she'd lacked any sense of humor whatsoever. So she hadn't been so easy to get along with. Ah, but then there was Alex's snobby ways. And

Darcy's constant ass kissing. Darcy, apparently, thought being a yes-girl would hoist her a little farther up the food chain. Alex had evidently assumed that the world should and would bow to her every wish.

Rainy saw through all the superficial crap every last one of them oozed. She knew that each of her assigned mentees were good where it counted, deep down inside. All she had to do was polish that goodness and bring it to the surface. Not such a simple task.

Kayla would never forget having to stay at the Academy when their first break rolled around. Rainy had insisted. Principal Christine Evans had agreed. The Cassandras were grounded, no going home for break. Kayla would never forget the indignation.

"Why do we have to go on a field trip?" Tory griped. "We're supposed to be going on break. I wanna go home."

"Because I said so," Rainy tossed back. "Any questions?" She surveyed the gloomy group. "I thought not."

Kayla hadn't been too keen on the idea of going on an overnight survival trip into the wilds of the White Tank Mountains, which really amounted to a trip into the farthest reaches of the Academy property. Not such a big deal looking back, but, at the time, it had felt like going to the ends of the earth…in the dark with a bunch of quarreling buttheads, when she should have been at home with her loving family watching her mother weave or her grandmother bake.

The Cassandras had no sooner foraged into the creepy, dark landscape than disaster struck.

"I can't find her anywhere!"

Kayla saw the fear on the other girls' faces. Rainy was lost. They had looked everywhere. It was so dark. She shivered. They were all terrified. What would they do now? Rainy was their leader...what would they do without her?

"Are you sure?" Kayla asked Josie. Josie never missed anything. God, if she couldn't find Rainy...

"All right," Alex piped up in that authoritative heiress voice of hers. "Here's what we'll do." She divided up the area to be searched and sent two girls into each quadrant, just like they'd learned in class. "Stick with your partner," she'd instructed, "and we'll find her."

Every one of the Cassandras had loved Rainy. Respected and looked up to her. They just hadn't been able to get past their irritation with each other long enough to show it. But that night, all those years ago in the middle of nowhere in the dark, they had worked together. When they'd found their beloved leader she was injured, a sprained ankle that prevented her from walking without assistance.

Everyone pitched in immediately. Tory told jokes to keep Rainy's sprits up. Josie, Darcy and Kayla had built a shelter while Sam and Alex started a fire to stay warm. Alex had busily splinted Rainy's ankle. Using the stars as her guide, Sam had figured out in which direction the school lay. The next morning they would be prepared for getting Rainy back to the safety of the Academy.

The whole transition had occurred like magic.

They were all suddenly working together as a team. When all was done the girls, exhausted from their labors, had settled around the campfire with Rainy to wait for daybreak. And then something else unexpected had happened.

"I have a secret to share with you," Rainy said in *a mysterious tone.*

Kayla, like all the others, leaned forward a bit, anxious to hear whatever their fearless leader had to say. They were all so awed by her. She'd been injured and lost and yet she'd never worried. She had felt certain her Cassandra sisters would rescue her. The realization that they had done just that warmed Kayla. Even on a cool night in the foothills of the mountains she felt that heady glow more deeply than the heat from the fire.

Rainy looked from one expectant face to the other. "I was never lost…or injured." She shucked the splint Alex had carefully applied and wiggled her foot. "I was only pretending."

Gasps echoed in the firelight. Eyes went wide, mouths gaped.

"But why?" Darcy wanted to know.

Rainy smiled at each of them. "Because I needed you to look past your differences and to see each other for who you really are."

The girls glanced at each other, awed and sort of bewildered at the same time. It was that very night, at that precise moment, that something special passed between Kayla and Alex. Something very special happened between them all.

"We're a team. Like sisters," Rainy continued. *"Nothing can pull us apart or divide us as long as we stick together."*

Cheers went up around the campfire. And the Cassandras were baptized in their unity.

Sisters...there for each other...forever.

"What did you want to talk about, Mom?"

Jazz's question jerked Kayla back to the here and now. She blinked away the sentimental tears that burned in her eyes. "Oh...you're ready." She smiled for her daughter, couldn't help wondering what kind of character-building adventures she would have if she attended the Academy.

Kayla got to her feet and draped her arm around her daughter's shoulders. Another few inches and she'd be as tall as her mother. How time flew.

"Come on, I'll tuck you in and we'll talk."

As her daughter climbed into bed Kayla glanced around her room and contemplated how much longer the little-girl décor would last. Before long a redo would be in order. Maybe that would make a good birthday gift, since Christmas was already taken care of. Jazz had asked for a laptop computer for Christmas. It was a bit extravagant but she could use it for school. Especially if she went to the Academy.

"Can we put up the tree this weekend?" Jazz asked as Kayla settled on the edge of the bed next to her.

"You bet."

"Aunt Mary already has hers up."

"I noticed." Kayla's sister always had the best tree.

"Am I in trouble?" Jazz asked, then chewed her

lip as if prepared for the worst. "I haven't been on the Internet anymore without asking first. I didn't even play computer games at Aunt Mary's. I did my homework just like you said."

Jazz's big hazel eyes peered up at Kayla. Kayla's heart squeezed at how very much like Mike's those gorgeous eyes were. He certainly couldn't deny his child. Any more than Kayla could, since every other feature besides those eyes were an exact replica of Kayla's.

"No, sweetie, you're not in trouble at all." She sighed, couldn't help herself. "But I had a visitor today."

"A visitor? Who?"

Jazz looked so innocent, her expression naively inquisitive. She had no idea her life was about to change in so many ways.

Kayla picked up the framed photograph from her daughter's bedside table. "We haven't talked about your father in a while."

Jazz took the photograph from her mom. "I wonder about him sometimes. Does he still live far away?"

Not able to break her daughter's heart by telling her the whole truth, she'd just told her that Mike was in the Air Force and stationed far away. God, what a cop-out that had been.

"Actually, he's moved closer now," she said cautiously. "In fact, he came by today and told me he'd like to visit with you if you wouldn't mind."

Jazz studied the picture a little longer, then set it aside. "Mom." She looked directly into Kayla's eyes. "I know you don't like to talk about him."

"Jazz, I—"

"I know, okay?" she butted in. "Every time I ever mentioned him I could see the way you looked." She shrugged those slim shoulders clad in pink flannel. "So I didn't bring him up much. But I know what happened." Her face clouded. "He didn't want us so he went away."

"No." Kayla shook her head. This was exactly what she hadn't intended to let happen. She should have been smarter. Should have realized her bright daughter would figure out her reasons for silence. "It wasn't like that. We were just young. But he's older now. He realizes that not being around was a mistake." She prayed he did. God, if he broke her baby's heart…. "He's your father. He does want to be with you. But being in the military makes it difficult for him. Maybe he thought it was better this way…until now."

Jazz shrugged again. "Maybe. What did you tell him?"

How strong her daughter was. Kayla was so proud, but she would not cry. She had to be strong too. "I told him we'd give him a call and set up a time to have lunch or watch a movie. Something like that. That okay?"

"Only if you're with us."

Kayla pressed a kiss to her forehead. "Count on it."

Jazz nodded. "Tell him we'll give it a try."

Kayla had to laugh. When had her baby grown up so?

"I'll call him now."

When she would have gotten up, Jazz tugged at her arm. Kayla turned back to her. "You have more instructions for me?" she teased.

Jazz's face turned serious as she shook her head.

Kayla's gut clenched. Had the reality of the conversation only now caught up to her child?

"I love you, Mom."

Relief flooded Kayla. "I love you too, sweetie."

After hugs and good-nights, Kayla made the call.

Mike answered on the first ring. He'd been waiting.

"It's me," Kayla's entire body, her throat especially, felt tight with emotion.

"I'm glad you called." She heard relief in his voice.

Oddly, that only made this harder for her. "We'd like you to come for dinner on Friday evening."

"Why not tomorrow?"

Kayla held on to her emotions. Anger wouldn't help right now. Tears wouldn't either. "She has choir practice after school. They practice twice a week. She'll be late getting home."

A beat of silence passed. "All right. Friday then. Seven?"

"Seven's good." Kayla tried to think what she should say next, but she just wanted to hang up. She needed to sever the connection before her composure crumpled completely.

"Thank you, Kayla. You don't know how much this means to me."

She managed a polite goodbye and hung up.

Mike Bridges would visit his daughter for dinner on Friday evening. Day after tomorrow.

Kayla climbed into her own bed then and pulled the covers up close around her. She tried to be strong, but she just couldn't do it. She cried. Cried for the mistakes she and Mike had made. Cried because she was awed by her young daughter's perceptiveness and strength. Cried for Marshall and all he'd lost.

Lastly she cried because she was lonely.

Nights like this she desperately wished she could put her arms around a big, strong man.

One exactly like Peter Hadden.

Before she could chastise herself for the weakness she drifted off to sleep.

Early Thursday Investigator Devon called Kayla to let her know her bike-pirating perp had rolled over on one of the biggest car thieves in the state. The guy hadn't been bluffing when he'd made the offer. Cars, bikes, anything with wheels were pretty much on his connection's agenda.

This was a major coup. Investigator Devon had concluded that Kayla's anonymous tip had come from a competitor who had known one of the three she caught would drop a dime on their main connection. The strategy was as transparent as glass—take the competition off the street.

Devon also wanted to warn Kayla that for his testimony Mr. Terrence Swafford would get a mere slap on the wrist. In fact, he would be taken into protective custody today and kept in an undisclosed location until the trial, after which he would receive a reduced sentence. Devon added that he felt compelled to give her the heads-up since this guy could pose a threat to her later on.

Kayla would also be expected to testify as to what happened the day of the bust. She had assured the investigator that the district attorney could count on her. She wasn't going anywhere.

And she sure as hell wasn't afraid of some loose-lipped bike thief who might be looking for a little payback. The only worry she had in that area was in keeping her daughter safe from scum like Swafford.

Just another reason Jazz would likely be better off at Athena. Security was tight when it came to protecting the students. She thought of Rainy. Well, most of the time, anyway.

"I've got to run a couple errands," she told Jim around 11:00. Jazz had choir practice again today so that gave Kayla a few hours to check out a couple things on Rainy's case. "Call me if you need me."

Jim, neck deep in reports, only grunted. When it was slow, like today, it wasn't uncommon for the deputies on duty to take a little free time to take care of personal business. If Jim needed her he would call her back in. He didn't ask where she was headed. He likely assumed she had last-minute Christmas shopping to attend to.

She was glad he didn't ask. Lying to her partner wasn't something that came easy to her. But sharing information with him about Rainy was definitely not a good idea. This had to be kept between the Cassandras. Well, and some aspects had to be shared with Peter Hadden. She had little choice there.

As she climbed into her Jeep she gave herself another mental kick for allowing Hadden to slip into her thoughts too often. After last night's too-close-for-comfort moment in his car she'd managed to dream about him in spite of her nerve-racking heart-to-heart with her daughter.

Who would have thought that Peter Hadden could kick worries about Mike right out of her head? She'd expected to have dreams about Mike trying to horn in on her close relationship with their daughter, not close encounters of the sexual kind with Hadden.

She had to get her head back on straight on the subject of Peter Hadden. Last night had ventured over the line. But she wasn't the only one having trouble. In fact, he'd been the one to bring up the awareness between them. She had to be the one to end it. Until she cleared up the mystery around Rainy's death she had no choice but to be involved with Hadden. After that they wouldn't see each other again.

Why get involved with a man she wouldn't even be seeing in the future?

By the time she reached Marshall Carrington's home in Tucson, Kayla had convinced herself she'd made the right decision. She had her immediate future under control, at least in her mind.

She'd called Marshall that morning and he had assured her he would be home all afternoon. He'd lectured his final class yesterday until after Christmas vacation. He had no plans for any research trips until the new year. He would love to see her.

Kayla wondered how he would spend the holidays without Rainy. If he was smart he'd plan some time away with friends and family. Anything to get out of the house. The notion that maybe she should invite him to join her family for the holidays crossed her mind but she imagined he already had invitations from his own relatives as well as Rainy's parents.

Would being with Rainy's family be too difficult for him? She should ask if he'd talked to the Millers recently. Then again, questions along those lines might disturb his tenuous grip on normalcy.

She parked in his driveway behind his luxury sedan. The best thing to do in a situation like this, she reminded herself, was to go with the flow. She'd feel out the situation and go from there.

"Kayla!"

Marshall stood in the open doorway waving as if he were profoundly happy to see her. She couldn't help noticing that the front of the house was undecorated. Rainy had always been eager to drape the Christmas lights and hang the seasonal wreath on her door. Would Marshall even bother with a tree without his wife to share the festivities?

"It's great to see you, Marshall." She gave him a quick hug. Memories of how things had almost gotten out of hand shortly after Rainy's death kept her from lingering too long in his strong arms.

"Please come in."

She followed Marshall inside and waited until he had closed the door before she began. "How are the Millers?" she asked before she could stop herself. It felt so strange to be in Rainy's house and not talk about her. The question just felt necessary.

Marshall gestured toward the living room, then started to move in that direction as he spoke. "They're coming down a few days before Christmas. We're going to Rainy's grave together."

Kayla sat down on the sofa and Marshall settled into one of the leather chairs facing her. "That's good. Rainy always did love Christmas." Memories of Christmas drinks and presents shared over the years with Rainy instantly flickered through Kayla's mind. God, how she did miss her.

Marshall nodded. "I'm having a special wreath made for her headstone."

"Jazz and I will stop by. I'm sure it'll be beautiful."

He pasted on a smile. It was obvious to Kayla that the smile was only there for her benefit. "I mentioned that my classes are finished until the new year, didn't I?"

"Yes. That's great. Are you planning to take some time away between now and then?"

He lifted one shoulder in a halfhearted shrug. "I thought I might. I'll be heading off to Bogotá in February. One of my contacts there has turned up some ancient artifacts he thought I might be interested in."

That he didn't mention the kind of artifacts suddenly struck Kayla as odd. But she refused to allow the doubt Hadden had planted to grow beyond a certain level. There had been a time when Marshall Carrington wouldn't shut up about his research, but a lot had changed in his life the past few months. It made sense that his priorities would as well. She felt confident that the wow of ancient artifacts dimmed considerably after one had lost the love of his life.

And yet she knew better than most that permitting herself to fall too deeply into a sympathetic role would jeopardize her objectivity every bit as much as Hadden's theories. She had to get to the point and be done with this unappealing business.

"Marshall, I've heard a rumor that I feel you should know about."

His expectant gaze fastened onto hers. "About Rainy?"

The hurt in his voice when he said his late wife's name tugged at Kayla's heart. She shook her head sadly. "No. Not about Rainy."

"You're still investigating her…death?"

"Of course. I won't give up until I know exactly what happened."

His gaze dropped to the floor. "Thank you, Kayla. That means a great deal to me."

The picture he made now broke her heart. Those broad shoulders were slumped in defeat, his usually animated features dormant from loss. Even those affecting gray eyes seemed listless and almost colorless, as if losing Rainy had taken away his body's ability to sparkle in any respect. The smile was nothing more than a prop. Nothing glittered about Marshall Carrington anymore and it was such a shame. His charm and ability to light up a room had been one of the reasons Rainy had fallen in love with him.

"Marshall, in your research…" God, how did she

say this to a friend? "Have you ever had contact with anyone who might be considered a...criminal?"

His head came up, his brow furrowed. The question in his solemn eyes almost undid her. "What do you mean?"

She swallowed. Rainy would feel betrayed by the mere idea of what Kayla was about to ask. But she had to, if for no other reason than to warn him that someone had an eye on him. Someone who wanted to hurt him.

Not Hadden. He had no reason to want to injure Marshall. Kayla had checked out Hadden thoroughly. He was on the up-and-up. But someone from Tucson's legal hierarchy.

"I believe that someone is attempting to sully your reputation by tossing around rumors that you're involved with some sort of smuggling."

The rush of red rage up Marshall's neck and face startled her. He was on his feet and glaring down at her before the realization of his reaction had fully assimilated in her brain.

Kayla had expected him to be offended, upset even. But not in her wildest dreams had she expected this level of unadulterated fury.

"What the hell are you suggesting?"

"Wait a minute." She stood, her instincts going to full-scale alert. "I'm not suggesting anything, I'm only telling you about the rumor I heard. I thought you might want to know that someone out there is—"

He moved a step closer, shaking a reproving finger at her. "My wife is dead. You said yourself you didn't believe it was an accident. Alex said the same. And yet, you would dare to come into my house and accuse me of wrongdoing?" The veins bulged in his neck. "Why the hell aren't you out there hounding Gracelyn? He's the one who wanted to take her away from me!"

This had gotten completely out of hand. She held up both hands in a *whoa* gesture. "Wait a minute. I'm not accusing you of anything. Nobody wants to get to the truth about Rainy's death more than I do."

"Then go toss accusations at Gracelyn! He's the one!" A muscle in Marshall's hard jaw ticked violently. "For all we know he may have decided that if he couldn't have her, no one would."

"Marshall." She took him by the arms. He tried to pull away but she held on. "Calm down. I'm on your side."

What the hell was wrong with him? There was no reason for him to explode at her like this.

He heaved out a ragged breath. "I can't believe it." He shook his head. "I've lost my wife and now someone is trying to make me look like a criminal." He turned a laserlike gaze on her now. "It's Gracelyn. I know it. He's trying to make me look guilty. Ask him, Kayla. Make him tell you the truth." He tugged free of her hold to grab her by the shoulders. "He tried to lure my wife away from me. He's capable of anything." He searched her eyes, her face. His own filled with a fierce urgency. "Don't let him get away with this. You told me you would find whoever did this. I'm telling you it's him."

"Marshall, I—"

"Please, Kayla. Do it for me."

"I didn't come here for—"

His lips silenced her. He kissed her hard. His arms went around her and locked as if he feared he might lose her too. She tried to push him away but she couldn't...or wouldn't. He felt warm and strong around her...tasted good and so comfortingly familiar. She just couldn't help herself. Needed this moment...his touch.

But it was wrong.

This wasn't about her.

It was about Rainy.

She drew back. Fought to catch her breath. "Marshall, this is—"

"But I'm so alone." He pressed his forehead to hers. "You can't imagine how it feels."

But she could. God, she could.

As much as she cared about Marshall, as much as she longed to comfort him the way he wanted, she would not go there. He was still Rainy's husband. Always would be, really. And this case was far from solved. Until that time she had to keep her objectivity about all involved.

Most especially where Marshall was concerned.

Though nothing Peter Hadden could say would convince her Marshall was guilty of wrongdoing, her training was too thorough to discount the concept completely without due consideration.

She had to keep her senses about her.

And that was impossible in Marshall's arms.

As if picking up on her thoughts he released her. "I'm sorry, Kayla." He ran a hand through his hair. "I seem to forget myself when we're together."

She managed a meager smile, fumbled for the right thing to say. They were both hurting, but getting involved wasn't the answer. "We'll get through this."

He nodded vaguely.

"I'll call you again soon. Don't hesitate to call me if you need me…anytime." She'd done what she came for. She'd warned him. Getting out of here now would be the best for both of them.

He exhaled wearily. "Thank you." He shook his head sadly. "For everything."

She dared to pat his arm, then she left.

Staying a moment longer would have been sheer insanity. She had to put some distance between them…pull herself back together. Her hands were shaking and her gut was twisted in knots. She shouldn't have let this happen.

Once in her Jeep she waited a bit before backing out of the drive. Took a few deep breaths. *Okay, girl, think. Focus.* Her cop instincts wouldn't let her totally ignore Marshall's ranting. He'd accused David Gracelyn once before of being after Rainy. Maybe there was more to that theory than Kayla knew.

Kayla couldn't be sure what made her decide to do it. She really didn't have time…but she suddenly felt as if she couldn't leave Tucson without going by Rainy's grave. She hadn't been by the cemetery since the funeral. She needed to go there now…at least for a few minutes.

A short time later she parked along a narrow road-side that cut through the prestigious cemetery. Most of the tree branches were bare at this time of year, making the landscape look even more barren. Nothing but headstones and artificial flowers for as far as the eye could see.

Kayla got out of her Jeep and started toward the place where they'd lowered Rainy into the ground four short months ago. It still didn't feel real. Rainy should be at her office, going over legal briefs, laughing about some client who'd pulled a dumb stunt. She shouldn't be lying deep within the cold ground. It just wasn't fair. She'd been too vital, too full of life to die so young.

But she had. Evil had snatched her off this earth in a single heartbeat.

Kayla crouched down next to Rainy's final resting place and wrapped her arms around her knees. "What do I do now?" she murmured. God, she wished she had at least some of the answers.

How could all this be happening? How could someone from Athena have had anything to do with Rainy's murder? How could the man Rainy had loved and married be mixed up with anything illegal? Certainly nothing would ever make Kayla believe that Rainy had cheated on Marshall. That was simply unthinkable. Never. Not Rainy. Absolutely no way.

Kayla blinked back the tears and considered the fading flowers Marshall or maybe Rainy's parents had left on their last visit. How could this be all that was left of Rainy?

The possibility that Rainy could have one or more children out there somewhere nudged at Kayla. She gritted her teeth against the outrage that boiled up inside her. She would find the truth—the whole truth. No matter how long it took. Regardless of how deep she had to dig.

A leaf crunched behind her.

Kayla froze.

That nagging feeling that someone was watching her prodded her even more strongly.

She wasn't alone in this place of the dead.

Keeping her movements unhurried, she pushed to her feet. Took one last look down at Rainy's final resting place and then wheeled around to face the threat.

No one was there.

Kayla surveyed from left to right. Jerked her gaze back to the left.

Ten, maybe fifteen yards in the distance she saw a figure dart behind a tree.

Kayla lunged in that direction in an all-out run. The occasional glimpse of movement was all she got to give her any sense of direction, but she made the best of it. Ran as hard as she could. Darted around trees…past headstones. She needed to know who the hell was tailing her.

There. To the left. Twenty yards away.

Kayla ran faster still. Her lungs burned with the need for more oxygen but she ignored it. Ran harder. Tuned out everything but the chase.

A door slammed and the squeal of tires punctuated the realization that whoever had been following her would get away.

Kayla skidded to a stop. Frustration pounded in her veins. She stared after the fleeing vehicle. Small. Black. Two doors. Couldn't make out the license plate.

Dammit.

She stomped her foot and wheeled around to head back to where she'd parked her Jeep.

That definitely hadn't been Hadden. She knew his vehicle. Knew him. And though she hadn't been able to discern whether the person was male or female, her every instinct had told her it definitely wasn't Hadden.

One of his cronies maybe? He worked here in Tucson. Lived maybe thirty minutes from the cemetery.

But why would he have someone tailing her here of all places?

Maybe it was someone who knew the Cassandras had taken out the Cipher. Or hell, for all she knew it could be someone commissioned by Athena Academy. But she wasn't prepared to believe that yet, any more than she was ready to go along with the idea that Marshall Carrington was a bad guy. Confused, hurting, desperate even, but no way a bad guy.

Time to give Marshall some credit. He was convinced that Rainy and David Gracelyn were involved. Kayla was certain that wasn't true, but there could have been something between them. Maybe Rainy had shared some aspect of her troubles with him. He could have useful information.

Only one way to find out.

She drove out of the cemetery and headed for Phoenix. She would have just enough time to drop by David Gracelyn's office before making the long drive back to Athens to pick up her daughter after choir. All she had to do was call Gracelyn's secretary and make sure he was in. She wouldn't make an appointment or give him any forewarning.

She needed him off balance. A mere cop would need the element of surprise when going up against an assistant attorney general and his Harvard law degree.

The idea was to get off-the-cuff, unprepared responses. Any advance warning of her arrival would have him mulling over what she might want. Considering his family played a major role in the support and funding of Athena Academy, he likely already knew about Kayla's investigation. There was no doubt that he knew how Marshall felt about him.

That put him in the category of hostile witness. And yet she couldn't imagine that David Gracelyn would ever in a million years hurt Rainy. The Gracelyns had all loved Rainy. Allison Gracelyn, David's sister, had been one of Rainy's closest friends. But Kayla needed to know once and for all where he and Rainy had stood prior to her death. The exact nature of their relationship.

Even the suggestion of an affair would cast a whole new light on the matter…as well as a completely new focus on the husband. Adultery was one of the primary motivating factors for when men and women killed their spouses.

She couldn't see Marshall doing such a thing,

much less having the contacts to call in an assassin like the Cipher.

But, a cop's job was to turn over every single rock, no matter how small and unlikely that rock looked to the naked eye.

By the time she arrived at David Gracelyn's office in Phoenix, Kayla's tension level had reached the breaking point. Between Marshall's unexpected reaction—she didn't even want to think about the kiss—and the chase in the cemetery, she felt ready to snap. Rather than giving her time to calm down, the long ride had agitated her further.

She got out of her Jeep, determination urging her on. She wasn't leaving Gracelyn's office until she had the truth.

Chapter 7

Kayla didn't have to wait to see David Gracelyn. Not only was he in, he was glad she'd come. The receptionist showed Kayla to his elegant office.

Assistant attorney generals had it made, she decided upon entering his distinguished digs.

"It's good to see you, Kayla. Please, sit." He gestured to a brocade wing-back chair that flanked his desk. "Would you like coffee? Water, perhaps?"

His smile was pleasant and reached his eyes. Tall, with brown hair and eyes, David wasn't so much handsome because of his good looks. It was the whole package—the air of confidence and elegance. The mark of a Gracelyn.

Despite his smile, there was a solemn quality

about him that spoke of deep pain. She wondered about that, Marshall's accusations filtering through her mind.

She declined his offer of refreshments. "Thank you for seeing me, Mr. Gracelyn." Though she'd known him for a long time, his position prompted her to address him formally.

She thrust out her hand. He shook it briskly and scolded, "You know better than to call me mister. We've known each other far too long for that kind of formality."

They had known each other for many years—that was true—but that didn't make them close. The Gracelyns ran in more aristocratic circles. Kayla's family personified the term *working middle-class,* their love of the simpler ways flavored with Navajo influence. Had it not been for Athena Academy her path likely would never have crossed his.

David was a kind man, a good ten years Kayla's senior. Allison, his sister, had been a senior at Athena Academy when Kayla started in seventh grade. Allison had been Rainy's best non-Cassandra friend. Her parents were among Arizona's elite. David, her only sibling, had always gone out of his way to make those in his company feel relaxed and welcome. Allison, on the other hand, came off a bit haughtier, less touchable. Still, Rainy had cherished her, so she couldn't be as snobbish as Kayla at times thought.

David's pleasant expression abruptly cluttered with concern. "Is this visit about Rainy? When I heard you were here I thought it might be police business, but…" His words trailed off as if he wasn't quite sure how to finish the statement.

Instinct told Kayla that Marshall was right, at least to some degree. This man had clearly been in love with Rainy.

"I have some questions for you, if that's all right." She settled into the chair he'd indicated. "About Rainy," she clarified.

He resumed his seat and braced his forearms on the gleaming mahogany desk that stood between them. "Of course. I'm happy to help in any way I can." He blinked, glanced away for a moment. "Allison told me that there was some uncertainty as to the circumstances surrounding Rainy's death. I'm not sure I understand, but…" His gaze met hers once more. "Surely you can't be thinking foul play."

Kayla studied his reactions closely. "I'm afraid I do."

His head moved side to side, the despair he felt mounting visibly. "I just can't believe anyone would want to harm her. Not Rainy. I've no doubt that she had a few enemies. Most attorneys do…but Rainy didn't have *those kind* of enemies."

Kayla moistened her lips and took a deep breath. Rather than comment on his suggestion, she dove in headfirst with the real reason she'd come. "Marshall is convinced that you and Rainy were having an affair."

The announcement took him aback. "That's just not true."

Maybe not, but Kayla felt her own conviction slipping. Mincing words wouldn't help. "Pardon me for saying so but even I get the distinct impression that you had very deep feelings for her."

He stiffened, ever so slightly. "She and my sister were the closest of friends. Our families—"

"David." Kayla didn't see the point in allowing him to dig that hole. "This isn't about Allison, this is about you and Rainy. I know a man in love when I see one. You loved her."

Silence seemed to suck all the air out of the room for several seconds. Kayla resisted the urge to shift in her chair. Her presence might not be welcome after this.

"It's true." He leaned back into the supple leather of his chair. "I've been in love with her for years." A far-away look claimed his features as he went on, "We fell hard for each other shortly after my mother's death."

Kayla's heart slammed hard against her sternum. Could she have been so wrong about this? She just couldn't believe Rainy would have cheated on Marshall.

"But it didn't work out," he added, a keen sadness in his voice. "We were both too young and foolish to recognize what was best for us."

As relieved as she was to learn their relationship had ended long ago, that didn't give her all she wanted to know. "So you and Rainy hadn't been involved since," Kayla pressed. She needed more recent history. The pain she'd seen in his eyes when she first entered his office was far deeper than that suffered from a lost love so very long ago. David had been in love with Rainy. Still was.

"Last year," he confessed, "we worked on a trial together." He stared down at his hands as if the right words would somehow fall within his grasp. "We spent a lot of time together…talked." He let go a weary breath. "I fell in love with her all over again. I think she felt strongly about me as well."

Disappointment speared Kayla all over again. She didn't want to hear this about her dear friend. Rainy was too strong to be weak where her marriage was concerned. She'd always been the strong one. Always. This just didn't fit. And yet, Kayla had to hear it all.

"But," he continued, "Rainy loved Marshall." David's watery gaze fastened on Kayla's. "Though her marriage was less than idyllic, she would not cheat on her husband."

Extreme relief bloomed in Kayla's chest. She should have known better than to doubt Rainy. A frown nagged at her brow as she processed the rest of what David said. "What do you mean her marriage was less than idyllic?"

He took a few moments to gather his thoughts or to choose his words carefully before he answered. "She wanted children desperately."

That much Kayla had learned.

"Marshall didn't seem to care one way or the other." David lifted his hands in a gesture of uncertainty or indifference. "He wanted a child if that's what would make Rainy happy but he didn't want to bother with the extreme measures. When she didn't conceive, he wanted to move on. To forget about it.

Rainy was intensely disappointed. I think the whole situation put a strain on their marriage."

David leaned forward, clasped his hands together on his desk. "I don't have any hard feelings toward Marshall. Maybe I should. But he didn't steal Rainy from me, he merely took what I foolishly let go." The true depth of his regret showed in his listless eyes.

It hurt just a little that Rainy would share these intimate details with David and not her friends. Did Allison know? Kayla had known Rainy wanted children, but not this. An ache churned through her at the idea of how her friend must have agonized over the situation. Kayla'd had no idea. Even Marshall hadn't indicated that things between him and Rainy had digressed to this point. But then, why would he?

"Had she confronted Marshall about this?" It felt like a betrayal to Marshall to ask, but she had to. The cop in Kayla could not do otherwise.

David shook his head. "I don't think so. At least, if she did, she didn't mention it to me."

Kayla's instincts went on point. "Do you recall her seeming upset or acting any differently than usual?" Her heart thumped hard. How long had Rainy known? What steps had she taken before invoking the promise?

"Those last few months…especially over the summer…" He hesitated, clearly grappling to maintain his composure. "She always seemed preoccupied. Distant. I thought maybe she'd begun to feel guilty about our time together though it was completely innocent."

Maybe on Rainy's side, but on David's it had gone

way beyond friendship. He'd fallen hard for Rainy…
again.

"The last couple of times I saw her, she was upset.
She wouldn't talk about it."

A weight settled on Kayla's chest. Rainy had been
upset because she'd discovered the truth. Maybe
weeks before asking for help. She'd known what
someone had done to her all those years ago. Kayla
had to look away from David then. He'd loved her,
maybe as much or more than Marshall had. All this
time Kayla had thought Marshall was the perfect
husband. How could he have been indifferent to
Rainy's needs…to her distraction those last weeks of
her life?

Or was it easier for Kayla to take that position considering what Hadden had told her and now, with
this new evidence? Did it make her less guilty for
enjoying Marshall's kiss for a second? Something
was wrong.

No. She couldn't judge Marshall so harshly just yet.

But was that her objectivity speaking…or the
woman in her? She would be lying to herself if she
claimed not to have been affected by his kiss…his
touch.

Christ, she was losing all objectivity here.

"Thank you for your time, David." She stood, certain she couldn't listen to any more of his heartrend-
ing stories about Rainy. Obviously there was nothing
of benefit to her investigation that she could learn
from his personal torment.

Had Rainy secretly loved him? Would she have

gone to David if Marshall hadn't been in the way? Had Marshall suspected as much? The rage Kayla had witnessed today was so unlike the man she'd known all these years.

Some aspects of Rainy's final days she might not ever understand.

Her grandmother would say that there were some things a mere human didn't need to know. Maybe this love triangle was one of those things. But if the information would help her bring down the ones responsible…help her find Rainy's child…

Kayla drove back to Athens, her heart floundering in her chest. Maybe she wasn't objective enough to conduct this investigation properly. She could talk to Jim, let him help. Or Hadden.

She dismissed both possibilities.

She owed it to Rainy to do this one personally. The promise. She couldn't back out on that promise now. No matter how hard the going got.

Rainy was counting on her. Rainy's child or children had to be found. The motivation behind this evil legacy had to be uncovered, those behind it brought to justice.

Kayla had to do her part. Alex and the others had already done theirs.

Her cell phone vibrated, reminding her that she'd set it on silent vibrate before going into David Gracelyn's office.

"Ryan."

"Mom, where are you?"

For an instant panic gripped Kayla's heart.

"What's wrong?" She glanced at the clock. 6:15. Had she made a mistake about the time to pick up her daughter at choir practice? Had something happened?

"Nothing, Mom," Jazz said, relieving her mother's mushrooming anxiety with the simple statement. "My friend Lexi wants to know if I can spend the night with her so we can study for the science test tomorrow."

"Jazz." Her daughter knew how much she hated last-minute sleepovers like this. They always put someone involved at a disadvantage. The girl was probably standing right beside Jazz, listening, hoping.

"It was her mom's idea," Jazz put in quickly. "Honest. She said she'd make homemade pizza and everything. No TV, just studying."

Kayla hoped her lack of cooking skills wasn't the motivation behind her daughter's mention of *homemade* pizza. Mary had taken to the cooking skills their mother and grandmother had taught. Kayla was just hopeless. But she could outweave her sister any day of the week. She just didn't have time for any hobbies lately.

"Please, Mom." Jazz evidently took her silence for hesitation.

Granted, Kayla could use the time to try and track down Betsy Stone. The woman apparently never went home, and certainly never responded to her messages.

Kayla caved, just like she always did. "All right, but this had better be the last time you give me short notice like this."

Her daughter's squeals of delight were sufficient

justification. The echoing peals of joy were no doubt from Lexi, who had been listening. Oh, well. Anything to make the kid happy.

Kayla tucked her phone back into her pocket and took the turn that led to Athena Academy. Like Christine, Betsy resided in one of the staff bungalows on school property. Not that she was ever there. It was late but Kayla intended to check her house as well as the infirmary for any sign of the elusive woman.

Maybe Kayla would just wait outside the nurse's house all night. After all, her daughter would be with a friend. She had no reason to go home.

That thought depressed her. The little house she and Jazz called home would be empty, too quiet and too lonesome. If Kayla turned on the television or her favorite CD she could make some noise, but she'd still be alone.

Not even a whole bottle of wine would chase that empty feeling away.

Peter Hadden's image traipsed through her mind before she could stop it.

She rolled her eyes and made a scoffing sound. What was wrong with her lately? She was only twenty-nine. It wasn't like she was an old maid, not by today's standards. Maybe it was Rainy's death, her missing offspring. Or Marshall's desperate loneliness.

Suddenly and with complete certainty, Kayla knew that she didn't want to end up that way.

Alone.

Annoyed at herself for launching the pity fest, she drove to the infirmary. The place looked utterly deserted. When classes were in session, the infirmary was open 24/7, but with most students gone for the holidays, hours were limited now.

Instead of climbing back into her Jeep she opted for walking to Nurse Stone's bungalow. It was smaller and several houses away from Christine's place. The principal's lights were on. Kayla considered dropping by to talk with her but decided to give Christine some time to come to terms with her own confession before she intruded. She felt certain emotions would still be tender. Christine had been harboring that dark secret for a long time.

Kayla knocked on Nurse Stone's door but didn't get a response. The house was silent and dark.

Not to be deterred, Kayla took a seat on the top step leading to the bungalow's porch. She would wait all night if necessary. Betsy Stone had put her off long enough. She'd claimed on the two other occasions when Kayla had interviewed her that she knew nothing, but she had to. There was no way around it.

Christine stated that Betsy had had an affair with Dr. Bradford. Cleo Patra, the surrogate who had carried a baby that could possibly be Rainy's child, also claimed that a Nurse Stone had worked with Dr. Reagan during her pregnancy. The description matched Betsy Stone. No way could the elusive nurse lie her way out of this. Kayla had the proof she needed now to push her harder.

The idea that Betsy was involved made perfect sense. Betsy Stone had access to all the students' files. She would have known what to look for in the event Rainy's selection as an egg donor had required certain characteristics.

She needed to find Dr. Reagan's files. She also needed to find Carl Bradford. He appeared to have dropped off the face of the earth a couple years ago.

That made him a primary suspect.

Could he be in hiding?

The hair on the back of Kayla's neck suddenly stood on end.

She stilled, listened, her hand going instinctively to the weapon at her side.

The whisper of foliage against fabric reached her. She eased up from the step and moved silently in the direction of the corner of the house.

Kayla flattened against the aged siding. She forced her respiration to calm and listened harder.

Someone was here. Close.

Nurse Stone?

Why would she sneak around in the dark?

Where would she have left her car?

Kayla moved along the side of the house, pausing to listen every few seconds. The sound never came again. In fact, she didn't hear any kind of sound. Not even the crisp night air stirred the barren limbs of the trees surrounding the staff housing area.

Nothing.

Keeping her movements stealthy, she eased all the way around the house, listening, watching. Still nothing.

She made another round of the house, this time looking in the windows. Everything seemed normal.

When she felt certain she was alone, she moved back to the front of the house and waited in the shadows of the porch.

Most of the staff members who lived on campus were away for the holidays. It wasn't impossible that Betsy Stone had taken a trip to wherever her family resided. She didn't always report in to Christine during the school's downtime. Kayla would have to question Christine about any family Betsy had and look into that possibility if the woman hadn't shown by daylight.

She shook herself, ridding her body of the lingering sensations of not being alone in the dark. Looking at the situation from a rational standpoint, it wasn't impossible that she was feeling paranoid since Rainy's murder. She'd worked plenty of investigations in the past, even a couple of murder cases, and hadn't gotten spooked. But Rainy was more than just a case, she was a lifelong friend. A good friend. Maybe that was the reason Kayla felt under constant scrutiny.

But that wouldn't explain the person she'd chased through the cemetery. Whatever the reason, she didn't like the feeling of being watched. The sensation gave her a new outlook on how suspects felt when she and her partner were on a stakeout. Only, she wasn't the guilty party here.

Or was she?

The idea that Mike might have hired someone to follow her in hopes of pinning some bad rap on her to help him gain custody of their daughter slammed into her brain with all the subtlety of a broad ax.

What if Mike didn't just want to see Jazz? What if he wanted her all to himself? Those meager monthly payments could stop and maybe being a single father would make him look less self-serving to his superiors. Getting custody of Jazz might help to mend his damaged reputation. After all, being a father could go a long way in changing people's opinions about a man.

He would take Jazz over Kayla's dead body.

She shivered.

There were people who could arrange that very situation.

Shit. Now she was really dancing to the tune of paranoia.

Maybe she'd take a walk down to Christine's anyway. Talk for a few minutes. Ask about any family Betsy Stone might have. Anything to get her mind off Mike and stalkers.

As she strode along the sidewalk she mentally kicked herself for being such an idiot. She was not afraid of Mike Bridges. She doubted his damaged reputation could be mended if he showed up in front of his commander with a whole gaggle of kids. For all Kayla knew, Jazz might not be his only child.

Something else she didn't want to think about.

She tapped on Christine's door and waited. The sound of the television filtered through the wall. One of those legal dramas everyone who had time for television loved.

She rapped again and this time while she waited she surveyed the darkened area around the bungalows. The inky drive that cut in front of the small homes. The thick copse of trees that provided shade during the long, hot summers. In the distance, the dormitory she'd once occupied stood, scarcely visible and tomb-silent in the meager moonlight. If Jazz attended Athena she would stay there. Instantly the memory of midnight snacks and giggles echoed through Kayla's mind. No matter how closely they were monitored, the Cassandras always managed to have the occasional midnight rendezvous.

Kayla smiled. Their lives had been so different then. Who would have thought they'd have grown up and lost Rainy. That familiar ache pierced her. Each of them had achieved a level of professional success any woman would find satisfying. And it wasn't as if their personal lives were any more screwed up than the average person's in this day and time.

But they'd felt so special in their Athena days. Like the rest of the world couldn't touch them. Somehow above it all.

They'd been wrong. Evil had touched them through Rainy. Whoever had set that evil in motion had to be found and stopped. What if more students had been touched by it? There was just no way to know yet.

Kayla looked away. She felt torn. Jazz would blossom here. No doubt about that. But would she be safe from men like Dr. Reagan and Dr. Bradford?

Would she really be safe anywhere?

Just another worry for a parent.

She expelled a sigh. Every parent went through

these same scenarios, or very similar ones in any event. Protecting her child was priority one.

She frowned. Why hadn't Christine answered the door? She tried to peer in a window, but the blinds were closed.

Kayla pivoted and banged a little harder this time.

Cocking her head, she strained to listen.

Over the sound of the television program she heard…a muffled groan or cry.

Adrenaline lit like a wildfire in her veins.

She tried the door.

Locked.

Not wanting to waste time picking the lock she reared back and kicked the door in.

It flew inward, banged against the wall.

Christine lay on the floor. She reached out toward Kayla then wilted into a heap.

Kayla rushed to her.

"Christine, are you—"

And then she saw the blood.

Far too much for comfort.

"I'm calling for help."

Not leaving Christine's side she stabbed the speed dial number for 911 on her cell.

Once she'd passed along the necessary details she focused her attention on doing what she could for Christine.

As she attempted to slow the blood spilling from her friend's abdomen, she wondered aloud, "What the hell happened here?"

Christine gasped in pain, then stuttered, "I—I—"

Her eyes looked glassy. Her skin was too cool to the touch.

Kayla swore silently. Not good. She took the necessary steps for rudimentary treatment of shock, careful to keep her right hand over the wound. Despite her best efforts blood still seeped between her fingers.

Christine struggled to say something…but her words were nothing more than choked gasps.

"It's okay," Kayla assured. "Just relax. Help is on the way. We'll figure this out later."

Christine's eyes closed. Her awkward, writhing movements ceased.

Fear rocketed through Kayla.

"Stay with me, Christine."

As she checked the woman's vitals with her free hand she did the only other thing she could…she prayed.

Chapter 8

At eight o'clock on Friday morning Christine Evans was still holding her own in Intensive Care. The surgeon had said that, if she made it through those first critical hours after the surgery, she would probably survive. But he couldn't give any assurances.

The bullet had done some serious damage, and the blood loss was extensive. Basically it was a miracle she was alive at all. Kayla couldn't help thinking she was hanging on so she could identify whoever had attempted to end her life. She just hoped her friend made it. Burying two friends in one year would simply be too much.

Kayla had called the Cassandras. A forensics team had swept the crime scene, under her partner's watchful eye. She wanted to get back over there first thing this morning and go through the steps herself. A murderer just didn't walk into a person's home and take a couple of shots without leaving some sort of evidence. All one had to do was look closely.

Oftentimes a person familiar with the environment would notice things a trained professional wouldn't. Kayla had been in Christine's bungalow enough times to know the way things should be. That wasn't the only place she intended to look. The killer might have been looking for access to students' files or other sensitive records.

Since Christine couldn't tell her what had happened, Kayla had to go on speculation. First she had to rule out robbery, then revenge or an act of passion. Her gut told her that none of those would be the perp's motive.

Every instinct she possessed screamed at her that this was about Rainy. About the egg harvesting. But she had to view this like any other case. The fact that she had close personal ties to the school as well as the victim didn't change things. Standard operating procedure dictated the steps.

To hell with SOP. As soon as Christine's doctor made his rounds and gave Kayla an update, she was going directly to Athena Academy. Maybe following instincts wasn't the course most cops would take, but, in Kayla's experience, when she didn't follow her instincts, things usually turned out disastrously.

Half an hour later the surgeon checked in on his patient and advised Kayla that it would likely be

The Silhouette Reader Service™ — Here's how it works:

Accepting your 2 free books and gift places you under no obligation to buy anything. You may keep the books and gift and return the shipping statement marked "cancel." If you do not cancel, about a month later we'll send you 4 additional books and bill you just $4.69 each in the U.S., or $5.24 each in Canada, plus 25¢ shipping & handling per book and applicable taxes if any.* That's the complete price and — compared to cover prices of $5.50 each in the U.S. and $6.50 each in Canada — it's quite a bargain! You may cancel at any time, but if you choose to continue, every month we'll send you 4 more books, which you may either purchase at the discount price or return to us and cancel your subscription. *Terms and prices subject to change without notice. Sales tax applicable in N.Y. Canadian residents will be charged applicable provincial taxes and GST. Credit or debit balances in a customer's account(s) may be offset by any other outstanding balance owed by or to the customer.

If offer card is missing write to: Silhouette Reader Service, 3010 Walden Ave., P.O. Box 1867, Buffalo NY 14240-1867

NO POSTAGE
NECESSARY
IF MAILED
IN THE
UNITED STATES

BUSINESS REPLY MAIL
FIRST-CLASS MAIL   PERMIT NO. 717-003   BUFFALO, NY

POSTAGE WILL BE PAID BY ADDRESSEE

SILHOUETTE READER SERVICE
3010 WALDEN AVE
PO BOX 1867
BUFFALO NY 14240-9952

GET FREE BOOKS and a FREE GIFT WHEN YOU PLAY THE...

7 7 7

Lucky 7

SLOT MACHINE GAME!

Just scratch off the silver box with a coin. Then check below to see the gifts you get!

YES! I have scratched off the silver box. Please send me the 2 free Silhouette Bombshell™ books and gift for which I qualify. I understand I am under no obligation to purchase any books, as explained on the back of this card.

300 SDL D356   **200 SDL D36N**

FIRST NAME   LAST NAME

ADDRESS

APT.#   CITY

STATE/PROV.   ZIP/POSTAL CODE

7	7	7	**Worth TWO FREE BOOKS plus a BONUS Mystery Gift!**
🍒	🍒	🍒	**Worth TWO FREE BOOKS!**
♣	♣	♣	**Worth ONE FREE BOOK!**
🔔	🔔	🍒	**TRY AGAIN!**

www.eHarlequin.com

(S-B-12/04)

DETACH AND MAIL CARD TODAY!

touch and go for a few more days. The coma she was in was a good thing, since it allowed Christine's body to concentrate solely on healing itself. The doctor explained that many times after catastrophic trauma, a coma would be induced if a patient didn't lapse into one on her own. Like last night, he couldn't offer any real assurances other than her chances of recovery were well within the range to offer hope.

The trip from Phoenix to Athens was spent in deep supplication for her friend's speedy recovery.

As she pulled up in front of Christine's bungalow on the Athena campus, she punched in her partner's cell number and waited for him to answer.

"Got any news for me?" It was likely too early to have any feedback on the forensics search, but if the guys found anything other than the blood trail Christine had left in her attempt to get to the phone, Jim Harkey would know it, since he'd been there.

"Nada."

Definitely not what she had wanted to hear. "Dammit."

"My sentiments exactly," he echoed. "Her blood, nothing else. No sign of forced entry, other than what you did to the front door getting in. No indication whatsoever that she'd had company. Nothing. Prelim on the slugs indicates a silencer was used."

They wouldn't be getting any breaks on this one. There would be plenty of prints to run, some of which might belong to the Cassandras who'd visited Christine's bungalow a few months back, on that fateful night when they'd learned of Rainy's accident. And there would likely be many others. As principal of the academy, Christine often entertained distinguished guests and parents of potential students as well as staff members. The lack of sound would lessen the probability that anyone saw or heard anything.

The memory of the invitation Jazz had received shook loose from the far corner of her mind to which she'd banished it. The danger at Athena Academy had moved to a new level. Something else she had to consider as soon as her life calmed down for two minutes.

Not going to happen, a little voice reminded.

Probably not. Her life had always been anything but calm. Why would the routine be any different now?

Kayla gave Jim her agenda for the morning and promised to check back in with him in a couple of hours. She emerged from the car, dragging on her jacket in deference to the cool morning air. She had a feeling the temps wouldn't reach the fifties as the weatherman had suggested. Christmas was scarcely more than a week away so she had no room to complain. The winter had been relatively mild thus far.

Christmas. Man, she had to get a tree up. Jazz was counting on decorating this weekend.

Then the significance of the day broadsided her.

Friday.

They had dinner with Mike tonight.

Another round of hot curses spilled past her lips. Just her luck. She needed an evening with him like she needed a root canal.

Kayla unlocked the padlock her partner had

placed on Christine's damaged door and then ducked beneath the yellow crime scene tape.

The smell of coagulated blood hit her nostrils the moment she entered the living room. She would never get used to that odor. Her fingers located the switch and flipped on the overhead light.

It wasn't easy coming back to the scene of a crime that involved a friend or loved one, but Kayla had to look things over for herself. Jim was a damn good cop, the forensics guys the best, but she had to do this. Had to be certain nothing was missed.

She moved through Christine's bungalow twice, taking her time, surveying from ceiling to floor and all places in between. One of her instructors at the police academy had reiterated over and over again how it was the little things that solved most crimes.

In the kitchen she hesitated before moving on. Knowing full well the forensics techs had already done so she opened the dishwasher and peeked inside. Empty.

She closed the appliance and leaned against the counter, took a moment to survey the small, galley-style kitchen one last time. A dish towel lay on the counter directly across from her position. Hanging from the overhead cabinet was a rack that held a half dozen or so stemmed wineglasses. But the rack and the glasses weren't what captured her attention. It was the tiny reddish speck on the white counter next to the dish towel.

Kayla crossed the narrow expanse of tile to peer down at the speck. She looked from the speck to the array of wineglasses hanging above it. She withdrew a plastic glove from her jacket pocket and slipped it onto her right hand. Careful not to touch the rim of the glasses, she tilted each one and sniffed. At least two had not gone through the dishwasher. The scent of wine still lingered in the bowls. The fleck of red lay directly beneath one.

Next she picked up the towel and sniffed. Aside from the scent all towels had after lying on the counter a day or so, the distinct aroma of wine was unmistakable.

If Christine's guest had been invited in and they'd shared some wine—tests performed at the E.R. indicated she'd had at least one glass—then it was no wonder there were no signs of forced entry. Her shooter hadn't been a foe. He, or she, had been a friend.

Playing devil's advocate, Kayla stood back and surveyed the small area of counter. It was possible Christine had had wine alone or with someone else prior to the shooter's visit.

But why would she store unwashed wineglasses? Why simply dab them out with a dry dish towel and stick them back in the rack?

Okay. If she'd had wine last night, where was the opened bottle? It wasn't listed on the forensics inventory her partner had rattled off to her.

She opened the refrigerator. No wine. It wasn't anywhere else in the house because she'd already walked through twice.

No way. This would be too easy. She pivoted and

crouched down in front of the sink cabinet. Sure enough, behind those innocuous-looking oak doors stood a half-empty bottle of red wine.

Kayla shook her head slowly from side to side. She snagged her cell phone from her belt and entered Jim's number. Whoever had shot Christine had some brass ones, that was for sure. While she'd lain there struggling on the living room floor, her shooter had painstakingly cleared away the signs of his presence—except for the wine. What had stopped him? Maybe Kayla's knock on the door.

Or maybe Kayla was wrong. The wine could have been something Christine had opened days ago, but not likely. Anyone who drank wine knew that it wouldn't last more than a few days at room temperature after being opened. Not even red, when it was best served at room temp.

She explained to her partner that she needed one of the techs to stop back by and pick up the wine and glasses. She didn't want to risk contaminating the evidence by trying to haul it in herself. Though whoever had done this had likely wiped the bottle as well as the glasses in an effort to clear away any prints, there was always the chance at least a partial would be found. Not to mention DNA evidence left behind on the rims of the glasses.

Prints and DNA were pretty much useless without a suspect to compare them with, but Kayla would take any evidence she could get. One way or another she was going to bring down whoever was responsible for this.

If she were a betting woman, she would wager that the culprit behind Christine's shooting was someone who wanted to stop the investigation into Rainy's murder.

The idea that it could have been Betsy Stone entered her mind. That was one lady she needed to get her hands on. That she was conveniently away when this kind of thing went down was just that…too convenient.

Since Kayla couldn't ask Christine about the AWOL nurse, she'd ask Rebecca, the vice principal. Kayla needed to bring her up to speed on the investigation anyway. They hadn't talked much last night. Both had been too worried about Christine.

But there were things that had to be done today.

Locating Betsy Stone was the first in a long list.

When Kayla arrived at the administrative offices another brick wall jumped out in front of her.

"What are you saying?" she demanded, too stunned to fully assimilate the vice principal's words.

"Everything is gone," Rebecca repeated. She plowed the fingers of one hand through her long, gray-streaked hair. "I can't believe it. This has never happened before."

The academy's computer banks had been wiped. Not a single bit of information remained. Nothing.

"How soon can you have the backup files?" Kayla hadn't found anything of note yet in her review of the files, but the fact that they'd been wiped indicated there was something to find. She would be working this case full-time now, which would help in her search for clues as to how the egg-mining incident came about. But she needed those files.

"Monday if we're lucky."

Since Athena Academy was still covered under the government's umbrella of unofficial projects, there would be backup files. But like everything else it took time to get anything from the government. Calls had to be made, paperwork completed. A royal pain for the vice principal, who no doubt felt overwhelmed as it was.

Rebecca took a deep breath and visibly grappled for calm. "I'll let you know the minute they're downloaded." She searched Kayla's eyes. "Do you have anything yet on who did this? Is it possible that the two incidents could be connected?"

Kayla shook her head. "It's too early to tell. We don't have anything yet." She didn't mention the wine or the lack of forced entry at Christine's bungalow. At this point even Rebecca was a suspect. Being promoted to principal would be a big step up for her. Every imaginable motive had to be eliminated.

"Please keep me informed." She looked around her office as if she didn't know where to begin or what should be done next. "I've got a million things to do."

"I'll get out of your way then." Kayla managed a weary smile. She didn't really believe Rebecca Claussen was capable of attempted murder, but it was way too early to rule anyone out. Even mild-mannered science teachers-turned-vice principals.

"Just one other thing," Kayla said, remembering

the other crucial information she'd needed. "Can you give me the telephone numbers and addresses of any family members or friends Betsy Stone has listed in her personnel file? Also," Kayla tacked on as an afterthought, "I need to know if you hear from Betsy Stone."

Rebecca obliged without protest or inquiry. The latter surprised Kayla, but it shouldn't have. Nobody wanted to be under suspicion. If Kayla was focused on Betsy, maybe she wouldn't drag Rebecca into the scrutiny.

Kayla took the info and left the administration building. She wasn't usually so cynical, but this was getting to her. Rainy was dead. Christine was hanging on by a thread. What the hell was going on here? She surveyed the buildings that made up the Athena Academy. It had once been a mental health clinic and dry-out spa for the rich and famous. Who'd have thought all these years later, after massive renovations and being blessed with such a worthy cause, that insanity would still be thriving somewhere deep within those walls.

She had to get to the bottom of this, find the one who had started it, and put a stop to the evil once and for all. Athena Academy would not be safe until she did. Not for her daughter, not for anyone.

Kayla climbed into her Jeep and sat there for a while. The sun had climbed to the midmorning mark. Her vehicle faced east. Maybe that was a sign that she needed to consider all she'd learned so far. After all, east was the traditional Navajo thinking direction.

And she definitely needed to do some serious thinking.

While Rainy was a student at Athena, she'd had what those in charge believed to be an appendicitis attack. But that was a calculated deception. In reality she had been transferred to a hospital in Phoenix where a Dr. Henry Reagan, the prime suspect, had harvested Rainy's eggs, damaging her ovaries.

Ads had been placed in a tabloid soliciting surrogates. They now knew that at least one woman, Cleo Patra, a Vegas showgirl, had responded to that ad and been implanted with a fertilized egg. Justin Cohen's sister was believed to have responded to the ad as well, and later died in childbirth. Betsy Stone had been her nurse.

Cleo Patra had successfully delivered her baby but someone had stolen the child. Cleo insisted that a Nurse Stone had assisted Dr. Reagan. She claimed to have seen her on several occasions. Kayla had no proof that Betsy was guilty of anything. Betsy insisted she had worked for Reagan to supplement her salary and had never seen anything strange going on in the office. But after Christine's confession that she had caught Dr. Carl Bradford searching through the files, and that she'd later caught Bradford and Stone together, Kayla had even more reason to believe Nurse Stone was guilty to some degree in this sinister plan. Unless she, too, had been Bradford's pawn.

And now the nurse had seemingly disappeared.

Somehow Rainy had connected all the scattered dots. She had learned at least part of what Kayla and the Cassandras now knew. That knowledge had gotten her killed. Had put them all in danger in one way or another during the past few months.

But it wasn't going away. Now that they knew the truth, intuition warned Kayla that they wouldn't be allowed to live with that knowledge any more than Rainy had been.

Rainy was dead. Someone had attempted to kill Christine. What if Nurse Stone was already out of the picture as well?

Kayla had to find her.

Kayla picked up her daughter from school. It was the last day until after the new year.

"Can we do the tree?" Jazz asked the moment her bottom landed in the passenger seat. "All my friends already have their trees decorated."

Of course they did. Kayla was always the last one to get around to the decorating thing.

"Sure." Kayla pulled out onto the street. "You know your dad is coming for dinner this evening."

"Yep." Jazz made a face that said she hated to ask but intended to just the same, "Is it okay if you don't wear your gun for dinner?"

Kayla frowned. If her weapon had ever bothered her daughter before she'd never mentioned it. More proof that things were changing.

"I guess that'd be okay," Kayla relented. What the heck? It wasn't like she wore the thing 24/7. Shooting Mike most likely wouldn't be necessary. Yet.

"Did you cook?"

Kayla glanced across the seat. If her daughter's eyes hadn't been as round as saucers and her voice hadn't sounded so incredulous, Kayla might have let the remark pass.

"What's that supposed to mean, young lady?"

Jazz bit down on her lower lip, in an effort to hold back the giggles, no doubt. "Maybe we should go out."

Kayla yanked one of her long braids. "Not necessary," she shot back. "Lu Wan's is delivering our dinner."

Her daughter's face lit up. "I love Lu Wan's!"

The truth was, she and Jazz both loved anything oriental when it came to cuisine. So did Mike, she'd recalled. Though Kayla was far from happy about this arrangement, she had to do the right thing. Tonight might as well be tolerable.

With more than two hours to spare before the food and the father arrived, she and Jazz picked up a tree at a local lot and did the decorating thing. Kayla watched her daughter and her heart filled with gladness. How had she been so lucky? She couldn't help thinking of Rainy and how she'd wanted a child so badly. She'd had the terrific husband but no child. Kayla, conversely, had the terrific kid but no husband.

Life could be so ironic.

With the thought of Rainy's husband came Peter Hadden's assertion that Marshall Carrington was somehow involved in smuggling. She wouldn't believe that. Rainy would have known. Or would she?

The memory of her discussion with David Gracelyn joined the rest of the worries whirling around in her head. If Rainy was unhappy with Marshall would she have bothered to pay attention to what he'd been up to recently?

That was something Kayla would simply never know.

She thought of Christine Evans and Nurse Betsy Stone, both women she had known for years. Respected figures at Athena Academy. Both with secrets. One hanging on to life by a thread, one nowhere to be found.

Her gaze settled on her daughter once more. Though her entire family was quite modern, they still kept close to their hearts many Navajo traditions, such as enjoying the simpler things and the love of family. Other than her misstep that last year of school at Athena, attendance there had made a tremendous impact on her life. A very good impact. She was stronger and was a better person for her time there.

But Rainy was dead.

Then and there Kayla made the decision that had been weighing so heavily on her heart. She would send her daughter to Athena Academy—but only if she solved this old evil that still loomed over the school like a dark cloud.

Finding that truth was more than a matter of her job, more, even, than a matter of the promise…it was her quest. She must succeed in this quest to ensure her daughter's future.

For the first time in a long time Kayla felt at peace with what lay before her.

The doorbell rang just then, and a whole new layer of tension and trepidation wrapped around her.

Mike was here.

Jazz was about to spend her first evening with her father.

Jazz opened the door and Mike towered in the threshold. He wore his Air Force uniform, for Jazz's benefit, Kayla suspected. He wanted to impress his daughter.

"For you." He held out a large bouquet of lovely cut flowers in Kayla's direction.

Uncertain what to say, she accepted the sweet-scented peace offering.

"And for you." He pulled a smaller, similar bouquet from behind his back and offered it to Jazz. "Pretty flowers for a pretty lady."

So it began.

Mike laid on the charm and Jazz soaked it up like a sponge. Dinner arrived a few minutes later and they ate. Mike told an amazing assortment of military stories and Jazz loved every moment of it.

Kayla tried hard not to resent how much her daughter appeared to enjoy her father's company, but she just couldn't help herself. It was so unfair. All this time she'd managed without him, and now he was here, as big as life and stealing the show. She felt like an actress who'd won the role of a lifetime only to have it jerked out from under her at the last moment by a devious understudy.

But he was here. He was Jazz's father. To pray that he would go away would be both unfair and unkind on a basic level. She couldn't do that to her daughter.

Jazz was a bright child. As jealous as it made Kayla to watch her revel in her father's attention, Jazz knew who had been there for her all these years.

Suddenly Kayla realized what really bothered her about Mike's presence. She'd gotten over him long ago. She really wasn't afraid of him, not really. What she was afraid of was being second-best in her daughter's eyes.

Jazz looked toward her at that moment, as if Kayla had somehow telegraphed that last thought. She smiled widely, appreciatively.

She loved her mother. She appreciated Kayla's tolerance of the situation. It was all there in those big hazel eyes.

Kayla didn't have to worry about being second-best to Mike Bridges.

By ten Kayla had gotten pretty comfortable with Mike's presence. Her tension had softened and she decided she could tolerate an occasional visit. Thinking beyond that was more than she could deal with, so she didn't.

When Mike had said good-night to Jazz, Kayla walked him to his shiny red SUV.

"So you're heading for Nevada tomorrow?" She'd heard him tell Jazz that he had to be back on the base this weekend, but she needed to confirm it.

"That's right. I'll be in touch with you about Christmas."

Kayla tamped down the irritation that wanted to

surface. "Just keep in mind that Christmas day is spent with my family."

He nodded. "I'll work around it." He opened the driver's side door of his vehicle. "You've got my number."

Then he was gone.

Kayla stood there in the darkness and watched his taillights fade in the distance.

Jazz had told him about the church play next Sunday, the day after Christmas. He'd likely show up for that if he could get the leave time.

Again she tried hard not to resent his participation, but it wasn't easy by any stretch of the imagination.

A sound whispered across her auditory senses.

She turned slowly and stared into the inky blackness of her backyard. The thick cluster of trees blocked out any light from the star-filled night.

Wishing she hadn't given in to her daughter's request that she not wear her gun at dinner, Kayla backed into the shadows at the side of the driveway. Slowly, noiselessly, she maneuvered her way toward the rear of the house.

The tiny hairs on the back of her neck stood at full attention and goose bumps skittered across her skin like tiny pearls spilling across the floor.

For months she'd been seized by this overwhelming sensation of being watched. She'd even considered that Mike might have someone watching her, trying to gather evidence. But he'd been here tonight. Why would he have had someone keeping an eye on her tonight? Then she'd wondered if it was Hadden, but that didn't appear likely at this point.

Another sound raked across her senses. Closer. Maybe half a dozen yards from the corner of the house.

The idea that Christine Evans had been shot in her own home just last night didn't deter Kayla from moving in that direction. She didn't like being stalked, for any reason. If this was some ambitious private investigator Mike had hired, he was about to find out what it was like to two-step with a real cop.

If it was Christine's shooter, well, since she was unarmed Kayla would have to improvise.

A thud on the other side of the privacy fence that separated Kayla's yard from the neighbor's behind her had her racing in that direction.

She scaled the dog-eared wood fence in two seconds flat. The neighboring yard was empty but the gate swung back and forth on its hinges on the street side of the property. Kayla headed in that direction but took a good look first left then right before bursting through the gate. She was unarmed after all.

Nothing.

Whoever had been in her yard was gone now.

A car engine started somewhere in the distance. Brake lights flickered briefly as the vehicle zoomed through an intersection.

Black. Two doors. She couldn't make out the license plate. Just like the cemetery.

Kayla skirted her neighbor's yard rather than barreling back through it. Back in her house she found Jazz engrossed in her favorite computer game.

"I don't have to go to bed now, do I?"

The plea in her eyes won any battle Kayla might

have hoped to launch before she uttered the first protest.

What the heck? It was Christmas vacation.

She hadn't completely forgotten what it was like to be a kid.

"One more hour," Kayla qualified.

"Thanks!" Jazz gave her a big hug. She looked up at her mom then. "And thanks for not freaking out about...Dad."

Dad. God, that would take some getting used to.

"I'm a highly trained officer of the law," Kayla informed her, hoping to conceal her real feelings with humor, "I don't *freak* out."

Jazz gave her one of those *yeah-right* looks. "I gotta get back to my game."

Kayla propped her shoulder against the bedroom door frame and watched her daughter kick some cyber butt. She wondered if Jazz would want to go into law enforcement like her mom. Or maybe the legal side of things. Or even forensics. There was investigative reporting, the military or even private investigations.

All Athena graduates had their choice of futures. Her daughter would have that too.

Kayla would not fail her.

She had a promise to keep, to Rainy as well as her daughter.

Chapter 9

Monday morning brought a call from Rebecca Claussen.

The backup files for Athena were in. The download had completed at 9:30, just half an hour ago.

Kayla stared through the glass wall of Christine Evans's room in ICU. Christine lay in the bed with half a dozen lines snaking out from her toward the machines that monitored her fragile hold on life. She remained in stable condition. The doctor had made his rounds and insisted that her condition looked quite good, the prognosis more favorable with each passing hour.

But she wasn't out of the woods yet.

Things could still go either way.

At Kayla's prompting the sheriff had elicited the help of Youngtown's police chief. Between the sheriff's department and Youngtown's finest, a guard stood posted outside Christine's door 24/7.

Comfortable with Christine's care and security, Kayla headed for Athena Academy. She wanted to get into those files as quickly as possible.

The weekend had turned out pretty well considering.

Dinner with Mike had gone better than she'd anticipated. Jazz's grown-up attitude continued to amaze Kayla. She had to keep reminding herself that her daughter was only eleven…okay, she'd be twelve in a few weeks. But still, that was so damn young. How had she gotten so smart in such a short time?

She'd been cordial to her father, attentive. She hadn't overreacted or withdrawn. The whole concept amazed Kayla. She wasn't sure what she'd expected but it wasn't that. She had worried that Mike's transition into their lives would be disruptive, problematic. The ease with which he waltzed into the situation felt almost surreal.

Her grandmother had always said that when something appeared too good to be true it usually was. Trepidation trickled through Kayla. She hoped, for Jazz's sake, that her grandmother's wisdom wouldn't prove accurate this time.

Sunday dinner with her folks had gone smoothly as well. Mary had taken it upon herself to inform the family about Mike since Kayla had been tied up with the investigation into Christine's shooting. Thank God for big sisters.

Kayla's mother and father actually considered Mike's involvement in Jazz's life to be a pleasant surprise. Wow. Kayla still had trouble swallowing the overwhelming acceptance. Maybe she was the only one who'd had trouble coming to terms with this new twist. But then, her folks didn't know everything. She hadn't told them about Mike's recent troubles with the Air Force. Maybe she should have.

And then what?

Made this tougher than it was already?

No. It was best to move forward, not look back.

One thing was certain: for her Mike Bridges was still on probation. She wouldn't be letting down her guard any time soon.

Kayla parked in the admin parking area and headed straight for the files room. Rebecca had insisted that she make herself at home there. She'd also promised to have her secretary continue the search for Betsy Stone. Kayla had contacted every single relative and reference listed in Betsy's file. No one had heard from her in years. Apparently she didn't consider family a priority.

Jim was running a formal background search on Betsy, but so far he hadn't turned up anything Kayla didn't already know. Thankfully, Kayla could focus solely on this case since the shooting. That was the only good thing to come out of it. Another deputy was taking her regular shifts.

Kayla had mentally tossed around a number of

scenarios over the weekend. Her investigation of egg harvesting had revealed two things consistently. Those involved in the process were either desperate to have a child of their own, or were hoping to find the closest thing to a perfect egg donor as possible. The point was to select a donor with preferred human characteristics. Physically and mentally superior.

Rainy had been strong, healthy as the proverbial horse. No defects. She had come from a family with the same traits on both sides, in other words good stock. She possessed the other desired qualities as well. Extremely intelligent with no mental instabilities. All of which came in a beautiful package. From what Kayla had ascertained about Thomas King, the suspected sperm donor, the same could be said for him.

Considering the extreme—and illegal—measures that had been taken to select the perfect specimens, it only made sense that the resulting offspring would be provided with all the best life had to offer in order to follow through with the intended theory.

Kayla entered the main files center at Athena Academy and sat down before the computer screen. The job that lay before her couldn't be called simple. The number of files she would have to review was daunting. But she knew with complete certainty that the task would be worth the effort.

In the past few months Kayla had focused on searching for any sort of inconsistency in the files. Anything that stood out. But now she had another approach—looking for a student who resembled Rainy.

A child created with Rainy's fertilized egg might

have been sent to the finest schools on the planet. And if that child was a girl, that would no doubt have been Athena Academy. Kayla mentally kicked herself for not thinking of this earlier. Maybe she had. Perhaps she'd been looking for that connection from the beginning without actually spelling it out to herself.

It was a long shot. She couldn't be sure…it was only speculation. The child, the baby girl Cleo Patra had given birth to, might not be Rainy's. But Kayla had to try. It was the best idea she had right now.

The whole concept made sense. Those involved would consider the step pure genius. Create the perfect child, then send her to the perfect school—the same one her mother had attended. What better way to gauge results?

To narrow down her search criteria she selected students who would have attended Athena between twelve and eighteen years after Rainy's eggs were mined. That dropped the number of candidates to a more reasonable level, just under four hundred.

Kayla thought about the information Tory Patton had provided on Thomas King, then limited the criteria further by selecting only those students with either blue eyes, like Rainy's, or green, like Thomas King's. Though she knew it was possible for the offspring to have inherited an ancestor's eye color other than that of a parent, it was the next logical step to her way of thinking.

With the number of names reduced to around one hundred, she then threw in a third eliminating criteria, hair color. Rainy'd had chestnut-colored hair while Thomas King had blond. The list of names thinned to well under one hundred.

It was possible she had already disqualified Rainy's child with her rudimentary criteria, but it was all she had to work with at the moment.

Since she already suspected that surrogate mothers would have borne Rainy's babies, the offspring could have been adopted.

For attendance at Athena Academy, thorough background investigations were conducted on all potential students. Adoption information would be listed even if a parent didn't want it to be.

Unfortunately not a single student under the current criteria base had been listed as adopted. Damn.

Kayla grumbled in frustration. She needed more.

But there was no more, leaving her no alternative except to review each one of those files in-depth.

No problem. Christine's shooting was certainly related to Rainy's murder, making both a part of Kayla's ongoing case. Jazz was with her aunt Mary. Kayla had all day.

Since the files were listed in alphabetical order, that's how she began. Each file included a picture, which she scanned, looking for a hint of Rainy in every face. She reviewed every single word regarding each student, then verified all pertinent personal data such as address, number of siblings, occupation of parents. Every damned detail. It was the only way.

And even then she might be looking at the wrong candidates.

A needle in a haystack.

But for now, it was the only direction in which she had to go. Anything was better than nothing.

She wouldn't give up.

O.

O'Shaughnessy, Dawn.

Kayla stared at the image of the young, blond-haired woman with the gold-green eyes.

Her heart thundered, forcing the blood to roar in her ears.

It was incredible. The facial structure…cheekbones, mouth, even the straight slant of her nose was all Rainy.

"Jesus Christ."

The hair and eyes were exact replicas of Thomas King.

The age was perfect.

Kayla had used Athena resources as well as law enforcement ones to verify her suspicions. The parents listed for Dawn O'Shaughnessy had never existed. The street address was false, the mailing address was a post office box that had changed hands a dozen times in the intervening years. The social security numbers for all three amounted to identity theft of the deceased.

Her hunch—shot in the dark, really—had paid off. Dawn O'Shaughnessy not only had the right looks, her background was as trumped-up as Santa Claus's, no offense to the upcoming holiday.

Damn, that reminded her, she had a couple of gifts she still had to pick up.

Kayla scrubbed at her forehead.

Last-minute shopping would have to wait. Right now she had to find this Dawn.

DNA testing would easily confirm that she was Rainy's child. Permission to conduct such testing was another matter altogether. She could only hope the girl would be as determined to learn the truth as Kayla was.

Her next step was to call the Cassandras and pass on the news. Before she reached for the phone she e-mailed Alex a copy of the file. Alex's FBI contacts could be useful in finding the girl.

As usual, Darcy, Sam, Tory and Josie were unreachable. Kayla left messages for all four. Hearing Alex's voice went a long way in soothing Kayla's frazzled nerves.

"It's her," she told her Cassandra sister. "I know she's Rainy's daughter. Did you look at that picture?"

Dawn O'Shaughnessy had only attended Athena Academy for one year, her junior year. That didn't really surprise Kayla. To keep the girl at the academy much longer would have been a risk. Selecting that particular year for her attendance had proven well thought out. As a junior Dawn would have had flying lessons as well as numerous other advance survival and self-defense skill courses at her disposal.

She had excelled in all.

"It's incredible," Alex said, her voice scarcely more than a whisper. "The resemblance between her and Rainy is remarkable once you get past the golden hair and extraordinary eyes."

"We have to find this girl."

"I'm working on it already," Alex assured her. An extended pause set Kayla's nerves further on edge. "But I feel like I need to be there. For Christine…and for you."

Kayla closed her eyes and held back the emotions that wanted to overflow. "That would be good. I could use your help." And your support, she didn't add.

"I've talked to Justin, and he wants me to fly over tomorrow. You know this affects him as well."

She was right. Justin Cohen's sister had been one of the surrogates, if their theory proved true. Although according to hospital records, the child she'd carried had died, too. Then again, look how accurate Rainy's records had been….

Would Dawn have any ideas about her past? Wherever she had gone to college or now worked was a total mystery. At this point it looked as if the girl simply vanished after her one year at the academy.

There was always the chance she could be dead.

Kayla pushed aside that theory. She needed her alive. She wasn't going to allow herself to believe otherwise.

"Call me when your flight arrives," Kayla reminded Alex.

As she disconnected the call, she felt stronger already just knowing that Alex was on her way.

They were getting close now.

Kayla could feel it.

She packed up her notes, shut down the system she'd been using. At this point there was no reason to share what she'd discovered with anyone else. Especially since she wasn't sure who she could trust, and what she had was clearly circumstantial. She hated to think of Rebecca Claussen as anything other than an ally, but she wouldn't take the risk. Peter Hadden's tall, handsome image popped into her head. She was actually surprised that she hadn't heard from him this weekend, after Christine's shooting. Maybe he was tied up on a big case.

Or maybe he'd decided that working with Kayla wasn't worth the effort. Then again, after what he'd said to her in his car that night, maybe he was simply too embarrassed by his own admission.

It was dark already when she returned to the parking lot, but her mind wasn't really fixed on how late it was. She kept playing Peter's words over and over. He was attracted to her.

She hesitated, her hand on the Jeep's door. *Peter?* Since when had she started referring to him as Peter?

Dumb, Kayla, she chastised as she opened the driver's side door. Really dumb.

She hesitated before climbing into the vehicle. That creepy sensation of being watched engulfed her.

Kayla surveyed the deserted parking area. Had everyone gone home already? Rebecca hadn't even popped in to say good-night. Was she still inside? But her car wasn't in the lot.

Kayla sat down behind the wheel of her Jeep and closed the door, instinctively depressing the lock button.

The incidents were growing closer, increasing in frequency. Whoever was tracking her was growing bolder.

Kayla started the engine and shifted into drive. Tail or no tail, she had things to do. Intimidation, if that was the intent, wasn't going to slow her down. She touched the weapon at her side. Not in this lifetime.

With even more certainty, she had reason to believe Christine's shooting as well as this persistent shadow were connected to Rainy's murder. Someone knew Kayla was getting closer to the truth.

How close would she be allowed to get before more aggressive steps were taken to intervene?

Only one way to find out.

Kayla drove straight to Christine's bungalow. She passed slowly, then abruptly stopped halfway down the street that would lead to Betsy Stone's home.

She climbed out of the Jeep. Strode straight up to Christine's home and performed a perimeter check. A guard hadn't been posted, since it was unlikely further evidence could be gathered from the scene.

Kayla turned all the way around, scanned the moonlit area. Her shadow stayed out of sight, but he was there. She felt his presence.

Kayla walked the distance to Betsy Stone's place. As with Christine's, she walked the perimeter, checked the doors and windows. Nothing had been disturbed.

Nurse Stone had not returned to her small, cozy home.

Kayla didn't have to speculate on that conclusion. Last time she'd stopped by she'd taped the doors, front and back, as well as the windows. If anyone had entered the premises the transparent tape would have been broken or detached. In each instance the tape was exactly as she'd left it.

Wherever the good nurse had disappeared to, she hadn't returned to her home or the campus as far as anyone knew.

Was she running for her life, or on the run?

Or dead?

Kayla had to find her, if she was still alive. She was the key.

Then and there Kayla made another decision. Whether Betsy Stone showed or not, she intended to get a search warrant on her home first thing tomorrow. If there was any evidence inside those four walls, Kayla wanted it before someone else got hold of it. But she had to get it legally, or anything she found would be inadmissible in court.

The possibility that Christine's shooter could have already pilfered Stone's house punched a hole in Kayla's hope, but she had to be sure. Overlooking any lead or aspect, no matter how remote, was bad police procedure. Kayla prided herself on good cop work, and she wasn't about to change now.

When she'd looked her fill she drove to Mary's house. She hated missing dinner with her daughter but it was too late to worry about that now.

She braked to a stop at the curb, her full attention zeroing in on the red SUV parked behind her brother-in-law's truck.

Until she'd gotten out and walked up to the vehicle so she could make out the license plate she told herself that it couldn't be. Had to be a coincidence.

But she was wrong.

1PILOT.

Mike.

Fury exploded inside Kayla as she strode up the walk and onto her sister's porch.

The scene inside the house only fueled her already out-of-control fury and frustration—a volatile mix under any circumstances.

Mike, looking as much at home as any member of the family, sat on the sofa next to Jazz. Mary's husband occupied his favorite chair. Mary's two boys were sprawled on the floor, heads cupped in hands, watching television.

"Hey, Kayla." Her sister greeted her, the door held open wide as if the scenario playing out inside her living room was completely innocent and totally normal. "I was worried."

The worry in Mary's eyes was the only thing that kept Kayla from going off then and there. The expression on her face signaled that she wasn't completely comfortable.

"Sorry, I was on a case." Her gaze shifted to Mike. "What's up?"

Mary ushered her into the room and closed the door. "Mike dropped in on us a couple hours ago," she explained, keeping her tone light and cheery. Too cheery. "He had the day off and thought he'd drive down."

Mike finally bothered to join the conversation. He stood and walked toward Kayla.

She worked hard at keeping her face free of the anger boiling inside her. "Really?" The tension in the one word was thick enough to cut with a knife. "How nice."

He flared his hands. "I tried to call you today but never could catch you at home."

"That's why I carry a cell phone," she inserted with an exaggerated smile.

A frown marred his handsome face. "I…ah…" He shook his head. "I don't have your cell number."

As much as she wanted to bite off his head and spit down his neck, he was right. Dammit.

"Anyway," he went on, "I left a couple of messages on your machine en route."

"You drove all this way not knowing if we'd gone out of town for some reason?" That just didn't sound like the self-serving guy she'd once known.

He shrugged. "I had to take the chance. Something's come up at the base and I won't be able to get away this weekend. I didn't want to have to wait until after Christmas to give Jazz her present."

Fury mushroomed inside Kayla all over again. He'd come bearing gifts? Perfect.

"Come look, Mom!" Jazz motioned for her to join her at the dining room table.

Mary looked utterly mortified.

Kayla had a bad feeling.

"Isn't it cool?"

On Mary's dining room table Kayla saw her daughter's gift from her newly interested father.

A state-of-the-art, big-name laptop computer.

Not one of the no-frills models Kayla had purchased. She recognized the compact machine at once. It must have cost at least two grand.

Son of a…

"It's exactly what I wanted."

Kayla smiled and made all the expected responses. What else could she do? Her daughter was clearly thrilled. But Kayla felt sick to her stomach. What was she supposed to do with the laptop computer she'd purchased? What in the world would she buy for her daughter now?

There was no way to top Mike's gift.

Kayla suddenly felt exactly like second best.

She nibbled at the dinner Mary thrust in front of her. Her mouth somehow tossed out the necessary answers whenever someone addressed her. But she didn't know how she kept it up. Only by the grace of God.

Finally Mike mentioned that he should get on the road. He couldn't be away from the base as long as he would have liked.

Poor bastard, Kayla thought with absolutely no sympathy.

She stiffened as he kissed his daughter goodnight. But it wasn't really his gesture that got to Kayla—it was the way her daughter responded. She hugged him so tight…as if she wanted to hang on…and on.

Kayla told herself she could be rational about this as she followed Mike outside. But the moment they were alone that possibility evaporated in a blast of red-hot anger that should have melted the soles of her shoes.

"How could you?" she demanded between clenched teeth. He'd upstaged her Christmas. Had outmaneuvered her.

"What're you talking about?" Mike laid on that innocent look just a little too thick.

"I had already bought her a laptop," Kayla snarled like a wounded animal. Only he, or maybe some criminal, could bring out the beast in her like this.

He held out his hands in bewilderment. "I had no idea." He dropped his arms back to his sides and cocked his head to eye her suspiciously. "What exactly are you accusing me of, Kayla? You think I did this on purpose?"

"Don't try that innocent gig on me, Mike," she ground out. "Remember, I know you. I learned your MO the hard way."

"Don't confuse me with one of your criminals." His face tightened with his own mounting anger. "I'm only trying to do the right thing here."

"Too little too late, hotshot." She planted her hands at her hips. "Do you think you can just come back here and act like the past twelve years didn't happen? Get real, Bridges, this is not a game. This is real. I'm not going to let you play games with Jazz's feelings."

"I'm not playing games." A muscle in his hard jaw flexed. "I have a right to see my daughter. I'm sorry if my showing up tonight was an inconvenience but to be honest, you weren't around, so what does it matter?"

Any hopes she'd had of keeping this civil vanished. "You bastard. I have a job to do. Don't you dare hold that against me. You've used your career to get out of every personal responsibility you've ever had. You have no right to come here and judge me."

"I have as many rights as you do," he threw back. "Ask any lawyer."

Fear tightened around her throat like the greedy fingers of the grim reaper. "Don't even think about it, Bridges," she cautioned. "I'll dig up your every escapade. You think your name is mud now, just try me." She glared at him, infusing every ounce of determination she possessed into that lethal stare. "You will regret it."

"I tried to reach you," he restated, visibly backing off.

The about-face startled Kayla. Was this some kind of new tactic? "So you said. Just remember, we do this my way. Next time you want to see Jazz you don't show up until we've squared it. Got it?"

He hesitated, but only for a split second. "Got it."

"I guess you'd better get on the road."

He nodded, his gaze averted, his posture still rigid in spite of his composed tone. "I'll be in touch."

Kayla didn't move until he was gone from sight. She closed her eyes and grappled for calm. What the hell was he thinking? Instinct warned that it was not nearly as simple as he wanted her to believe it was. The fear that had gripped her throat relaxed marginally, just enough for her to draw in a much-needed breath.

She definitely could not trust him.

"Why'd you do that?"

Kayla whirled around at the sound of Jazz's voice. Her daughter stood on the porch staring at her, tears glistening on her cheeks, hurt shining in her big eyes.

"Jazz, you don't understand." Kayla started toward her. "Your dad and I—"

"I understand," she accused. "You want him to go away like before. You don't want him to come around any more."

Kayla's heart bumped against her sternum, sending a shattering ache reverberating through her. "No, sweetie, that's not true." When she started up the porch steps Jazz backed away.

"I know you don't like him," she said, her voice shaky with emotions. "But I do."

Kayla exhaled a heavy breath as she crossed to where her daughter hovered in the door, half in, half out of the house. "I know you do. I'm not trying to make him go away." She held out her hand to her daughter but Jazz dodged her touch. "Let's go home now. We can talk about this tomorrow when we've both settled down."

Jazz shook her head. "I'm not going with you. I'm staying here."

Before Kayla could say more Jazz ran inside. Mary, who'd waited by the door, clearly torn between interfering and keeping her mouth shut, stepped out onto the porch.

"Let her be," she offered gently. "This is all so confusing for her. Let her spend the night with me."

"But, Mary, we need to work this out." Kayla fought back the sting of tears.

"Of course you do, but not tonight. Let her sleep on it." Mary managed a faint smile. "You know what they say, absence makes the heart grow fonder. She'll wake up in the morning asking for you. You know how kids are."

Kayla could only hope. She shook her head. "Why is it I'm the bad guy?" It just wasn't fair. "He flits around all over the world while I'm here taking care of business, then when he finally shows up I'm the one doing everything wrong."

Mary hugged her close, smoothed a hand over her hair. "Shhh," she urged. "Don't do this to yourself. You know this isn't your fault. It'll work out." Mary drew back then, her cheeks damp with the emotion she could not restrain. "Mark my words, sister, all will work out if you allow nature to take its course."

Kayla released another of those soul-shuddering breaths. "You're right. I'm overreacting."

Mary patted her arm reassuringly. "You're human. Go home. Get some sleep. I'll deliver your precious daughter to you tomorrow after choir practice—or you can pick her up."

Kayla had forgotten about that.

"I'll pick her up. Kiss her good-night for me, would you?"

"I will."

Leaving with that heartache unresolved between her and her daughter was one of the hardest things Kayla had ever had to do. But she was the grown-up here. Her daughter didn't fully understand. It would take time and patience on both their parts.

Tomorrow things would be better.

Chapter 10

Kayla parked in her driveway but didn't get out of the Jeep. Her heart felt heavy with regret that she hadn't been able to make up with Jazz. But a part of her was still furious with Mike.

No doubt she would get inside and find a couple of messages from him, but why hadn't he bothered to call her office? Anyone there would have been happy to patch him through to her. The bottom line was he hadn't wanted to locate her. Not really. He'd wanted to avoid the whole confrontation and simply show up...and steal the show.

That's what he'd done, all in one fell swoop. Jazz was charmed and Kayla was the bad guy.

She closed her eyes in an attempt to push aside the

hurt and anger. Being a parent just kept getting harder…her every move lately felt wrong.

A soft tap on her window jerked her head up and her eyes wide open. Her hand was on the butt of her weapon before her brain assimilated what she saw.

Peter Hadden.

Detective Hadden, she amended, annoyed at herself for thinking of him in any other capacity.

"You planning to stay a while?"

His smile had the usual effect. She felt her tension melting despite her determination not to let him get to her on any level.

She opened the door and got out, automatically depressing the lock button as she closed it. The act had nothing to do with her certainty that someone was keeping a watch on her. An unlocked door, home or automobile, was an invitation to thieves.

"What're you doing here?" Was the wrong man popping into her life tonight destiny or what? First Mike and now *him.*

And what was so wrong with this handsome detective? another voice challenged. God, there it was. The part of her that suffered with loneliness and wished she had a physical relationship in her life. Why was it a woman didn't feel complete without a man in her life? Was this God's sense of humor at work? Or maybe it simply boiled down to basic biology.

That's all she really needed, wasn't it? Just some good sex to stave off depressing nights like tonight?

"I wanted to ask how your friend is doing."

He was lying. He hadn't driven all this way just

to find out information he could have gotten over the phone. He might be a great detective, might even fool the suspects he interrogated, but whenever he lied to her she could tell.

"She's stable." Hanging on by a thread, she didn't say. "Still unconscious, so we don't know any more about what happened than we did when we found her."

He nodded, his expression somber. He knew the way this worked better than she did. No cop wanted a case to stand still. Not moving forward equated to going backward. In some aspects of the overall investigation Kayla had made definite headway, but in others she was still running blind.

"Can we talk?"

Something changed in his expression then, and the transition set her on edge. "What's up?"

He inclined his head toward her house. "You could invite me in?"

She would have liked to think that the query was an invitation based on the other night's confession of attraction, but she sensed that there was something more on his mind.

A new kind of apprehension working its way into her composure, she shrugged. "Sure, why not?"

He followed her onto the porch, waited patiently while she unlocked the door. She flipped the wall switch and a lamp next to the sofa bloomed with soft light. She cringed. She hadn't picked things up in a while, and Christmas decorating paraphernalia was scattered everywhere.

"Would you care for a glass of wine?"

She hadn't meant to make the offer but she could damn sure use one herself. It wasn't like she could have a drink without asking him and taking the edge off this night had just gone from a nice idea to an outright necessity.

"I'd love one."

She peeled off her jacket and tossed it onto a chair. Her utility belt, including her weapon, followed. She didn't need to worry about it lying around tonight. Jazz wouldn't be here. A fresh stab of pain sliced through her heart. This evening had definitely sucked.

In the kitchen she pulled the half-empty bottle of white wine from her fridge and dug through her cabinets until she found two stemmed glasses. She thought about the wine and glasses at Christine's house. Prints had been lifted from both the glasses and the bottle, but no match in any of the databases had been found. No real surprise there.

Someone Christine knew, most likely, had entered her home, shared wine with her, then shot her. Kayla wouldn't have been so certain about that were it not for the way the glasses had been stored. Christine Evans was too particular to have put the glasses away dirty and to have stuck a bottle of red wine under the sink. In fact that quick cleanup had been so sloppy, Kayla felt certain she'd interrupted the perp.

Kayla's thoughts went back to Nurse Betsy Stone. It could have been her. Damn, she hated to think the nurse was capable of attempted murder, but she'd certainly been involved with what happened to

Rainy. Criminal activity escalated more often than not. There was every reason to believe at this point that she could be involved in most anything.

With the glasses filled, she made her way back into the living room where Peter Hadden waited. He'd occupied himself with looking at the collection of framed photos she had sitting about. Most were of Jazz, from infancy to this last Thanksgiving. A few of family. Then one or two with Jazz and Kayla together. Not a single one of the *father.*

God, she had to get past the whole Mike issue. It wasn't like his sudden appearance was the end of the world.

Enough was enough. She glanced at the answering machine as she passed it, two messages. Just like he'd said.

"Your daughter is really gorgeous," Peter said as he set a photograph back on the mantle.

Hadden. Not Peter.

"Thanks." She handed him the glass in her left hand.

"Thank you." That high voltage smile flashed, sending a little shock wave straight through her.

Flustered, frustrated, and just plain fed up, Kayla took a long drink of her wine. She had to regain control here.

"She's with your family tonight?"

Nosy, wasn't he?

"Yeah. We had a fight." She gulped another swallow, hoping against hope the alcohol would hurry up and do its woefully needed work.

"About Mike Bridges."

She almost choked, coughed then cleared her throat. "You got a crystal ball in your pocket, Detective?"

Maybe he was the one who'd been following her. Nah, that couldn't be right. What would be his motivation?

"I called looking for you over the weekend and your partner said I shouldn't give you any grief because you had enough already with the shooting of Christine Evans and Jazz's father showing up."

Kayla considered whether capital punishment applied when one cop killed another. Jim must have really been worried about her. She had complained a number of times about Hadden's annoying interference. She narrowed her gaze. More likely the fine detective had wormed it out of her pushover of a partner.

"That's right," she admitted. "He's decided he wants to know his daughter after all this time." Why the hell was she even telling Hadden this? "His timing stinks, but then it always did."

Hadden set his glass on the nearest table. "I wish I didn't have to dump more bad news on you."

Kayla went still. "What?" She set her glass next to his. Had he learned something else about Rainy or Marshall? If he was here to try and convince her that Marshall was a bad guy, well, he could just save himself the energy.

"Kayla, Marshall Carrington is dead."

She blinked. Her mind refused to accept the words her ears clearly heard. "What did you say?"

"I'm sorry to have to tell you this, but he was

killed in a smuggling operation. The authorities in Bogotá haven't given us all the details yet, but the FBI is looking into the incident. The consensus is that the deal went sour and Marshall was caught in the middle."

Bogotá? FBI?

She shook her head in denial. "He said he wouldn't be going to Colombia until after the new year." This didn't make sense.

"The trip got moved up. His contact in Tucson called and passed along the instructions Friday afternoon."

"But I just talked to him—"

Hadden wrapped his strong fingers around her arms and gazed down at her with genuine sympathy. "I know you didn't want to believe the worst about him, but what I told you is true and it cost him his life."

She shook her head again. "This is crazy. I need to call—" She couldn't think what to say…how to proceed. This couldn't be real. No way. There had to be a mistake. "Who identified the body?" That's it. It was a mistake. Marshall had been confused with someone else.

"A Bureau agent identified him, Kayla. There is no mistake."

She jerked free of his hold. "Why would he be involved in smuggling? It's not like he needed the money!" She froze, her mind screaming but her body unable to respond immediately. "Are…are you thinking that what he was involved in had something to do with Rainy's murder?"

"I don't know. We believe he kept that part of his

life completely secret from Rainy, but his associates could have known about her."

"How long…" God, even asking the question felt like an outright betrayal to the man she had adored and respected. "How long was he supposed to have been involved with this smuggling?" A frown nagged at her brow. "And what the hell was he supposed to be smuggling?"

"There's not a lot I can tell you," Hadden cautioned. "I can say that he'd been involved for at least two years, maybe longer. I can't share more than that at this point. But," he pressed her with his piercing blue gaze, "trust me when I say there's no evidence that ties his activities to Rainy's death."

He still refused to call it a murder.

She turned away from him, unable to deal with the truth she saw in his eyes. All that she'd believed in was suddenly going to hell. Rainy was dead. Athena Academy was somehow involved. Christine Evans and Betsy Stone were up to their necks in secrets, one fighting for her life in the hospital, the other missing, maybe even dead. And now Marshall. Jesus, that didn't even include Mike's sudden interest in her daughter.

The idea of what might be next was too terrifying to contemplate at the moment.

"I really am sorry, Kayla." Hadden moved in close behind her. Her body reacted instantly to his nearness. "I didn't come here to gloat. I wanted to be the one to tell you because I knew you'd be hurt."

Anger flared inside her. She swiveled to face him.

"Well, you were right. Bully for you. What do you want now? A medal? Thanks, Detective, but you aren't likely to find any compensation here."

The angst in his expression told her she'd accomplished her mission. She'd cut him to the bone. Somehow the realization gave her no satisfaction.

"I should go."

Before he could walk away, a truckload of contrition heaped onto Kayla's shoulders. "Wait." She closed her eyes and blew out a weary breath. "I'm the one who's sorry." She'd have to call the girls. Alex…

Who would call the Millers? She wasn't sure Marshall had any close family living. Did he have an attorney?

She opened her eyes once more and lifted her gaze to Hadden's. He did look as if he cared how she felt. Or was that wishful thinking?

She so needed something good to be real tonight.

The hurt from seeing Mike with Jazz and that damned laptop. Watching Christine lie in ICU on the edge of death. Discovering the identity of a young woman who might be Rainy's child. Marshall's death. It was just too much.

His arms were suddenly around her and Kayla didn't resist. Couldn't possibly have held back. She needed his strength, his warmth. Needed him.

For a long while he held her that way, allowing her to lean against him. But that would never be enough.

Without having to say a word, he suddenly understood that she needed more. He lifted her face to his and he kissed her, long and thoroughly. He took his time, didn't rush, allowing the sweet sensations to wash over and over her again and again.

Kayla couldn't remember how long it had been since a man had held her…kissed her this way. Didn't even want to think about it. She just wanted to feel.

He lifted her into his arms and carried her toward the hall. "Second door on the left," she murmured between kisses.

That was all the instruction he required.

Peter Hadden lowered her to her feet in the middle of her cluttered bedroom. One by one he released the buttons of her police-issue shirt, then pulled it free of her slacks and pushed it off her shoulders. He ushered her to the edge of the unmade bed, then knelt before her to remove her shoes and socks.

Kayla said nothing. She simply reveled in watching him. His unhurried movements. His close attention to every single detail, like the way he massaged her bare feet. The feel of his long fingers soothing, caressing almost undid her completely.

He released the button at her waist. She stood just long enough for him to lower the zipper then tug down the slacks. At last she was naked save for her bra and panties. The way he skimmed her body with his eyes, his expression awed, she couldn't possibly feel embarrassed, only flattered…desired.

With slow, infinite finesse he kissed her belly, teased her flesh with his tongue.

Her body quivered in anticipation. She couldn't take it.

Tugging him to his feet she assumed control. She wasn't nearly so patient and careful in removing his clothes. Buttons flew loose from his shirt. He kicked off his shoes and she dragged down his trousers and briefs.

Finally they were on the bed together, his weight bearing down on her. The panties and briefs disappeared. The bra fell away. He was touching her all over, with those skilled hands and that wicked tongue.

His kisses went on and on, pleasured every part of her and she paid him back in kind.

When neither of them could take the building tension any longer, he entered her…held completely still for one endless moment. When they could breathe again he started to move…she met his every thrust until they came together in a searing blast of frantic release.

The second time they reached for each other, both had grown bolder, more creative, allowing for an even deeper physical satisfaction. This time it was about pure pleasure, not the desperation of the first time.

His breath ragged from his recent climax, Hadden slumped against her back. The smooth, damp feel of his skin set hers on fire all over again. She snuggled deeper into the covers, arched her bottom against him and relished the feel of him on top of her, his still-hard sex pressed firmly against her buttocks.

She should have known it would be like this. Maybe that's why she'd resisted the attraction for so long.

There had been other men in her life, but some-

how, she had known Peter Hadden was different…
special. *Too good to be true.* She shivered, suddenly
uncertain of herself.

"I may not survive this night," he murmured
against her ear. "You are incredible."

Kayla couldn't prevent the smile that tickled her
lips from widening into a grin. "Don't talk," she
warned. "Catch your breath so we can go again."

He pressed his lips to her shoulder. "Fine by me."
He kissed lower, flicked his tongue in slow circles on
her flesh. "This time you can be on top first."

"You like that, do you?" she asked, forcing away
her feelings of vulnerability.

She started to turn over, but he stopped her. "Hold
still."

She obliged, unsure she actually wanted to wait
for anything. Considering the second round had been
markedly more delicious than the first, she could
only imagine how round three would be.

"What's this?"

He touched a sensitive place on her back just
above her shoulder blade.

"What does it look like, a mole?" She had noticed
a tender spot now and again at the edge of where her
bra strap hit, but each time she'd tried to see the cause
in the mirror it simply looked like an irritated mole.

"I don't think this is a mole. I think…hmmm."

"What?" She pushed her way into a sitting position, forcing him to move off her. "What is it?"

"Let me wash my hands." He climbed off the bed.
"Do you have some peroxide and maybe some Q-tips?"

"In the bathroom." Frowning, Kayla watched him trot to the adjoining bathroom. But the view had her frown fading fast. He had a great ass. Truly superb, muscled buttocks that made her insides contract with want...even after two sessions of phenomenal sex.

"Look under the sink," she shouted when she heard him rummaging through her medicine cabinet. Maybe a third round wasn't a good idea after all.

Prompted by the sound of water running she decided maybe she should at least pull on her panties. By the time she'd tracked them down and tugged them up her legs he was back, peroxide, Q-tips, and cotton balls in hand.

Her gaze instantly dropped from that well-defined chest to a six-pack abdomen and then lower still to runner's legs and a semi-aroused sex. The air hissed out of her lungs.

Oh, yes. There would have to be a round three.

Whatever tomorrow might bring...she was going to enjoy this. The damage was done. She'd slept with him. What difference did it make if it was once or four times?

"Sit." He gestured to the edge of the bed. She obeyed. He settled onto the bed behind her. "This might sting a little."

"What the hell is it, Hadden?" She absolutely would not call him by his first name and make this any more personal.

"We'll see, *Ryan,*" he mocked.

Her face flushed with the idea that he knew exactly

what she was doing. She felt him probing with one of the Q-tips and she focused on that for the moment.

"Ouch!"

"Sorry."

Sorry or not, he kept prodding. She gritted her teeth to keep from complaining further. No way was he going to call her a wimp.

"Got it."

He dabbed peroxide onto the wound. "Check this out while I get the antibiotic ointment and a bandage."

He handed her a cotton ball with a tiny object, about the size of an apple seed, on it. What the hell?

Carefully she set the cotton ball on the dresser and put on a T-shirt. She needed a magnifying glass. She picked up the cotton ball, then moved into her living room and fished for the magnifying glass she kept in her desk. If need be she'd drag out Jazz's chemistry set. But a microscope might not be necessary.

Ten minutes later, her wound covered with ointment and a bandage, she'd dug out the microscope and both she and Hadden had taken turns viewing the object.

"It's a tracking device," she pronounced, bewildered.

"I agree." He drew back from the child-size microscope and looked at Kayla. "When do you suppose you picked this up? And where?"

Thankfully he'd pulled on his pants, otherwise she might not have been able to concentrate. She raked her fingers through her hair and wracked her brain for an answer. "I don't know. I..." The mem-

ory of fainting at the academy back in August shortly
after Rainy died slammed into her memory. She'd
gone there just after Rainy's funeral to make a copy
of Rainy's medical file. She'd passed out, right by the
copier. At first she'd thought it was from stress, but
later she and the Cassandras had discovered that the
Cipher—the assassin who'd killed Rainy—had a device that used a frequency to cause people to pass out.
He'd used it to cause Rainy's accident. He'd later
tried to do the same to Alex, while she'd been driving. And he had likely used it on Kayla. And now she
could guess why.

Betsy Stone had been keeping an eye on her when
she awoke. Kayla just bet that Betsy had implanted
the device.

Christine had been there too, when Kayla woke
up. Could she have been in on it?

"How long do you think it's been there?"

He thought about that a moment. "More than a
few weeks. Couple months maybe. It's hard to say.
Your bra strap probably irritated it."

If his guess was even close to accurate, the timing fit.

She bagged the device in a Ziploc sandwich bag.
The idea that Betsy Stone had planted the device on
her while she was unconscious, probably a victim of
the Cipher's technique, made her blood simmer with
rage. No wonder her shadow had been able to follow
her every move. She had no doubt now that the numerous anomalies were connected. Rainy's death,
Christine's shooting and Kayla's shadow were all

related. "I'll have Fred Kaiser over at the lab take a look at this to confirm our suspicions."

"Good idea."

She set the bag on the counter and looked up at him. As furious as she was at the idea of Betsy Stone having done this to her—certainly no one else had had the chance—there was nothing she could do about it tonight. And she definitely didn't want to answer any more of Hadden's questions. Like him, when it came to his cases, there was only so much she was at liberty to disclose.

"So, what now?" she asked. Her heart started to hammer as she saw desire flicker in his eyes.

"It's not that late." He was right. Just past midnight. "I guess we could get some sleep since we both have a big day tomorrow."

She locked her arms around his neck and tilted her mouth toward his. "You're kidding, right?"

"Right." His mouth closed over hers and everything else drifted into insignificance.

Kayla overslept the next morning.

"Dammit." She snapped her utility belt into place and shoved her weapon into its holster.

What the hell had she been thinking last night? She grabbed the bag that contained the tracking device. She'd drop it off first, then check on Christine.

Then she intended to find Betsy Stone, dead or alive.

"The morning after is the worst part."

Her gaze collided with Hadden's. He lounged against her kitchen counter, second cup of coffee in hand. She had to look away from his damaged shirt. She couldn't believe she'd ripped it off him. Those desperate moments tumbled one over the other through her mind.

No matter how embarrassed a part of her was this morning, her body still hummed with lingering pleasure. Damn, the guy knew how to make love to a woman.

"I have to go." She couldn't talk about last night right now. Didn't even need to be thinking about it. She had to find that nurse. Alex and Justin would arrive sometime today. And she had to touch base with Sam, Darcy, Tory and Josie about Christine and Marshall. God, she still couldn't believe Marshall was dead. But it was true. And with his body still in Colombia, God only knew when a funeral would happen. "Lock up for me, would you?" She had to get out of here.

Hadden stepped in her path when she would have left the room. "I'll call you."

She nodded. Didn't want him to make promises he might not be able to keep. Her experiences thus far with commitment had been less than reliable. That's why she didn't do long-term relationships.

He took her by the arm before she could get away. "I will call, Kayla. Count on it. I'll be in the area for a day or two on another case. I hope we can have dinner."

"Gotta go."

Kayla left the handsome detective from Tucson in her kitchen. She had to have been out of her mind to have allowed things to go so far with him.

She did a bone-jarring, ninety-degree turn in Reverse out of her driveway and rocketed forward in the Jeep.

She hadn't even been out on a date with the guy and she'd slept with him!

Christ!

Was that stupid or what?

Blocking any further thought on the subject before she could start answering herself, she whipped out her cell phone and checked in with her partner. He needed to know where she would be this morning.

Next she called Mary's house, but her sister had already taken Jazz to choir practice.

Dammit. She'd wanted to talk to her daughter this morning.

She'd just have to make sure she picked her up at noon and that they spent some quality time together. Sorted out this mess. Maybe she'd even call Mike and apologize. Scratch that. She wasn't going to surrender that easily. He had to understand that his participation in Jazz's life had to be a team effort. He had to work with Kayla, not against her. Let him apologize.

The drive to the lab near Casa Grande took up precious time. Kayla didn't hang around and chat with her pal Fred. He promised he would have a full analysis for her by lunchtime and would call her cell phone. She smiled grimly at the thought that whoever was tracking her would be on a wild goose chase until they realized the game was up. Just over half an hour later, having broken a number of traffic laws, she was back in Athens.

Athena Academy looked desolate this morning. Only a few more days from Christmas, it was most likely everyone was gone for the holidays. Rebecca Claussen wasn't in yet so Kayla decided to check out Betsy Stone's place just in case she'd returned.

She parked her Jeep at Christine's bungalow and made her way on foot through and around the copse of trees that dotted the rear of the small housing area. There was still no vehicle in sight at Betsy's house, but it could be in the garage. If Betsy was in there, Kayla didn't want her to have any warning that she had company. She supposed there was some chance the woman didn't realize her cover had been blown. It took some courage to keep doing her job when Kayla had confronted her on two other occasions with certain facts. The seemingly unfazed woman had simply denied the accusations and gone on about her business. Or maybe the woman was just plain cocky. If Kayla's suspicions proved accurate, Stone had been at this for years. She'd had plenty of time to get comfortable with lying.

When Kayla reached the rear entry door to Betsy Stone's bungalow a smile slid across her face, the first job-related one in several days.

Someone had been in Betsy's house. The tape Kayla had placed across the edge of the door beneath the locking mechanism had been pulled loose from the jamb by the opening of the door.

Kayla's pulse rate jumped into double time. She hoped like hell it was Betsy.

Kayla prayed the back door wouldn't squeak as

she slowly turned the knob and ushered the wooden door inward. It obliged.

Sounds echoed from somewhere beyond the kitchen. A bedroom maybe?

Kayla moved noiselessly across the room, her weapon drawn and leveled. As she cleared the living room and started into the hall the sounds grew louder, more distinct. Whoever was in there, he or she was definitely doing some damage. The rip of fabric combined with the friction of ransacking splintered the air.

Kayla paused outside the door of the first bedroom she reached. The perp didn't let up, had no idea he or she was about to have company.

Tightening her grip on her weapon, Kayla swung around the doorjamb and leveled her weapon on the first thing that moved.

Betsy Stone.

Chapter 11

Kayla watched Betsy Stone from the observation booth on the other side of the mirror flanking one wall of the interrogation room. She hadn't admitted to anything yet other than having driven to Texas to visit her niece. Dammit. Kayla suspected it was a lie, but since she hadn't been able to reach the so-called niece, she couldn't disprove Betsy's statement.

"You realize we can only hold her twenty-four hours on suspicion," Jim said, "then we'll have to charge her or let her go."

"I know." Letting her go would be a huge mistake. Betsy Stone had been preparing to run when Kayla had found her. The woman's purse had contained her passport as well as a couple thousand dollars cash. Kayla couldn't figure out what had brought her back to her place on campus unless that's where she'd left the passport. Kayla hadn't found a thing of interest in her search. The house had been a bust, as had the woman, other than the passport. So far.

The destruction Betsy Stone had been up to in the bedroom could have been an attempt to make it look as if her home had been ransacked. With her missing and her place torn apart, anyone looking for her might tie her disappearance to Christine's shooting.

Kayla had proposed just such a scenario to her suspect moments ago, but Betsy had refused to respond.

"I'm gonna try one more thing," Kayla said, more to herself than to her partner. She couldn't let Stone slip through her fingers. She knew too much.

"Need my help?"

Kayla thought about that a moment, then said, "Yeah, I do."

She filled Jim in on her plan before sauntering into the interrogation room where Betsy Stone waited, her entire demeanor amazingly serene.

For almost a full minute Kayla stood there and peered down at her suspect, giving the woman ample time to grow apprehensive about what would happen next. Betsy Stone wore her usual conservative attire, slacks and a sweater. Her bottled-blond hair was secured at her neck to keep it out of her way. The only thing missing was the stethoscope she'd accessorized with for as long as Kayla could remember.

"Ms. Stone," she said finally, using the formal address to set the necessary tone, "I've just come from another interview room where we're holding a material witness."

Betsy looked up at her and shrugged. "I have no idea what you mean, Kayla." She rearranged her face into a frown. "Why did you bring me here? You surely know I didn't have anything to do with Christine's shooting. I wasn't even home. I only just returned from Texas."

Kayla kept the smirk off her face. She had one ace up her sleeve and it was now or never. "The witness I was referring to is Cleo Patra. She's from Vegas. Sound familiar?"

Giving Stone credit, she didn't even flinch. "I'm afraid I have no idea who you're talking about. Does she claim to know me?"

Kayla pulled out the adjacent chair and sat down. "Actually she does. About twenty years ago you worked with a Dr. Henry Reagan in providing prenatal care for the child she surrogated."

Stone blinked her blue eyes a couple of times in bewilderment. "I've already told you I worked with many women during my time with Doctor Reagan. I don't remember a Cleo Patra—one surely wouldn't forget that name. But I saw so many people, it's entirely possible that I did work with her."

"Really." Kayla pushed back her chair, allowing the legs to scrape across the tile floor. She stood, folded her arms over her chest and walked around the room, pretending to mull over the nurse's comment. She took her time, didn't rush, let the woman stew.

Eventually Kayla stopped, leveled her gaze back

on Stone's. "You don't know anything about Cleo Patra or Kelly Cohen receiving fifty-thousand dollars to become surrogate mothers."

Stone moved her head adamantly from side to side. "I have no idea what this woman is talking about." Disgust glinted in her eyes. "How could you believe anything a slut like that would say?"

Kayla quirked one eyebrow. "Slut? I'm not sure what you mean."

Stone averted her eyes. "I do remember her coming into Dr. Reagan's office," she admitted. "She was nothing but trash. She's probably making up her testimony just to get the attention." She smirked. "Cleo Patra, *please.* She's likely as unreliable now as she was then."

Kayla braced her hands on the table and leaned toward the nurse, who'd finally started to get a little nervous. "Actually, her testimony isn't all we've got to go on, Ms. Stone. Christine Evans gave a statement before the shooting indicating that she'd caught Dr. Carl Bradford going through student files around the same time Rainy's emergency surgery took place. And she caught Bradford cheating on her—with you." Kayla smiled at the slight telling flare of the woman's pupils. "It doesn't take much of a leap to put together the error in Rainy's medical files along with the damage to her ovaries from the egg harvesting to a surrogate named Cleo Patra under the care of Dr. Reagan—who, conveniently enough, performed Rainy's supposed appendectomy. Hmm. Now, why would a gynecologist be the physician of record for an appendectomy?"

Stone shook her head again. "I don't know what you're talking about. I didn't—"

Kayla put her face in the nurse's. "Yes, you did. You and Bradford selected the best candidate. Reagan took care of the rest. I know that's how it happened. Don't lie to me. It's over, Betsy, we've got you."

"No jury is going to take that whore Cleo Patra's word over mine," Stone argued, though her voice lacked conviction. The slightest hint of panic had niggled its way into her expression.

Kayla straightened. "You could be right. So, let's make this easy. Cleo has already agreed to a polygraph, we'll want the same from you. That should tell us what we need to know."

Stone's eyes rounded. "You know those things aren't always accurate."

Kayla turned her palms upward in a gesture of indifference. "If you're telling the truth you have nothing to worry about."

Stone's hands shook before she clasped them together in front of her. "I...want a lawyer."

Jim walked in just then. "Let's go, Ryan," he said to Kayla. "Christine Evans just regained consciousness. She wants to give a statement about the identity of her assailant." He flicked a suspicious glance in Betsy's direction. "She apparently knew the perp."

Kayla headed for the door. "Think about what I said, Ms. Stone."

"Wait."

Kayla stilled, turned slowly so as not to act too enthusiastic. "I really have to go. We can finish this later."

Betsy exhaled a shaky breath. "I'll tell you what I can." Her gaze fastened on Kayla's. "But you'll have to promise me protection. They'll kill me if they find out I talked."

Kayla looked to Jim and smiled. "You go ahead without me."

Jim closed the door and headed for his real destination, lunch. Christine Evans hadn't regained consciousness, unfortunately. But Kayla had suspected that Betsy wouldn't want to risk that whoever had shot Christine might have revealed something that would incriminate her. Or that the shooter's identity could be tied to her in any way.

"He made me do it," she said right off the bat but Kayla didn't believe her for a second. "Carl Bradford told me that I'd lose my job if I didn't help him. He'd already pitted Christine and me against each other. I just didn't know it." Her shoulders slumped. "I didn't do anything wrong. All I did was help him review the files so he could select the best candidate. Dr. Reagan took over from there. That's all I know. I was told nothing more." She looked up at Kayla, a plea in her eyes. "I was just a pawn. They used me."

Kayla had to suppress the urge to punch the woman. She'd helped do this to Rainy.

"Why?" Kayla asked, her tone lethal.

"I…I don't know what you mean." Stone looked scared now. Really scared.

"Why did Reagan and Bradford do this? Who backed their work…commissioned it? Why Athena

Academy?" She moved in close to the woman again. "I *need* to know."

"I don't know why," she trilled. "I just did what he made me do…that's all…" She dropped her head into her hands. "That's all I'm guilty of."

Kayla sensed she was lying. But she couldn't make her confess to anything else just yet. "And what about the tracking device? I know you did that."

Betsy's head shot up, her expression startled. "You just don't understand, if I had refused I'd be dead now. I couldn't say no…not to him."

"To the Cipher, Lee Craig?"

Stone's surprise morphed into shock. "How did you know…?" She blinked, glanced around the room like a caged animal. "You have to protect me."

Kayla ignored her plea. "I'm going to have you transferred to county lockup. It's the only way I can protect you."

To her surprise Stone nodded in agreement.

Kayla moved toward the door without saying anything more. She wanted to shake the woman, somehow make her understand that what she'd done had culminated in Rainy's death. But she had to tread carefully. Alienating Betsy at this juncture would be a mistake. She knew far more than she was telling.

"Kayla."

The woman's voice sounded small and uncharacteristically fearful. Kayla hesitated at the door and turned back to her. "Yeah."

"They'll kill me if they get to me, just like they

tried to kill Christine. You have to believe that, if you believe nothing else I say."

Kayla felt certain she would never forget the look in Betsy Stone's eyes when she said those words. She was terrified. Whatever else she knew, she understood that her life was in jeopardy because of it.

With orders in place to relocate her to county lockup, Kayla intended to check on Christine, then pick up Jazz for lunch. After she'd had her talk with Jazz, she'd pay another visit to the nurse and see if she had suddenly remembered something more. At the last minute, she'd confessed to having risked returning to the bungalow for her passport. As Kayla had suspected, she'd hoped that ransacking the place would make it appear she'd gone missing, throwing both the cops and her former colleagues off her trail.

Sitting in county lockup was no walk in the park. Kayla imagined that environment would have the woman ready to make any kind of deal she could.

Kayla didn't want to make any deals, she just wanted the truth. She wanted to bring down whoever had done this to Rainy. She wanted to clear Athena Academy, ensure that the school was safe again.

Her cell phone vibrated. "Ryan."

"Kayla, Investigator Devon just called. He's going to need you to come in ASAP and have that interview with the D.A."

"Now?" She couldn't believe this. She was in the middle of an official investigation that involved attempted murder. Not to mention the unofficial one into Rainy's murder. Surely her chat with the D.A. could wait.

"Sorry, kiddo, but this new hotshot D.A. ain't gonna take no for an answer."

Frustrated, Kayla drove all the way to Casa Grande to meet with the D.A. in charge of the bike bust that was apparently turning into the sting of the decade.

The interview didn't take long. Kayla had a feeling it had more to do with his measuring the strength of her presence and ability to present her testimony. He was taking no chances on this case. Understandable, since the key witness against the big fish he'd nailed was a slimy thief himself.

"Thank you for coming in, Lieutenant Ryan." He shook her hand and offered that million-dollar smile that had likely gone a long ways in getting him into this high-profile office.

"Not a problem," she lied. "It's my job." She produced a smile of her own and tried her level best not to look impatient. She had things to do!

"Just so you know," he said, waylaying her once more, "we've written a clause into Terrence Swafford's immunity contract."

Kayla pushed aside her impatience for a moment. "A clause?"

"If he threatens you or anyone close to you he'll be in violation and then—" the young, clearly ambitious D.A. grinned "—his ass will be mine and there will be no bargaining."

This time her smile was the genuine article. "Thanks."

So maybe this little side trip hadn't been a waste of time after all.

She glanced at her watch. She still had time to get to the church and pick up Jazz.

As she neared Athens her phone vibrated once more. She hoped she wasn't late. Shortly after noon was the time she'd understood, but all this business with Marshall, Mike and Hadden had her second-guessing herself.

Heat rushed through her at the thought of Hadden and the way they'd made love last night. She had so needed that, as foolish as getting involved with the guy was.

"Ryan."

"Kayla, I've got that analysis for you."

Fred. "Great, what'd you find?" She rolled her shoulder, wincing at the small sore spot where the device had been removed.

"Definitely a tracking device," Fred told her. "I'd estimate that considering the tissue collection on its surface it's been implanted about three-and-a-half to four months."

Boy, he was good. That's why she loved him.

"I thought as much." That would tie in with when she'd fainted at the Academy. "I'll swing by and pick it up this afternoon if that's okay."

"There's something else."

The ominous tone in her friend's voice was more than his usual dramatic flare. "Oh yeah?"

"I've never seen a device like this. I had to show it to one of my colleagues in D.C." Which meant he'd uploaded a digital image for cyber-perusal. "He says it's the latest technology."

Kayla's heart rate picked up a few extra beats. "Does that mean it's not available on the general market?"

"That's only the beginning." Fred laughed, the sound strained. "Kayla, he says this thing is ultra-secret military shit. He wants to know where the hell we got it."

And then she knew her worst fears were on the money.

This went way higher than a couple of staff members at Athena Academy. Josie's sister was right. Whatever Lab 33 was, that tracking device had to have come from there.

The government held a great deal of power over Athena Academy. Was this why they'd created an all-girls school in the first place, to lure in potential egg mining candidates? Had Marion Gracelyn discovered that evil scheme and lost her life because of it?

"You still there, Kayla?"

She swallowed hard and scrambled to find her voice. "Yeah, Fred, I'm here. Listen, put that thing up where no one can find it, would you? I'm going to need it."

"What do I tell my D.C. colleague?"

"Tell him a cop in Athens got it from someone connected to Lab 33."

"What the hell is Lab 33?"

"Just tell him, okay?"

Kayla ended the call and tossed her phone into the seat.

She could feel the news vibrating across the air-waves already. A cop in Athens, Arizona, had discovered a link to Lab 33. Fred's colleague in D.C. probably wouldn't know what that was, but he'd report it to his superior. That superior would report it to his, and so on. Within an hour or so, the information would reach the right ears. And someone at Lab 33 would know that Kayla Ryan was onto them.

She glanced in her rearview mirror. She hadn't felt her shadow around today. Maybe she'd better make it a little easier for him. Instead of going straight to the church, she swung by the house, then dropped by hers and Jazz's favorite Chinese restaurant.

If her shadow wanted to follow her now, he'd have to get a little closer. That's all the leverage Kayla needed.

She put their lunch in the floorboard on the passenger side of the Jeep. She closed the door and started around the hood but that familiar sensation of being watched stopped her. Goose bumps scattered over her skin and those tiny hairs on the back of her neck stood on end.

Well, well, about time.

Instead of getting into the Jeep, Kayla strolled back toward the small restaurant. She moved around the side of the building, past the Dumpster and the employees' entrance, and headed to the very back where the restaurant nestled up to an apartment building and a Laundromat.

She rounded the rear corner of the building but instead of continuing down the alley, she flattened against the brick wall of Lu Wan's.

Assuming a battle-ready stance, she waited.

The whisper of a soft sole on asphalt broke the silence.

Then nothing.

Kayla held her breath. She focused her full attention on the person around that corner. She couldn't be certain how close he or she was...but close.

An abrupt shuffle of footsteps told her he'd decided to cut his losses.

Kayla barreled around the corner and lunged into a dead run.

Target was maybe ten yards ahead.

Medium height. Thin.

Tufts of blond hair showed beneath a baseball cap.

"Halt or I will shoot!" Kayla leveled her weapon, not daring to slow in her pursuit.

Surprisingly the perp skidded to a stop near the Dumpster. Kayla hadn't really expected that to happen. She drew up short, coming to her own sudden stop.

"Don't move," she ordered. "Get your hands up where I can see them."

A pair of gloved hands went up. It was chilly out, but not that damned cold. The gloves weren't about protection from the weather. Kayla's internal alarm shifted to a higher state of alert.

Despite the bulky jacket and baggy trousers, Kayla suspected her shadow was female. It was as much about the way she held herself as it was the attire. A kind of sultry confidence that didn't scream femininity but definitely lacked any true masculine quality.

"Turn around."

She, or he, if Kayla was wrong, didn't move.

Kayla's pulse tripped into triple time. She braced herself for a tactical maneuver. "I said turn around!"

Only three or four feet stood between them, Kayla held her aim steady.

Slowly, her body moving in timed increments almost like the eight count of dance moves, the perp executed a one-hundred-eighty-degree turn.

The hair might have been stuffed beneath that cap but Kayla would have known the eyes anywhere. The exquisite line of her jaw…the straight sophisticated nose.

Dawn O'Shaughnessy.

"Caught me," she said flippantly, "whatcha gonna do now? Shoot me?"

For two beats Kayla couldn't respond. She could only stand there and stare into the eyes of the young woman she knew with every fiber of her being was Rainy's child.

"You're Dawn O'Shaughnessy."

"And you're a murderer. You and your friends," she snarled. Any softness Kayla had thought she'd noted in the woman's face transformed into a hard mask of determination.

"Don't believe everything you hear, Dawn." As much as Kayla would have preferred to lower her weapon, considering the woman's identity and attitude, she couldn't see taking the risk. "I imagine you've been told a lot of lies."

The girl stormed up to her, allowing the barrel of Kayla's weapon to press into her chest. Not the first spark of fear showed in her eyes. This woman was prepared to die if necessary. Kayla didn't doubt for a second that she was just as prepared to kill.

"You and your friends killed my uncle."

"I'm afraid you've got me at a loss." Kayla's brain worked double time to figure out who Dawn was talking about.

"He was the only family I had. And you'll all pay."

"I don't know what you mean. Your uncle—"

"Lee Craig," Dawn snarled.

Who the hell…? And then she knew. The Cipher.

"He was your uncle?"

"That's right."

Kayla's heart missed a beat. She knew where this was going. "You've been following me using the tracking device Betsy Stone implanted."

That Dawn didn't look surprised to hear Kayla had connected the tracking device to Nurse Stone told her two things: she already knew Stone had been compromised and whoever wanted to stop Kayla and the Cassandras from learning the truth was running out of time. Things were escalating rapidly.

"Are you ready to die, Lieutenant Ryan?"

Dawn's penetrating gaze bored into Kayla's. Somehow she couldn't help finding the situation just a little ironic. She'd spent months trying to bring to justice those behind Rainy's murder and now Rainy's own child wanted Kayla dead.

Though the other woman didn't appear to be armed, one of them wouldn't be walking out of this alley. Kayla knew instinctively that it was as simple as that. She had one chance here at preventing bloodshed.

"Don't you want to know why my friends and I tracked him down?"

Dawn's gaze narrowed with mounting suspicion. "Nothing you have to say interests me."

She said the words with a total lack of emotion and yet Kayla saw the lie in her eyes. The faintest flicker of uncertainty and curiosity.

"Lee Craig—the Cipher—killed Lorraine Miller Carrington. She was a dear friend," Kayla explained.

"Too bad."

Kayla bit back a scathing retort. That's what Dawn wanted, animosity. "That's right. It was too bad. Rainy Carrington was one of the finest people I've ever known. And she was your mother."

The statement visibly startled the younger woman. "Lying won't save your ass, Ryan."

"Then check it out," Kayla urged. "If you know the Cipher, then you probably know the people who sent him. Those people took something from Rainy about twenty years ago." She searched Dawn's eyes as she spoke, looking for any hint that she was making headway. "That something they took was eggs from her ovaries. A man named Dr. Henry Reagan and another, Dr. Carl Bradford, orchestrated at least part of the procedure. They used those eggs to produce offspring through a sperm donor and surrogate mothers. You're one of those children."

Kayla waited a full five seconds for that information to sink in before reiterating, "You're Rainy Carrington's daughter."

The side door of Lu Wan's suddenly flew open.

For a split second Kayla's attention splintered.

A man wearing a white apron sauntered into the alley, simultaneously lighting up a cigarette.

Dawn leaped into the air, jerking Kayla's gaze back in that direction.

Her left foot shot outward and the weapon in Kayla's hand flew from her grasp.

Dawn's feet hit the ground running.

Kayla snatched up her weapon and raced after her.

Down the street…past the few other shops that made up the tiny community of Athens.

Dawn cut into another passage that ran between two buildings with Kayla right on her heels.

Shoving her weapon back into its holster she pushed hard…harder…came almost within reach of her. Using her weapon to stop the woman was out of the question.

Dawn flung herself toward a towering chainlink fence that separated commercial property from residential.

Kayla grabbed on, scaled after her. She manacled the other woman's ankle just as she straddled the top of the fence. Dawn kicked to free herself. Kayla held on, dragging herself upward with her free arm.

The back of a hand collided with Kayla's cheek.

She grunted but didn't back off. She reached the top of the fence, flung her arm around Dawn's waist.

Dawn twisted.

They both went over…falling…slamming into the ground, then struggling against each other.

Rolling to a grinding stop, Kayla pinned Dawn onto her back.

The seemingly unarmed young woman suddenly had a weapon in her right hand.

"Back off!"

Kayla froze.

"Get off!"

Kayla held her ground. "Think about what I said, Dawn. Cipher and his people killed your mother."

Dawn rammed the muzzle of the weapon beneath Kayla's chin. *"Get off!"*

Kayla held up her hands to show her surrender. "All right." She pushed to her feet and backed away.

Dawn scrambled up, her gaze and the aim of her weapon never deviating from her target.

"Toss your weapon over there." She jerked her head toward the clump of grass a few feet away.

"They lied to you, Dawn."

"Shut up and do it!"

Kayla drew her weapon from her holster. She held it firmly. Giving up a weapon was the stupidest thing a cop could do.

"I guess you'll just have to shoot me," she suggested, hoping like hell the girl wouldn't. She'd had other opportunities and had chosen not to. Then again, maybe her orders hadn't included killing

Kayla until now. Kayla's last images of Jazz flashed through her mind in rapid succession. That her final moments with her daughter had been angry ones ripped at her heart.

Dawn blinked, then did something totally unexpected.

She turned her back and sprinted away.

Kayla started to yell for her to stop. But she knew that wouldn't happen this side of the grave.

Instead, she let her go. She put her weapon away. There was nothing else she could do.

Jim and another deputy showed up. Kayla told her partner what she could, which included everything but the woman's identity and connection to Rainy Carrington. For now, she had to keep that to herself.

As Kayla climbed back into her Jeep the smell of Chinese food met her with a vengeance.

Her gaze flew to the digital clock on her dash.

12:45 p.m.

She swore.

Jazz.

She was half an hour late picking up her daughter.

She backed out of the parking slot and burned rubber. As an afterthought she one-handedly tugged on her seat belt.

Driving as fast as she dared she reached the small church in only four minutes.

She'd been that damned close and still she was late.

She didn't bother dusting off her clothes or checking her face to see if she had a shiner blooming there. After double-timing it up the front steps she forced herself to slow, to pull together her wobbly composure as she entered the solemn house of God.

"I am so sorry I'm late picking up my girl," she said to the choir director the moment their gazes met. She gestured to her disheveled appearance. "Police business."

The choir director's pleasant expression fell slightly. "I thought you already picked up Jazz."

Fear clenched around Kayla's heart. "No. No. I just got here."

The director looked around as if searching for someone to confirm her statement. "I'm certain she's gone. I think I saw her get into a car."

Kayla heaved a sigh that allowed her heart to start beating once more. "Mary must have picked her up." She should have thought of that. Jazz would have called Mary since she was likely still angry with Kayla.

The director's smile lifted back into place. "Sure. She must have gone with your sister." She pressed a hand to her chest. "My goodness. What a scare. There were so many children and so many cars. I just knew everyone was accounted for."

Kayla felt about as miserable as she no doubt looked. "Sorry."

She walked as quickly as she dared down the quiet corridor. Once she got through the doors she ran to her Jeep, grabbed her cell phone and stabbed in her sister's number.

"I'm sorry I was late. Thanks for picking up Jazz." Deep in her gut that funny feeling had started all over again. Regret, guilt, she told herself.

"What?" her sister's voice echoed across the connection.

A flood of anxiety washed over Kayla a second time in as many minutes. "Jazz. You picked her up at church, right?"

"I thought you were going to pick her up."

Full throttle terror banded around her heart. "Dammit, Mary, did you pick her up or not?"

"No, Kayla. I didn't pick her up. I haven't—"

Kayla's phone fell from her useless fingers and bounced twice on the ground. She turned all the way around in the middle of the street. But there was no one to call to for help.

Where was her daughter?

Chapter 12

Kayla's phone started to vibrate against the asphalt at her feet.

Still in shock she stared down at it as if it would somehow explain what was happening.

The grating sound echoed again and she jerked out of the trance she'd lapsed into.

She had to find Jazz.

She grabbed the phone and jumped into her car.

"Ryan," she snapped as she started the engine.

"Lieutenant Ryan, how nice to finally hear your voice."

A wave of nausea rolled over Kayla. She didn't know the voice. That alone told her this was no friendly call.

"Who is this?"

"I'm surprised you haven't guessed by now. You seem to have figured out everything else. And here I thought that you would be a bigger problem than Christine and Betsy."

Carl Bradford?

Fury obliterated her fear.

"Where's my daughter, you son of a bitch?"

"Now, now, is that how you were taught to speak at the police academy? I know you weren't taught such crude language at Athena."

"If you hurt her, Bradford, you're dead." Her voice cracked with the mixture of rising hysteria and shuddering fury. "Know that right now. I will kill you if you harm her in any way."

The thought of what he and Reagan had done to Rainy twisted in Kayla's chest like barbed wire. She squeezed her eyes shut to hold back the tears burning there.

"Perhaps, but you see, Lieutenant, I'm the one holding all the cards, so let's not waste anymore time exchanging meaningless chitchat."

"What do you want?" She went completely numb with the exception of the rage roiling inside her.

"As if you don't know. Please, don't patronize me, Lieutenant. I have no patience for such trivialities. Follow my instructions precisely and you might see your daughter one last time before she joins your dear friend Rainy."

Kayla restrained the clawing desire to scream at him. To reach through that phone and break his sick neck. "Tell me what you want me to do," she said with a sudden, unexpected calm. The abruptness of it made her dizzy. For the first time in her life the idea of taking someone else's life appealed to her like the thirst of blood to a vampire. She was going to kill this man. Whatever it took, he was dead.

"Ah, now that's more like it. I'm sure you'll recall that there's a special place you girls used to go. Meet me there and I'll allow you and your daughter to die together. Come alone, Lieutenant Ryan," he cautioned, "or else I will have no choice but to cut her tender throat on the spot. I think you know I won't hesitate to do so."

A single click punctuated his final threat.

Kayla stared at the phone, her heart sinking all the way to her feet. His intentions were crystal clear. He wanted her as well as her daughter dead. Kayla for what she knew, Jazz for simply being her child…for being Kayla's entire life.

She couldn't let him get away with this.

The only question was, could she risk going in alone? There would be no objectivity…her ability to reason was already greatly compromised.

But could she take the chance and call for help?

Kayla rammed the gearshift into drive and rocketed onto the street. She had to assume that someone would be watching her. Quite possibly Dawn O'Shaughnessy. Or that her cell was bugged or locked into some sort of monitoring system.

Kayla would have to do this another way.

When she arrived at the main entry gate of

Athena Academy she paused for the guard at the guard shack though she knew he recognized her vehicle.

She stretched out her hand to him, her wallet open, displaying her driver's license as ID.

"You didn't need to stop, Lieutenant." He looked at her wallet, confusion marring his brow.

Oh, but she did. She kept her wallet thrust at him until he reluctantly accepted it. "Do you have a cell phone I could use for a few minutes, my battery is dead. I'll only be an hour or so. I'll drop it back by on my way out."

"Sure." He passed her wallet as well as his cell phone to her. "Just remember I go off duty at four."

Kayla managed a brittle smile as she drew the two items into the Jeep with her. "I'll be back in a flash," she promised. Anyone watching her would not realize she'd just picked up an alternate means of communication.

She eased forward, her heart pounding like a drum in spite of the relief gushing through her. With a few flicks of her fingers she'd entered a number. She held the phone to her ear as discreetly as possible while she maneuvered the road that would take her to the foothills of the White Tank Mountains.

"I need your help." She gave the location and an abbreviated version of the situation. "Approach with caution." Then she disconnected. She couldn't afford to say more. There was no time to devise a plan. Chances were help wouldn't even arrive in time. But someone had to know she and her daughter were in danger. However Bradford intended to cover up their disappearance, she didn't want him to succeed.

She tightened her fingers on the steering wheel. She'd either just made the biggest mistake of her life or she'd saved her daughter's life. There was no way to predict which just yet.

Kayla didn't know how Bradford knew about this special place. She and the Cassandras had gathered here when necessary for private consultations. Rainy had made them all promise to never speak of this special place unless it was to call a meeting there.

But that had been years ago…when they were kids. Kayla hadn't even thought of that spot in years. Obviously Rainy hadn't either, since her final call to the Cassandras had been for a meeting at Christine's bungalow. But then, they were much older now. A warm living room with a comfy sofa was far more appealing than a scrub of brush in a thicket of trees in the dead of night.

Her heart wrenched at the idea that her daughter was out there…scared to death…wondering why this was happening to her. Kayla would make that bastard pay for this.

She could only assume that one of Bradford's cronies, such as Nurse Stone, had kept track of where the Cassandras went, even when they didn't know it. Maybe even with a tracking device like the one Hadden had dug out of Kayla's back.

She prayed the guard wouldn't find her actions suspicious. She'd driven through that gate enough times without stopping in the months since the guards had been posted. All the guards recognized her. This one had likely noted the direction she'd taken. But then, he also knew that she was investigating Christine's shooting. He probably wouldn't consider anything unusual under the circumstances.

The gate and the guard were all well and good, but the fact of the matter was that there was simply no way to protect five hundred acres of academy property from intruders. Bradford had gotten in. He definitely wouldn't have come in through the gate.

Of all people, she knew how easily someone could slip in and out of Athena if he or she really wanted to. Wasn't that why no one had ever learned what happened to Marion Gracelyn? Years from now would others still be wondering what happened to Christine Evans? To Kayla and Jazz? Without a small battalion of soldiers it would be impossible to guard every possible access to school property.

Bradford could have a whole team of thugs out here.

She refused to think the worst until she'd assessed the situation. She couldn't do it. Focus on the next step, she told herself. Do this one step at a time and pray help arrives in time. Bradford would likely have someone monitoring dispatch at the office. Calling her partner had been out of the question. She could only hope Bradford hadn't thought of the option she'd utilized.

When the service road ended, Kayla parked her Jeep and got out to make the rest of the journey on foot.

The White Tank Mountains towered over the valley where Athena Academy ruled. The freestanding range of mountains rose sharply from its base, offering deeply serrated ridges and inspiring canyon walls. Folks loved walking those slopes, climbing to those peaks. Kayla had always equated the mountains with peace and serenity, a monument to all her people believed in.

But there was nothing peaceful or serene here today.

As she crossed the wash trail left behind by the infrequent heavy rains, she thought of how the bedrock revealed by the flash floods looked as barren and defeated as she felt just then.

She didn't care that this fragile desert landscape of cholla, ironwood, and creosote had always given her a safe feeling of being home.

None of it made her feel safe and welcome today.

Her daughter was out there, held by a madman.

The only thing she wanted was to make sure his black heart stopped beating here and now.

Her skin prickled and Kayla drew her weapon. She slowly scanned the open landscape but discovered nothing. She wondered if her shadow had followed her here. Why not? This was what she'd wanted. To lure Kayla to her death or to find the right moment to execute her. But now it had gone too far. Kayla had learned too much and had outwitted her pursuer, leaving Bradford feeling desperate.

Desperation was a bad thing. It caused people to do things they wouldn't otherwise do. Taking Jazz had been an extreme measure but one that assured him that his orders would be followed.

Her fingers tightened around the butt of her

weapon. Maybe she wouldn't ever know who had commissioned Bradford and Reagan to carry out these heinous crimes, but she would end Bradford's participation. Officially Reagan was dead of a heart attack but he could have been murdered. Maybe she could beat it out of Bradford before she killed him.

The need for revenge for what he'd done to her daughter this very day…for what he'd done to Rainy all those years ago…sang in Kayla's blood.

As she neared the base of the mountains she slipped into the thicket of trees, used the patches of thick growth to move toward the larger copse of trees where she and her Cassandra sisters had met so many times all those years ago.

It wasn't until she'd gotten within thirty yards of her destination that she saw Jazz. She sat on the ground. Her hands appeared to be bound behind her back.

A new flash of white-hot rage surged inside Kayla.

A man who must be Bradford stood over her daughter, holding court and seemingly alone. But she knew better. The bastard would have backup around here someplace.

As she watched he surveyed the landscape, look-ing for her, she surmised. He would know she was close if by no other means than the passage of time. She'd driven straight to the campus. He would be ex-pecting her about now.

She crouched down and moved from one rock outcropping to another, used bushes, trees, whatever was available for cover as she journeyed closer to her target. The sun warmed her back, making it hard to remember that it was almost Christmas. That her daughter would forever associate this terror with Christmas gave Kayla all the more reason to want to wring the breath out of him.

Bradford appeared to go to no particular trouble to determine her whereabouts. He looked around now and then but nothing more.

Additional measures were definitely in place. No way would he be so nonchalant otherwise.

The thought fully evolved into Kayla's mind at the same instant the cold hard muzzle of a weapon bored into the back of her skull.

"On your feet, Ryan."

Kayla didn't have to turn around to identify the voice.

Dawn O'Shaughnessy.

Kayla had never known anyone else who could sneak up on her like that. The girl was good.

She stood slowly, careful not to make any sudden moves.

"Lose the weapon," Dawn ordered.

Kayla pitched her piece into the grassy stand a few feet away. She would have fought to keep it under other circumstances, but with Jazz's life at stake she wasn't taking any chances. "I guess you decided not to give any thought to the information I passed along."

She had hoped Dawn would be moved by the realization that her associates had murdered her mother. Clearly that had been wishful thinking.

"Don't talk."

She nudged Kayla in the back to get her moving. Her heart fluttered wildly as she journeyed closer to where her daughter waited like a lamb bound for slaughter. Seeing her so terrified turned Kayla inside out. She could scarcely bear to look. But she could not turn away.

Jazz suddenly turned her gaze in that direction, as if sensing her mother's nearness, and Kayla almost lost control completely. Tears streamed down her baby's face. Her mouth had been taped shut. Kayla gritted her teeth and promised herself again that Bradford would die today.

"Well, I see our guest has arrived."

Kayla's gaze shifted to his. Tall, trim, with silver hair and gray, piercing eyes. Those damned eyes seemed to look right into her soul. He gave her the creeps.

"This gives new meaning to the term private practice," Kayla mused aloud. "Is this why you closed your practice in Phoenix? Afraid someone would see you for what you are? Hiding is much more becoming for scum like you, Bradford."

"Enjoy your final moments," he suggested with a broad smile. "I know pretending you're in control makes the situation more tolerable for you, Lieutenant."

"You don't know anything." She flung the words at him like poison darts, wishing like hell that's all it would take to end his rotten life. She crouched down and drew her daughter into her arms. Jazz shuddered, sobbing against her. Tears spilled past Kayla's lashes. Why did Jazz have to be caught up in this? She wished Mike had been the one who'd taken her. The thought had entered her mind when she'd first realized Jazz was missing. Then Bradford's call had come.

"I love you, sweetie," she murmured. "It's gonna be all right."

"For God's sake, Ryan, don't lie to the child!" Bradford sneered.

Jazz shook in her arms. Kayla clenched her jaw to keep from responding. Instead, she sat back on her heels and gently peeled the tape from her baby's mouth. She pressed her finger to her trembling lips when she would have spoken.

Then Kayla pushed to her feet. With her eyes she told Jazz to stay put. She smiled down at her child one last time before turning to face Bradford.

"Do you really think you're going to be safe with me out of the way?" Kayla challenged.

Bradford chuckled. "Why, of course. The others are far too busy with their lives well away from Athens to bother with continuing this useless pursuit."

Oh, he just didn't know. The Cassandras had backed Kayla up every step of the way. All that she had gleaned regarding Rainy's murder and Athena Academy's involvement had resulted from their joint effort.

"Just tell me why," she ventured. Turning the question into a challenge he wouldn't be able to refuse she added, "if you know the details, that is. I'm certain you played only a small role in all this."

He acknowledged her remark with a nod. "Clever,

my dear. But remember, I've studied the behavioral sciences my entire career. I know what makes you tick. You believe you can goad me into telling you what I know." His head moved side to side. "I'm afraid you've overestimated your power of persuasion."

She shrugged. "You're going to kill me anyway, why not indulge my final wish. I want to know why you did this to Rainy."

He brought the palms of his hands together and pressed his fingers to his lips. "Ah, sweet Rainy. She was absolutely superb. Perfect in every way. Far superior to the rest of you."

Kayla didn't rise to the bait, she simply listened, all the while hoping the second part of her plan would fall into place soon.

"The sperm donor was equally perfect. An amazing specimen of the male species."

"Unlike yourself," Kayla suggested.

Fury contorted Bradford's face. "This is precisely why you should be dead already." He flicked a glance in Dawn's direction. "If someone had done their job as ordered this meeting would never have been necessary."

So Dawn was supposed to have killed her. Interesting that she hadn't. Kayla banished the distracting thought.

"Think about it, Bradford," she persisted. "Even if you kill me, even if none of my friends return to Arizona to hunt you down, what about Christine Evans and Betsy Stone? They know what you've done."

Bradford smirked. "Do you really think I would allow any loose ends? Christine will not survive the day. I've already arranged heart failure." He sighed. "Tragic. And wholly unnecessary. If you hadn't showed up at her home she would have died as planned. I'd calculated it out to the last detail. It was so shamelessly simple."

"I have your prints, you know," Kayla pointed out. "On the wineglasses and the bottle you stuck under the sink." She was the one shaking her head this time. "You really should have put that bottle of red wine in the fridge. And the glasses—" she shrugged "—why didn't you just take them with you? Not a good move."

Anger lit in his gray eyes. "I'm certain I can arrange for that evidence to disappear as easily as I took care of Betsy Stone."

Kayla felt a prick of panic. "Betsy Stone is in protective custody."

"Even those in county lockup are allowed access to legal counsel. She didn't even argue when I insisted she swallow both cyanide capsules. I was long gone before she seized—shock likely delayed the usual immediate physical response. Poor thing. I'm sure the autopsy will reveal an abrupt yet painful ending to her pathetic existence."

Panic fluttered in Kayla's stomach. Betsy was dead. Christine would be as well if Kayla didn't survive this encounter. She had to keep him talking. She needed more time.

"You still didn't tell me why. Who came up with this foul scheme?"

He scoffed. "Foul scheme? Really, Lieutenant, I

would have thought someone such as yourself considerably more knowledgeable. Science is never foul or scheming, it simply is. Without science where would we be?"

"I know you didn't come up with the master plan on your own," she tossed out. "Dr. Reagan was no better than you, just another minion following orders. What was the point? Black market babies? Genetics?"

Bradford's face suddenly cleared of any and all emotion. "I'm afraid that this stroll down memory lane has become quite tedious."

"Just tell me, Bradford," she urged, moving a step closer to him. "Tell me who did this to Rainy."

He withdrew a handgun from inside his jacket and aimed it directly at her. "I'm afraid I wouldn't even trust the devil himself with that information. And since you're going to hell post haste, I'll just keep that to myself."

"Let my daughter go," she urged, the panic gaining a foothold now. "It's me you want out of the way." Building anxiety punched a big hole in her bravado.

"That's true." He nodded succinctly. "But you see, the plan is to get rid of both of you and then pin it on Major Mike Bridges. He couldn't have his family, so he killed them." He shook his head sadly. "Happens all the time. Such a shame. His showing back up in your life at this particular juncture provided a definite advantage for me."

"Don't hurt her," Kayla warned. "Just let her go."

"Mommy!"

Kayla held up her hand, urging her baby to keep quiet.

"Step out of the way, Ryan, and I'll make it quick. I want you to take the image of your child's death to your grave with you. It's my gift to you."

Kayla had to do something and lunging toward him would only temporarily delay the inevitable.

"You mean like the gift you gave Dawn." Kayla jerked her head toward the young woman who stood only a few feet away, her weapon still trained on Kayla. "I can imagine every child's wish would be for their mother to be murdered before she even had a chance to get to know her."

"Rainy should have left it alone," Bradford snarled. "Her death was necessary."

"And if Alex and Josie and the others don't just walk away, are you going to kill them all?"

"We have ways to conceal our deeds."

She nodded. "Like with Rainy. Your assassin, the Cipher, caused her to have that accident. She died without ever having known about her child. Without having seen her daughter. Do you have any idea how badly Rainy wanted children? Do you even care how what you'd done tore her apart?"

"Rainy Carrington was of no consequence once we had what we wanted from her. Just like Reagan. He outlived his usefulness as well." He leveled his weapon. "Now, step aside."

Kayla dove for his midsection.

A shot exploded.

She and Bradford hit the ground.

She scrambled to get free…to see if Jazz was hit.

Bradford made no attempt to stop her frantic movements. Kayla stared down at him. His eyes were open wide as if in surprise. Crimson had spread across his white shirtfront.

He'd been shot. His own weapon remained clutched in his hand. Kayla snatched it away from him and spun around. Her daughter was fine, her knees hugged to her chest in a protective manner. Thank God.

Kayla's gaze swung to Dawn O'Shaughnessy. She hadn't moved, her posture still in the firing stance, her weapon clasped in both hands, ready to fire again.

Kayla lifted Bradford's weapon, took aim at the younger woman. "Drop it," she ordered.

Dawn looked at her for several seconds before she moved.

She didn't utter a single word. She simply turned her back on Kayla just like before and walked away, eventually disappearing into the rocky landscape.

Kayla resisted the urge to run after her. She had to make sure her baby was all right. Couldn't leave her here alone…even if Bradford was dead…there could be others.

Suddenly her daughter was in her arms.

Kayla dropped to her knees and held her child tight against her, chanted the words bursting in her chest over and over. *I love you. God, I love you. Thank God you're safe.*

"Looks like I missed all the action."

Kayla looked up to find Peter Hadden crouching down to check Bradford's carotid pulse.

"He's dead," she said flatly, too damned emotionally drained to infuse any inflection into her voice.

"Definitely." Hadden stood, peered down at the motionless body and then stepped around him. "What happened?" He looked down at Jazz, who peeked up at him from against her mother's shoulder.

"He kidnapped my daughter," Kayla repeated what she'd told him on the phone. She got to her feet, bringing Jazz up with her. "He knew I was closing in on him. He's the one who shot Christine and he was involved in Rainy's murder. He used my daughter to lure me here." Kayla squeezed her eyes shut and held on to her child even tighter. She thanked God over and over again for sparing their lives.

"So you killed him?" Hadden suggested, his gaze settling on the weapon he assumed she'd used.

Kayla knew she couldn't answer that question without further consideration. "I…I don't know exactly what happened. He had the gun. I lunged at him…a weapon discharged…and he was dead." She gestured behind him. "My weapon's over there somewhere."

Hadden grunted thoughtfully. "Self-defense."

Kayla felt suddenly exhausted. The adrenaline was draining, leaving her as weak as a kitten. "Yeah. Self-defense."

"How about I drive you two to the hospital and get you checked out." He placed a warm, strong hand on Kayla's arm. "I'll call someone from campus security to come guard the body until someone from your office and forensics can get over here."

The hospital.

"Oh, God." Her gaze collided with Hadden's. "Christine. We have to let her security know that her life is in danger. Bradford—" she nodded to the dead guy "—said he'd made the arrangements already."

"Doing that now." Hadden flipped open his phone and made the call. Next he called the guard shack and summoned security.

Kayla ushered a trembling Jazz toward her Jeep.

"I'll drive," Hadden insisted.

He escorted both Kayla and Jazz to his car. "Why don't you sit in the back with Jazz?"

Jazz looked up at him as if startled by his use of her name.

"It's okay, sweetie," Kayla assured her. "Detective Hadden is a friend."

As Jazz scooted into the back seat, Kayla's gaze locked with Hadden's across the top of the car.

He was a friend.

A very good friend, whom she'd turned to instinctively in her worst hour.

But she still couldn't tell him about Dawn.

Not yet.

Maybe not ever.

Chapter 13

Hadden delivered Kayla and Jazz to her home just as the sun dropped behind the mountains that evening.

She'd never felt so exhausted in her entire life. Jazz had fallen asleep against her in the back seat of his car. Kayla peered down at her now, so damned grateful that she was safe. Neither of them had been injured, discounting her bruised cheek where Dawn had slugged her.

From his position behind the steering wheel, Hadden turned back to her and asked, "Do you think I'll wake her if I carry her in?"

"We can give it a try."

He got out and went around to the passenger side of the vehicle. The door opened and in one fluid motion he reached inside and scooped her daughter into his big, strong arms. Jazz stirred but resettled against his broad shoulder.

Kayla scooted out and hurried to unlock the front door. She led the way to Jazz's bedroom and quickly turned back the covers.

"Rest, sweetie," she whispered against her child's forehead as she tucked her in with soft pink blankets and sheets alive with colorful butterflies.

Jazz murmured something inaudible then drifted back to sleep. Though both were physically unharmed, Jazz had been extremely upset. Rightfully so. The pediatrician on call had suggested a mild sedative to get her through the night. Kayla had refused any help of that kind since she needed to keep a clear head about her. There was too much she had to sort out…too many loose ends still dangling. Thank God Hadden had been in Casa Grande giving his statement to the D.A. regarding the shootout at the U-Store-It. She really hadn't expected him to reach her and Jazz in time to help but she'd needed to try. Mostly she'd needed someone to know.

She eased out into the hallway, pulling the door closed behind her. Voices in the living room dragged her attention there. Kayla heaved a weary sigh and headed in that direction. The voices were too low to make out. If she were to hazard a guess she would say her partner had arrived to demand to know what the hell had been going on.

Give the lady a cigar.

Jim Harkey stood, hands on hips, in the middle of

her living room looking madder than hell and ready to take it out on someone.

He pinched his lips together and shook his head when Kayla moved into the room.

"What the hell you doing, L.T.? Trying to get yourself killed? You should've called me for backup. I am your partner."

Kayla walked straight up to the big guy and gave him a bear hug. "I did what I had to do," she told him, a new wave of emotions rushing over her.

"I told him you had no choice," Hadden interjected, his voice the epitome of reason.

Kayla shifted to him, abruptly remembering the way he'd looked at her as he'd undressed her last night. God, had it been just last night? His arms had made her feel safer than she had in too long to recall.

Heat stirred deep inside her, in spite of the horrendous day she'd had. She needed that warmth right now. Needed it so badly. But that couldn't happen tonight…maybe not ever again.

"He's right." She turned back to her partner, not wanting to start melting right there in front of God and everyone. Continuing to stare into Hadden's blue bedroom eyes would definitely prompt exactly that reaction. "There was nothing else I could do," she assured her partner. "I couldn't risk putting in a call to you or dispatch. That kind of move might have been anticipated ahead of time. On the other hand, there was no reason for anyone to suspect I would call Hadden."

Jim sniffed, not completely convinced. "Investi-

gator Devon needs a statement from you." Jim gave
her a knowing look. "He's madder than hell that you
left the scene." When Kayla would have attempted
some acceptable excuse, he added, "But I smoothed
things over with him, told him that getting to the
hospital ASAP was necessary. All I can say is you'd
better act like you were injured when he comes fishing around for your report."

Kayla nodded. "Gotcha."

He snapped his fingers. "Damn. I almost forgot.
Betsy Stone committed suicide this afternoon." He
shuddered visibly. "The sheriff believes the attorney who visited her slipped her some cyanide capsules." A grimace furrowed his face. "Hell of a way
to go."

"Did they get a description of the attorney?" She
knew it was Bradford, but she needed to determine
if the authorities had identified him yet. She didn't
actually see that as a problem. He couldn't be connected to Athena Academy at this point other than the
fact that his death had occurred there. There was always the chance the episode could stir up those rumors Shannon Conner had started. Maybe she'd
better give Tory a call for some damage control.

"Got him on video and lifted prints from the interview room where they met," Jim said. "Funny
thing is—" he scratched his chin "—the guy looked
a hell of a lot like the stiff the M.E. hauled to the mor-
gue from that hoity-toity school you used to attend."

"It's him." Kayla folded her arms over her chest
in hopes of holding herself upright. Damn, she was

beat. "Carl Bradford kidnapped my daughter in an attempt to lure me into his trap."

Jim tipped her chin up and studied her cheek. "Did the old bastard do that to you?" He wouldn't bother asking why Bradford would have wanted to lure her anywhere. Jim understood that about her "unofficial" investigation into Rainy's death.

Kayla shrugged. "Who knows? Things were happening pretty fast and I was worried about Jazz."

Jim's gaze narrowed suspiciously. "It's over now, right?"

She offered a halfhearted shrug. "Pretty much."

Clearly that wasn't exactly the response he'd hoped for. "I guess I'd better get going." He sauntered to the door then hesitated. "Make sure you get ahold of Devon first thing in the morning." He gave her a meaningful look. "And try to stay out of trouble."

He worried about her. That touched her more than he could know. "Will do." She could feel an interview with the sheriff coming on. Two shootings in the space of one week. He didn't like those kinds of odds.

Kayla waggled her fingers at Jim as he opened the door. He gave Hadden a nod the way men do when they make an exit and don't want to bother with what they consider unnecessary pleasantries.

"Are you going to tell me what really happened?"

She turned to face Hadden, not really surprised that he didn't plan to give up on his pursuit of the facts. "I'm not sure how much I can tell you," she said in all honesty. "There are parts I don't even understand."

"Why don't you try starting at the beginning," he suggested as he took a step in her direction.

That sweet glow of heat he always generated shimmered through her again. This thing between them had gotten completely out of hand. But it damn sure felt nice.

"How about we talk about this tomorrow? I'm really beat." And right now, this instant, she could use some distance to try and recover her perspective on a number of things. Dawn O'Shaughnessy for one.

For a second or so she wasn't sure he would let it go quite so easily, but he finally caved.

"All right. For now," he clarified.

Relief made her knees weak. Or maybe it was the way he looked at her. Damn, he was handsome. And she could definitely deal with those big strong arms tonight.

But she needed that distance. Had to get her head back on straight. Too much had happened too fast. She also needed to feel her daughter in her arms tonight. Today had been far too close.

Hadden pressed a kiss to her forehead. "Call me," he murmured, "when you're ready to talk."

His thumb slid across her cheek before he let go.

He left. Kayla stood there, her eyes closed, her heart fluttering wildly. There was a lot she had to do before she could go where he threatened to take her.

Lots and lots to do.

First and foremost, she had to make sure she could take the risk. She needed to call the gang…fill them in on all that had taken place. Take care of Jazz. Find a way to apologize to Mike for behaving like a jealous kid. Boy, she had her work cut out for her.

A soft rap on the front door dragged her attention there. She scrubbed her hands over her face and took a deep breath in preparation for facing her family. She'd called her sister and her mother from the hospital to let them know that Jazz was fine. Mary had promised to call the choir director at church. Word traveled fast in a small town, especially when a child went missing.

Her new company would no doubt be the Ryan cavalry.

Sure enough, her sister and her family, along with Kayla's mom and dad, poured into the house. A five-course meal, all packaged neatly in covered plastic containers, was placed on her kitchen table. That's what the Ryans and their people did when they got nervous, they cooked. Well, all the Ryans except Kayla. She'd somehow missed out on that genetic trait.

No one wanted to risk disturbing Jazz, so little peeks were taken around the edge of her bedroom door and then the entire family rendezvoused in the living room.

"She'll be fine," Kayla's mother said with a nod. "She's a strong girl."

Kayla's father put his arm around his wife's shoulder. "Good and strong." His dark gaze settled on Kayla. "Like her mother."

Kayla tried not to cry but she couldn't help herself. Her parents held her and then Mary plowed her way through for a hug of her own.

"I was scared to death," Mary whispered.

Kayla couldn't answer.

Mary drew back and looked at her. "But I knew if anyone could save her, you could. The spirit is with you, sister."

Her parents seconded Mary's assertion. "Your grandmother's spirit guides you," her mother added.

Kayla's grandmother—her mother's mother—had always urged Kayla to follow her instincts. Apparently the lady had known what she was talking about.

"Now, you must eat," Kayla's father urged. "You need to replenish your strength."

Kayla swiped her eyes. "I don't know if I can."

Her mother laughed. "Please, Kayla, a Ryan can always eat. It's in the genes."

Kayla had to laugh with her when she noticed her father was already unwrapping her mother's broccoli casserole.

So she nibbled. Let her family fuss over her, as they needed to.

Oddly she couldn't help thinking of Hadden—and wishing he was there, too.

When her folks were convinced Kayla was really all right, hugs were exchanged and her family left in a flurry of parting queries: *Are you sure you don't want one of us to stay with you?* and *Is there anything else we can do to help?*

Kayla sagged against the closed door when everyone was at last gone. She wasn't sure she had the strength to figure out a response to another single question.

Hot tea. That would do the trick. Wine was out

of the question though she could sorely use some about now.

She had just put the kettle on the stove when a firm knock resonated from the front door yet again.

Kayla heaved a sigh and headed in that direction. What now? Surely Investigator Devon hadn't decided to get his statement tonight. She checked the viewfinder and her breath caught.

Alex and Justin.

Jesus, she'd forgotten Alex was flying in from D.C.

Kayla jerked the door open. "You're here." It was all she could think to say.

"Kayla, are you all right?" Alex surveyed her from head to toe. "We heard about what happened with Bradford."

Kayla pulled Alex into a hug, couldn't resist. "I'm okay."

"Thank God." Alex drew back to look at her. "And Jazz is all right?"

Kayla nodded. "She's a little shaken up but she's going to be fine. Come in. Sit." She gestured to the sofa. "I was about to have some tea."

"I'll help." Alex moved to her side. "Then you can fill us in on exactly what happened. You can't imagine how worried we've been."

As the two of them prepared the tea, Alex brought Kayla up to speed on how they'd arrived earlier that afternoon but hadn't been able to find her at the office or here. Alex had even gone by her sister's home as well as her parents'. What she hadn't known, of course, was that Jazz had been missing by that time and Kayla's whole world had turned upside down. Finally Alex had tracked down Rebecca Claussen and learned about the kidnapping and shooting, well after the fact.

Back in the living room seated around the coffee table, Alex's faced paled as Kayla related the story of what Bradford had done. Justin Cohen, the man clearly in love with Alex, and a brother to one of the women who may have surrogated a child of Rainy's, listened intently. A member of the FBI as well, he had been working with Alex to try and find the surrogates as well as any offspring that had resulted.

Alex picked up a framed photograph of Jazz from the coffee table. She sighed softly as she stared at the photo that had been taken at Thanksgiving. "I can't believe she's so grown up." Her gaze met Kayla's. "I'm looking forward to finally meeting her."

Kayla smiled, her heart bursting with joy at hearing Alex say those words. "She's a treasure."

"She looks exactly like you." She traced the image in the photo. "Just like you did when you started at Athena."

There was that.

Trepidation chased away those softer feelings. "I've decided to let her attend next fall."

Alex drew in a sharp breath as her gaze locked with Kayla's once more. "That's wonderful. I know she must be brilliant as well as beautiful."

Kayla somehow kept her smile tacked in place. "She is very bright."

Her friend's expression fell. "You're still worried

about what happened to Rainy and…" She shook her head, the movement as weary as Kayla felt. "All this other confusion."

"It was a big decision," she admitted. "But I know sending her is the right thing to do. I just have to get to the bottom of what happened to Rainy first."

Alex placed her hand on top of Kayla's. "We'll find the truth and then you can feel good about sending Jazz." A grin slid across her face. "Imagine, Kayla, at the adventures she'll have…the amazing young women she'll meet."

The smile was contagious. "I've been thinking about that." She laughed. "And some of the great times we had. All of us."

Alex nodded. "We were so lucky to have each other. The Cassandras."

Kayla remembered Justin then and wondered if their sentimental journey bothered him considering what had happened to his sister. But he seemed quite pleased to hear about Alex's life at Athena. Still, he had a right to know the rest of what had happened today.

"I suppose Rebecca filled you in on Betsy Stone."

Alex nodded. "Cyanide. Not a pleasant end."

Ditto. "She did confess to being involved with Bradford and Reagan. She claimed they forced her to take part. I had no doubt that she feared for her life. With good reason."

"What did Bradford hope to accomplish by kidnapping Jazz?" Alex asked.

"He considered my investigation the main threat to him. I live here, have the most opportunity to investigate Rainy's death and its connection to Athena. I believe he felt that if he got rid of me, the rest of you would let the whole thing die."

"Then he didn't know the Cassandras very well."

"I still haven't had any luck tracking down Dr. Reagan's files," Kayla mentioned in hopes of drawing Justin into the conversation. His sister had also been Reagan's patient, and a surrogate, and more information on her might be in those files. Reagan's files were crucial and Kayla sensed that his death was too convenient.

"We've hit a stone wall as well," Justin answered. He stared at the cup of tea waiting on the table before him. "But I have to admit at this point that it looks as if my sister did die from complications in childbirth."

"With Bradford dead," Kayla pointed out, "we may never know what really happened to Reagan or the location of his files. Bradford did say Reagan had outlived his usefulness."

"You killed Bradford?" Alex broached the question cautiously as if she feared Kayla's emotions might be too fragile to go there right now.

She took a deep, bolstering breath and said what she'd been dancing around all evening. "No. I didn't. The truth is, I'd be dead right now if someone hadn't intervened."

Alex blinked, stared at her expectantly. "That Detective Hadden who's been ridding your ass all this time?"

Kayla felt her face redden at Alex's too-close-to-home remark. She couldn't possibly know about last night. That was one venue she didn't plan to visit with anyone just yet.

"No. It was someone who'd been tracking my every move for months now."

A frown worked its way across Alex's smooth brow. "I remember you mentioned once or twice that you felt as if someone were watching you."

"I was right. I discovered a tiny tracking device implanted just beneath the skin on my left shoulder. I had it analyzed. It was state-of-the-art technology…top-secret, futuristic technology."

Alex tensed. "Lab 33?"

Kayla nodded. "That's my thinking." She picked up her cup of tea, her hands suddenly ice-cold and needing the warmth. "I figured out that Betsy Stone implanted it when I fainted at the Athena infirmary shortly after Rainy's death."

"The Cipher set it up," Alex remembered. "Just like he did my accident." She stared down at her own cup. "Like he did Rainy's."

"Now that I think about it—if they eliminated Reagan, maybe Lab 33 took his files," Kayla said, mulling over the idea even as she said it.

"That would make sense," Alex agreed.

Silence took over the group for a time. Kayla sipped her tea, needing the sweet heat to soothe her frazzled nerves to tell the rest of the story.

"Today I finally met the person who'd been shadowing me," she said, knowing there would be more questions than she could answer, but she couldn't keep this a secret any longer. She looked from Alex to Justin and back. "Female. Former Athena Academy student by the name of Dawn O'Shaughnessy."

Alex sat her cup on the table with a clang. "It was her?"

Kayla nodded. "The face—now there's something I won't forget." She cradled her hands in her lap and looked directly at Alex. "She's definitely one of Rainy's children."

Justin's shoulders stiffened. "How can you be certain of that?"

"Because I knew Rainy. Dawn is the spitting image of her, except for the hair and eyes."

They waited for her to continue.

"Blond hair, gold-green eyes. Extraordinary eyes. Those she inherited from her father."

Like Kayla, Alex had seen pictures of Thomas King. One wasn't likely to forget those eyes.

"I did a thorough background investigation," Kayla explained. "Just about everything about her past was falsified. She came to Athena in her junior year only, just long enough to get those skills that are offered at no other preparatory school, like flying."

"Did you speak with her?" Justin asked.

"Yes. She grew up thinking Lee Craig was her uncle. The Cipher." Adding that part wasn't necessary. They knew who Craig was.

"Where is she now?" This from Justin. The anticipation radiating from him now was palpable.

"I don't know. She saved my life and then she took off. She could be the child Cleo Patra carried." She didn't want to give Justin hope that the child his sister had died giving birth to had survived after all. At this point, all the evidence they had, meager as it was, indicated the opposite.

"She shot Bradford?" Alex looked totally confused.

Kayla nodded. "She saved my life. Mine and Jazz's."

Alex shook her head. "That doesn't make sense."

"No, it doesn't. From what I gathered listening to Bradford ramble on, she was supposed to have killed me days ago. He decided he'd just do the job himself when she continued to ignore his orders."

"I don't feel comfortable with this, Kayla." Alex pursed her lips and considered what she wanted to say next. "We need to talk this over with the other girls."

"I agree. Darcy will be here tomorrow." Darcy had called to say she was coming to see Christine.

"We can dive into the Bureau files," Justin suggested, "see what we can find on this Dawn O'Shaughnessy."

"That would be useful," Kayla encouraged. "Everything I turned up was crap."

"Have you heard anything more about Marshall?" Alex asked. A new kind of emotion joined the mix in her eyes.

Kayla shook her head. "Nothing yet. Peter—Detective Hadden—will let me know when the…body… is back in the States."

"I'm trying to find out what I can," Justin added. "But it may take some time. He was involved in a case that's ongoing, so security is tight."

Kayla remembered that Hadden had said the FBI were involved. God, she still couldn't believe Marshall was dead.

"It's so hard to believe," Alex murmured. Kayla started. Alex had seemed to read her mind, and Kayla choked up as she remembered how, back in their Athena days, they'd practically been able to finish each other's sentences. Things really were coming full circle.

Justin took Alex's hand, and Kayla almost got teary at the tenderness the tough agent showed her friend. "It may be days or even weeks before his body is brought home. The Colombian government isn't always cooperative."

Kayla shuddered. Well, when he did come home, they would still gather to acknowledge his life and death in a way that would make Rainy proud. No matter what he'd done, Marshall had loved their friend, and they would always respect him for that. Suddenly, a familiar sensation prickled Kayla's skin. She stilled.

Alex was the first to notice her heightened tension.

Kayla held up her hand then made a circling motion for them to continue.

While Alex and Justin went back to discussing ways to look into where Dawn had come from, Kayla eased toward the kitchen. Maybe it was nothing, but she'd felt a subtle shift in the atmosphere of her home. Felt that familiar tingling. Someone else was there....

She palmed her weapon and swung around the corner into her kitchen, her aim leveled on the first object she identified as out of place.

Dawn O'Shaughnessy stood in the middle of the room. No weapon visible, but that didn't mean anything, as Kayla had learned the hard way. Nor did locked doors, apparently, when it came to the young woman's determination to access her target.

"I want to talk."

Kayla put her weapon away and exhaled a tension-reducing breath. "Would you like some tea?"

The look Dawn sent in her direction spelled an unequivocal no. Kayla had to admit, she didn't act like the tea type.

Kayla led the way into the living room. Alex gasped as her gaze roved over Dawn's face. She didn't wait for an introduction. "She is Rainy's daughter."

Justin appeared uncertain how to cope with what his eyes saw. Kayla knew he was wondering if there was any chance his sister might have given birth to this young woman. He would always hope.

"She wants to talk," Kayla explained to Alex.

They all sat, except for Dawn. She didn't allow herself to get too comfortable or too far from the door.

"You were right about Lab 33," Dawn said abruptly. "I'm a part of Lab 33. I was raised there, trained there. The only family I've ever known was my uncle." Her face tightened at the mention of her uncle.

"He took care of you," Kayla suggested.

Dawn nodded. "He taught me everything I know."

How to seek, Kayla surmised, how to kill.

"What can you tell us about what goes on at Lab 33?" Alex ventured.

"Whatever others can't or won't do, haven't

thought of or wished they could accomplish, that's what Lab 33 does." She mentioned the technology her faux uncle had created, how he'd used it to mimic sudden lapses into deep sleep, as he'd done with Rainy…with each of them to serve his needs.

"Why are you telling us this?" Alex asked, her tone openly cautious.

"At first I wanted to kill all of you." She looked from Alex to Justin to Kayla and back. "The others as well." Kayla guessed that she meant Darcy, Josie, Tory and Sam. "But then I overheard some of your discussions about what Bradford had been up to. I never trusted him. Or Reagan. As you guessed, Lab 33 destroyed his files." She took a moment to consider what she would say next. "When you told me that Rainy Carrington was my mother, I knew I had to learn the whole truth." This she said to Kayla. "I decided to do whatever necessary to…know everything."

Kayla's heart threatened to jump out of her chest. She didn't want to risk spooking the young woman. She'd already run from Kayla twice. But she had to take a chance.

"I want to show you some pictures." Kayla got to her feet and crossed the room to remove an old, tattered photo album from a bookshelf. She offered it to Dawn. "Your mother is in there. Look at her and then think about what Bradford and Craig did to her."

Kayla and Alex exchanged anxious looks as Dawn pored over page after page. When she'd reached the end she tossed the album onto the nearest chair, seemingly indifferent.

"She's dead. I'll never know her."

Dawn made the statement with such cold, clinical objectivity that Kayla shivered. What had Bradford and Reagan created here? She was beautiful, extremely intelligent and capable. But where were the emotions?

"There's only one thing I want to know." She looked directly at Kayla then. "Tell me who my father is."

Another of those worried exchanges passed between Kayla and Alex.

"Dawn," Alex began, "I think it would be best for all involved if we started an investigation into Lab 33. The Bureau could see that you're placed into protective custody."

"I don't need protecting," Dawn said, her tone nothing short of lethal. Tension started to radiate from her like the summer heat rising off the rocks in the desert.

"Why do you want to know?" Justin looked squarely at her. As an agent he'd certainly had extensive training in detecting deceit as well as refocusing negotiations about to go wrong.

"Because I have the right to know."

"You wouldn't want to harm him," Alex countered.

"No." The single word was cram-packed with frustration.

Kayla held up her hands for everyone to stop. "Let's remember that we're all on the same side here, right?" She looked to Dawn for confirmation.

After about ten seconds she finally nodded. "I want to take care of Lab 33 myself. You have no idea what you'd be dealing with." She looked at each one in turn. "You and all your resources couldn't do what has to be done. You can't possibly comprehend what you'd be up against. I can handle it. I'm in deep. Clear for full access. *I* can destroy Lab 33."

A new kind of anticipation fizzed inside Kayla. "They're doing more experimenting like what they did to Rainy."

Dawn scoffed. "Far worse. That was only scratching the surface."

Kayla had to know. "Does what they do still involve Athena Academy?"

Dawn shook her head. "That was Bradford and Reagan's game. Lab 33 has many, many resources. Their reach is mind-boggling."

"Then how do you propose," Alex wanted to know, clearly skeptical, "to bring them down single-handedly?"

"Trust me," Dawn said flatly. "I can't offer you anything more than that."

The silence thickened for another pulse-pounding minute.

"And you'll keep us in the loop," Kayla pressed for some sort of guarantee.

Dawn considered Kayla for a time before responding. "You keep your knowledge of me under wraps and I'll see that you know what I know. I can't risk my cover being blown. Today was too close."

Kayla knew she meant the shooting. "I'll handle that. It was a justified shooting. If you hadn't shot him he would have killed my daughter and me. Even if you were forced to go to trial no jury would ever convict you of murder or even manslaughter for what happened today. Any D.A. worth his salt wouldn't even pursue charges."

"You keep up your end of this bargain and I'll keep up mine."

Kayla looked to Alex for agreement. She nodded.

"But I'll require a good faith gesture," Dawn went on. "Since you have nothing to lose and I have everything including my life on the line, I need some amount of proof that you're going to trust me."

"What is it you require?" Alex didn't bother beating around the bush.

"The name of my biological father."

"There's only one way to confirm he's your father," Kayla put in. "DNA testing."

"But you know who he is," Dawn argued.

"We know who we think he is," Alex clarified.

Dawn's expression reflected her impatience.

"Thomas King," Justin relented. "Navy SEAL Thomas King. He's a highly decorated hero."

Dawn took a step back, her eyes widening. She looked shocked. Kayla wondered if Dawn had been part of the team sent to eliminate King and Tory when Tory had gone to interview the Navy SEAL after his surprise rescue in the volatile Central American country of Puerto Isla. Tory had mentioned a blond female sniper who'd shot at them...but she'd also said the sniper had died. Perhaps Tory was wrong. If

Dawn had been that sniper, it just made the Cassandras' case stronger in Dawn's eyes. She hoped.

Dawn went to the table where Kayla's answering machine sat. She jotted something onto the message pad there. "If you need to contact me leave a word at this number." She turned back to the Kayla, Alex and Justin. "Don't do anything that will jeopardize my cover. Forget I exist for now."

When she would have disappeared the same way she'd come, Kayla stopped her with a question. "How will we know you're safe?"

Dawn turned back to her, those gold-green eyes glimmering with a knowing quality. "Don't worry about me, I'm pretty much kill-proof."

"If you need us we're here," Kayla said. She moistened her lips, sucked in a breath. "That's a promise."

For a seemingly endless beat Dawn stood there, her eyes full of uncertainty. And then she was gone.

For a long time, no one spoke. Then....

"What if we never see her again?"

Kayla shook her head. She had no answer for Alex's question. Dawn O'Shaughnessy was a complete mystery. "If she's anything like her mother, she'll keep her end of that bargain."

Alex suddenly pulled Kayla into her arms for a hug. "It's almost over." She drew back. Her usually cool exterior was not so cool now. "We're on the verge of bringing this whole empire of evil crashing down."

Kayla tried to work up more enthusiasm. She felt

utterly drained. "We still don't know exactly who is behind all that's happened."

"But we're getting closer. With Dawn's help we'll get there."

Justin walked over to the two of them and placed a hand on each of their shoulders. "I don't know about you two but I think it's time we ordered some dinner. We've got a lot to discuss. People to call."

He was right. She and Alex had to pull themselves together...had to follow through on their pact. The other Cassandras had to be updated on the situation. An agreed-upon strategy for their new role in this continuing investigation—the wait-and-see role.

Kayla couldn't have agreed more on the dinner suggestion as well. And she knew just the place to go.

Her kitchen. There was nothing else on the planet like Ryan cuisine.

Chapter 14

"I don't think he's coming out."

No kidding. That was just swell. Kayla flattened against the wall next to the front door of the subject house. Her partner had taken up a position on the opposite side.

"It's Christmas Eve, dammit," she muttered. "Don't these people have presents to open or something?"

Jim shrugged. "Beats the hell outta me."

Perfect.

Here it was 6:30 on Christmas Eve night, her folks were already gathering for Kismus and she was stuck trying to defuse a domestic disturbance.

"Maybe he had a little too much eggnog," Jim joked.

From the shouts going on just the other side of that

door, she felt relatively sure he'd had a little too much something.

"Let's give it another try." Kayla whipped around, kicked the hell out of the bottom of the door in an effort to make herself heard over the ruckus. "Open up! Sheriff's Department!"

She flattened against the wall next to the door once more in case the guy bellowing inside decided to shoot first and ask questions later.

The abrupt silence inside the house had her and Jim exchanging skeptical looks.

"Who the hell is it?" the husband of the woman who'd called in the complaint roared through the door.

"Santa," Jim muttered under his breath.

Kayla had to laugh. She stifled the hysteria and shouted, "Sheriff's Department, open up, Mr. Mitchell."

The door jerked inward and a mountain of a man towered in the open doorway. He appeared unarmed so Kayla took the lead. Jim moved up beside her, his hand resting on his sidearm.

"We received a complaint about the noise, sir," Kayla said with all the politeness she could muster for a guy wearing a wife-beater T-shirt and swizzling a can of beer while he waited for her to answer. His eyes, red-streaked from his alcohol binge, resembled road maps.

He gulped down the last of the beer in his can then crushed it in his fist. "What noise?" Two days' beard growth and a greasy mop of tousled hair suggested that hygiene was not a priority.

"Sir, my partner and I heard you ranting at someone inside. May we speak with your wife?"

He threw down the damaged can. "What the hell for? Did that bitch call you?"

Not good. Kayla stepped closer to the door. "I'm sure your wife wasn't involved with the complaint, sir, we'd just like to speak with her."

"Well, come on in then." The big burly ape suddenly grabbed Kayla by the shirtfront and jerked her inside.

Oh, hell was her first thought. *I'm gonna have to hurt this guy* her second.

She didn't want to shoot him. She'd only just gotten squared away after the last two shootings.

"Release my partner and put your hands up, Mr. Mitchell."

Ignoring Jim, the gorilla slammed Kayla against the closest wall. "She look okay to you?" He jerked his head toward his wife.

Shit. Kayla's hopes of getting through this without excessive force withered and died at the sight of Jim leveling his weapon on the brute who'd pinned her to the wall.

"Look at her," Mitchell repeated. "Don't she look just fine?"

Kayla glanced toward the sofa where a woman, midthirties maybe, sat. Her eyes were wide with fear. Her long brown hair disheveled. There were no obvious bruises, but that didn't mean a thing.

"Let go of me, sir, and we'll get this cleared up."

"You women," he snarled, "you think you can

treat us guys any way you want to and we're supposed to put up with it without a fight just because
you're women." He glanced at his wife. "Get me a
beer, bitch."

Merry Christmas, Kayla mused.

"Mr. Mitchell, I'm only going to ask you once
more to release my partner."

Mitchell didn't flinch, didn't even bother glanc-
ing Jim's way. "Bitches," he muttered, then burped.

Time was up. If Kayla didn't do something quick
Jim might just shoot this guy on principle.

Kayla heaved a sigh. "You know what, Mr. Mitchell, you're right."

He snickered. "Damn straight."

"We bitches," she added, "just don't know when
we've got it made."

Mitchell laughed loudly. "Now that's what I'm
talking about."

At that exact instant Kayla drove her right knee
into his unsuspecting balls.

Big, bad Mr. Mitchell was suddenly on the floor
howling in agony and curled into the fetal position.

Jim winced. "Man, that had to hurt."

"Book him, Jim," Kayla said, grinning from ear
to ear.

While her partner restrained the asshole on the
floor she walked over to the sofa and sat down next
to Mrs. Mitchell.

"Ma'am, are you all right?"

She nodded. Her hands were clasped tightly in
her lap.

"You're sure?"

She turned to Kayla then, tears spilling down her pale cheeks. "I'm glad you came so quickly."

Kayla placed a hand over hers. "That's what we're here for. Don't ever hesitate to call for help when you need it."

The woman swiped at her eyes and let go a shaky breath. "I didn't call you to help me," she said, her gaze connecting to Kayla's in a look that sent a new burst of adrenaline into Kayla's bloodstream.

"But he was hurting you? That's why you called, right?"

Mrs. Mitchell reached beneath the throw pillow next to her and withdrew a handgun. She offered it to Kayla, watched her accept it. "I'd decided to use it this time." The woman's gaze lifted back to Kayla's. "I called you to save him. I wasn't sure I could let him to do this to me again."

Kayla couldn't decide what to say, except the necessary. "I'm sorry, ma'am, but I'm going to have to bring you in as well for questioning. I hope you understand."

It was almost ten before Kayla and Jim headed back to their small Athens office. Mr. Mitchell was sleeping it off in county lockup and Mrs. Mitchell had been admitted to General for psychological observation.

Dammit. Kayla's family had probably given up on having her show up for dinner. Jazz would be intensely disappointed. She could imagine the whole clan of Ryans gathered around the table. Lights lining the driveway for welcoming the Christ child in celebration of the traditional Navajo Kismus. She was going to miss everything.

Oh, well, one of the many hazards of the job.

"Can you believe she was going to kill him?" Jim asked, dragging Kayla's attention back to the interior of her Jeep.

Kayla laughed dryly. "Sure looked that way."

"You're positive you're okay?" he asked, his tone somber.

"I'm good." She was a little shaken but she'd live.

Every home in Athens was lit up with Christmas lights. Beautifully decorated trees glowed from the front windows and wreaths hung on the doors. 'Twas the season to be jolly. No point in being depressed.

Kayla made the turn down Main Street toward the office. She had so much to be thankful for. Her daughter, her family. A great deal of the mystery behind Rainy's murder and the egg mining had been solved. Dawn had promised to keep the Cassandras in the loop as she progressed in her own investigation. Hell, Kayla had even worked out visitation arrangements with Mike. She had every right to feel damn good about her life right now.

"Kayla, there's something I should tell you," Jim said abruptly.

She parked behind the office they used as a station house for the small sheriff's department detachment here in Athens. "Yeah, what?" She shook off the worry that immediately launched. "It's Christmas Eve, don't sound so ominous."

She'd had all the bad she wanted for one night, especially this night.

"You know there's a lot of talk around the community about incorporating."

Kayla shrugged. "Yeah, so?" The way Athens was growing she'd expected as much. The only thing that prevented the little community from becoming an incorporated city was the official steps.

"You know that means a full city council and mayor." He opened his door and got out. "The whole works."

Kayla emerged from the Jeep. She knew what he meant. "Which would include a city hall and city police force," she said for him since he appeared to want to dance around that aspect.

"Uh-huh," he grunted.

"We'll still have our jobs." She figured that's what he was worried about. The sheriff would likely reallocate the assets used in Athens. Pinal County was a large, thriving area. It wasn't like the two of them had to worry about being laid off. Athens had been her territory for a long time now, she would miss being so close to home and her daughter, but she couldn't stop progress.

"A couple people mentioned a candidate for police chief."

She reached for the rear door of the building that housed their small detachment, but hesitated. "Anyone we know?"

"You." His face split into a broad smile. "They want you, Kayla. The sheriff's all for it."

Too stunned to speak, Kayla just shook her head. She jerked the door open and went inside, grappling with the unexpected news.

She stopped and turned back to him as the door closed behind him. "That's nuts. Why not you?"

Jim gave her that look. The one that said don't be stupid. "We both know who's the best man for that job," he told her bluntly. "I don't have the finesse required. I'm not chief material." His expression turned petulant. "But I do want to be your deputy chief."

Kayla had to laugh. "Okay, big guy. Consider it done. If, by some crazy stroke of fate, I'm asked to be chief of police when the time comes, I'll make sure you're my deputy."

The sound of a voice clearing jerked Kayla's attention down the corridor to the lobby. She blinked, looked again. What the…?

"Mom, what're you doing here?"

The next thing she knew her whole family, including the extended Ryan clan, had dragged her and Jim into the lobby. The room was packed with her loved ones.

"We decided if we couldn't bring Mohammed to the mountain, we'd—"

"I get the picture," she said, cutting off Mary's dramatic metaphor.

"Mom!" Jazz pushed through the crowd and wrapped her arms around Kayla's waist. "We didn't think you guys were ever going to get here. I'm starved!"

Just then the wonderful and varied scents of her

mother's cooking filled the air. In the room they used as a sort of conference room, every available surface was lined with food for the "big feed," another Navajo Christmas tradition.

Jim didn't waste any time; he grabbed a plate and headed up the line. Meat, beans, potatoes, breads, sweets, all the things her family pulled together for this special holiday.

"Merry Keshmish," her father said as he hugged her close. "I'm very proud of you, Kayla."

She kissed his cheek. "I know you are."

Kayla blinked back the tears and accompanied her father to the food line. She was starved.

By midnight the celebration was over. Everyone had hugged and kissed and said their good-nights.

Two more deputies had taken over, and each had been left with an overflowing platter of celebratory foods.

At home, Kayla watched as her daughter opened the one present she was allowed to open the night before Christmas, though technically it was Christmas already.

"Mom, this is great!"

Kayla had figured out the one thing she could get that would complement the laptop Mike had given their daughter. She'd traded in the laptop she'd purchased and gotten two state-of-the-art video cameras made for computers. She'd sent one to Mike and wrapped the other for Jazz. Now she and her dad could do the video-calling thing. See each other as they talked. Mike had been thrilled at the idea when Kayla had called and told him about it.

Jazz gave her another big hug and a mega kiss. "You're the best."

Kayla tucked a strand of hair behind her daughter's ear. "Nope. You're the best." Another of the prettily wrapped boxes beneath the tree contained the invitation to Athena Academy. She and Jazz would discuss what it meant tomorrow. That would be the most special gift of all.

"Time for bed."

Jazz didn't put up a fuss. She knew the rising sun would bring lots more Christmas fun and going to sleep was the fastest way to usher sunup.

Kayla kissed her daughter once more as she tucked her in, then she backed out of the room, closing the door as she went.

Time for a weary mother's kind of celebration, Kayla decided. She located the bottle of wine she'd picked up the day before and uncorked it. With the bottle in one hand and a glass in the other, she trudged into the living room to collapse on the sofa.

She filled her glass and stuck the bottle between her legs. Might as well keep it close. This was the kind of night that, as wonderful as sharing it with her friends and family had been, left her feeling lonely in the end. She was the one who'd have to crawl into an empty bed all by herself. That was a little depressing.

Oh well, there was always next year. Not that she considered having a man in her life the only way to feel complete, definitely not.

But it sure would be nice from time to time.

Just like the other night.

She could deal with that on a regular basis.

But she and Hadden hadn't spoken since he'd left that night after Bradford's shooting. He'd probably been too busy. She certainly had been.

Still, a call would have been nice. He'd said he would call.

A soft rap at her door tugged her from her troubling thoughts. Who the hell would show up at her door at this time of night? Maybe her sister, or even her mom. Both had sensed she was a little off tonight. As hard as she'd tried to be all smiles, her loneliness had apparently been visible to those who'd wanted to look closely enough.

Who wouldn't be lonely after a night of great sex with Hadden? Having him around could become addictive.

She set her wine aside and lugged herself up and across the room. Opening the door put her face-to-face with the man in question.

Speak of the devil. Anticipation made her heart beat faster.

"Merry Christmas," he said, his expression schooled.

"Your turn to play Santa?" she said, deadpan. It was after midnight after all. But, God, it was good to see him.

He smiled. "I know it's late."

"It's not that late." She opened the door wider. "Come in."

Hadden stepped inside and waited for her to close the door before saying, "This is for you."

She stared at the delicately wrapped box in his hands. The white wrapping looked like silk. A fragile pink organza ribbon completed the package.

"Thank you." She accepted the box feeling like a complete heel for not buying him a gift, but how was she supposed to have known?

He hitched a thumb toward the door. "There's a much larger box in the car for Jazz but I thought I'd better check with you before I brought it in."

Kayla couldn't open the box just then, she was too busy soaking up the sight of him. So tall, so gorgeous. So damned sexy. Navy trousers and a pastel blue shirt that complemented his eyes. Wow.

"Open it," he urged.

She shrugged. "I don't have anything for you."

He moved closer, pulled her into his arms. "Yes, you do." And then he kissed her, long and deep. No hurry, no hot frantic rush. It was just a kiss, soft and sweet and yet totally mind-bending.

"Open it," he whispered against her lips.

She licked the taste of him from her lips and nodded. She took him by the hand and dragged him back to the sofa. Sitting down was necessary since she wasn't sure if her legs would hold her up much longer.

The pink ribbon fell away as she tugged at the elegant fabric. The silk puddle around the small velvet box. She held her breath. Not a ring box. Way too soon for that. She opened it. The most beautiful necklace she'd ever laid eyes on winked at her.

The delicate silver chain held a tiny, equally del-

icate butterfly; its silver body glittered with tiny di-
amonds. It was so, so tiny and intricate.

She touched it. Her breath caught at its subtle
beauty. "It's exquisite," she murmured.

He lifted her chin so that he could look directly
into her eyes. "It reminded me of you."

Her chest tightened and she had to fight to hold
back the emotions brimming behind her lashes.
Okay. Slow down, girl. She'd been through so much
lately. Could she trust her emotions?

"Like capturing a butterfly…" He leaned closer,
threaded his fingers into her hair. "So delicate yet so
strong and determined to be free. I had to come back,
Kayla. Calling would never have been enough."

"And what do you think now that you're here?"
Her gaze dropped to his mouth. He had the most
amazing mouth. So sexy, so damned good at kissing…and a few other things.

"That I couldn't let you go," he whispered.

Kayla lifted her mouth to his. Whatever the future
held for her and those she cared about…she knew for
a certainty that this man would be a part of it.

Too good to be true?

God, maybe he was. But he was definitely worth
the risk.

'I think I can deal with that," she murmured, hope
blooming in her chest. "But there's something I have
to do first."

Kayla took Peter Hadden's hand and led him to
the couch, where he sat down, looking bemused.

Then she told him everything she'd held back

from him. About Rainy, the Cassandras and their quest for justice…and Dawn. Because if she was taking this chance, she was going to do it right.

No secrets. No hidden agendas.

Nothing but the truth.

And that was a promise.

Chapter 15

January

"I'll get the coffee." Kayla jumped up from the sofa, offered a tight smile to the Cassandras and hurried to her kitchen. She braced her hands against the counter and fought to hold back the tears.

No more crying.

They had buried Marshall Carrington that day. The sun had peeked from behind the dreary January cloud cover and poured over the Tucson cemetery as his coffin was lowered into the ground next to Rainy. It still didn't seem right that Rainy was gone. Probably never would. But Marshall was with her now. Whatever his sins, he had loved his wife and she had loved him. Nothing else really mattered. Kayla wanted to remember Rainy and Marshall the way they had been before…on their wedding day all those years ago. Marshall had looked at Rainy and smiled before he kissed her. Everyone in the chapel could see that he loved her more than life itself.

Kayla's tummy did a little flip-flop when she realized that she had caught Peter looking at her in a very similar manner.

She had to look to the future now. The past was gone, dead and buried. Rainy would want them all to get on with their lives. She would be furious if any of the Cassandras failed to do so.

Kayla had to smile as she imagined Rainy saying, "Get over it, Ryan. Life's too short to wallow in what can't be undone."

"Kayla."

She looked up as Alex wandered into the kitchen to join her. "I'm working on the coffee." Kayla reached for the carafe.

Alex placed a hand on Kayla's. "Let's skip the coffee." She draped an arm around her shoulder. "I think we'd all be happier if we went straight to the wine."

Kayla hugged her friend, held on tight for a bit. It felt good to have Alex back in her life.

After the funeral they had all driven back to Kayla's to visit for a while. Things had gotten a little sentimental as each had recalled fond memories of time spent with Rainy. With her composure back in place, Kayla drew back from Alex's comforting embrace.

"I guess we'd better get a move on or we're going to have a riot on our hands."

"I think you're probably right," Alex agreed. No one had felt like having lunch prior to the service, except the kids. Jazz and Charlie, Darcy's five-year-old son, had stayed with Kayla's sister Mary and her family during the funeral. Mary had taken them out to their favorite fast-food joint.

Alex gathered fruit and cheese from the fridge while Kayla put the glasses and the bottle of wine her partner had given her for Christmas on a tray. A few dessert plates and they were good to go.

"I thought you guys had gotten lost in there," Darcy said as Alex and Kayla returned to the living room with their laden trays.

Kayla set her tray on the sofa table. "We decided to skip the coffee."

As appreciative sounds rumbled through the group and Alex poured the wine, Kayla couldn't help thinking how happy Darcy looked. Now that she was no longer in hiding from her abusive ex-husband, she'd stopped dying her natural blond hair. The blond and brown combination fit right in with some of the new fad hairdos Kayla had seen in magazines recently. Not to mention the style made Darcy look five years younger…or maybe it was being in love that gave her that radiant glow. She and Jack Turner, the man in her life, were working on a partnership in a P.I./bounty hunting business. Darcy thought they might move to California for a brand new start. Thankfully, her scuzzball ex-husband, Maurice

Steele, would be going on trial for murdering one of his business associates soon. Darcy, who had uncovered the murder, intended to testify against him. Good for her.

"A toast," Tory said, drawing Kayla's attention to her. Kayla noted that Tory was beaming herself. She suspected the savvy journalist's radiance also had to do with love, but Tory wasn't revealing any sources. Yet.

"To the Cassandras," Tory announced, holding her glass high. "And those dear to them," she added with a smile aimed at Elle, Sam's twin sister. Glasses clinked.

They had all been surprised when Sam had shown up for the funeral. As a CIA agent, Sam rarely had free time. And they'd been shocked to meet her sister. They'd known Sam had discovered her long-lost identical twin, but seeing the two of them side by side was startling.

Getting Marshall's body returned home had taken less time than they'd expected, and no one had known until the last minute that it was actually going to happen. Kayla suspected Peter and Justin Cohen had both pulled some strings. The Millers, Rainy's folks, had taken care of the arrangements since Marshall had no close family of his own. Kayla had contacted the Cassandras, and thankfully they'd all managed to make it.

"To Rainy and Marshall," Josie offered on the heels of Tory's toast.

A moment of silence punctuated Josie's words. Kayla imagined that all were thinking of Rainy and how very much she was still missed.

A loud series of thuds shattered the silence. Kayla's gaze locked with Darcy's. They were at Kayla's daughter's bedroom door before either of them managed to speak.

"It's okay!" Jazz assured them, seeing Kayla's worried look as well as Darcy's. "Charlie accidentally knocked my rock collection off the shelf." Both kids were on their knees picking up Jazz's odd compilation of strangely shaped and colored rocks.

"Sorry!" Charlie exclaimed with a hopeful look at his mother.

Kayla and Darcy simultaneously breathed sighs of relief. Charlie had definitely gotten over his shy stage. He was a regular, rambunctious little boy now. Good thing, too, since he'd start school in the fall. Kayla's heart warmed as she considered that Jazz would start at Athena Academy. It was a big step but a good one in the right direction for Jazz's future.

"Kids," Darcy said with a chuckle as she and Kayla relaxed their protective mommy stances. "Gotta have strong hearts to survive them."

Kayla couldn't agree more.

"Is everything all right?" Alex wanted to know as the two returned to the living room.

Alex, Tory, Josie, Sam and Elle all looked so concerned Kayla had to laugh out loud. "No damage done." She couldn't wait for each to have children of her own. No one really understood what it was like until it happened to them. That might very well be sooner than one would think, considering every single Cassandra now had a man in her life. One who was far more than a passing fancy. Josie had recently moved in with Diego Morel. Now that was serious. Elle, Sam's sister, had mentioned Riley, Sam's team leader, and Sam had actually blushed. Unbelievable. Who would ever have thought cool, tough CIA agent Sam would blush about anything? Kayla couldn't help wondering if Elle would be going to work for the CIA as well. With her connections to the Russian secret service, the SVR, Elle would make the perfect double agent.

With the toasts behind them and enough fruit, cheese and wine in her belly to make even an ever-ready cop relax, Kayla sat back and enjoyed the great company. It was so good to have them all together, in spite of the sad circumstances that had brought them here today.

"I hope you'll give me an exclusive on the Predator spy plane when the testing is complete," Tory said to Josie after the long, contemplative silence. Tory's news show, *A Closer Look*, was giving the old-timers like *60 Minutes* and *20/20* a run for their money in the ratings.

"I'll talk to my new commander," Josie assured her. "I don't want Shannon Conner in my hair any more, and I can't think of anyone I'd rather have covering it."

Josie had worked hard to continue the work her mother had started years ago. Thank God her mother's name had been cleared and General John Quincy was finally getting his due. The guy had been obsessed with Josie's mother. Josie had learned that he'd sabotaged her mother's career all those years ago, and recently had messed with Josie's flight tests, causing the death of one of Josie's pilots. It was good to see that Josie as well as her family were happy these days. The weight of an unjust past had been lifted from their shoulders. Josie and her sister, Diana, appeared to be closer than they had been in years. Too bad Diana couldn't come. Josie had told the Cassandras earlier that Diana was using all her military connections to look into Lab 33. Uncovering Lab 33's dirty deeds was the only way they would ever know for sure what happened to any other children that may have been produced from Rainy's eggs, and they had no idea whether they'd hear from Dawn again or not. Kayla shivered when she recalled how much Dawn had looked like Rainy. There was still so much to learn about what had really happened.

"While we're talking about exclusives," Alex said, turning to look at Tory, "why don't you tell me what's going on with you and my brother."

Uh-oh. Kayla and the others kept quiet in anticipation of Tory's response. Alex had mentioned that Tory had come to Thanksgiving dinner with Ben, Alex's brother. She suspected that Ben and Tory were hot for each other. Well, maybe she hadn't said it exactly that way, but Kayla knew that's what she meant. Anyone with eyes could see that like the others Tory had someone.

Like everyone else, Kayla had always considered Ben Forsythe to be nothing more than a devil-may-care playboy. A great guy, but certainly not the type to commit, not even to a real career. But Alex now had her suspicions. Somehow, Tory and Ben had ended up together after the whole Thomas King rescue. Could Ben's playboy persona be a cover for something else? Kayla couldn't be sure, but like Alex, she had wondered about that. Considering how Rainy's eggs had literally been stolen from her body without anyone's knowledge, anything was possible. Not that Kayla intended to become one of those conspiracy theorists but her eyes had certainly been opened.

Tory took another sip of her wine then smiled mysteriously for Alex, "I never kiss and tell, Alex. How about you? How's the legendary Dark Angel?"

Giggles erupted through the group, as much maybe from the warm fuzzy feeling of the wine as from Tory's challenge. The Dark Angel was a nickname for Justin Cohen, stemming from the two times he'd broken into Athena Academy as a young man, searching for answers about his sister's death. Alex was the one blushing this time. She and Justin's relationship, though a long-distance one, was still going hot and heavy.

"Let's just say," Alex returned smugly, "that despite our geographical differences Justin and I are quite happy."

"So we all have serious love interests," Sam suggested, accidentally, or maybe not, giving away the depth of her own feelings.

Kayla poured herself another splash of wine. "Guilty," she allowed. No reason not to 'fess up. It was the first time she had admitted out loud that what she and Peter had was serious. Now that she had, it felt good. Jazz's father was behaving himself, had apparently learned his lesson and wanted to be a good father for the first time. There was no reason why Kayla couldn't have a serious relationship and be proud of it.

Alex thrust out her glass. "Let's have one last toast," she announced. "To the Promise."

Each woman present, including Elle, who probably knew of the Cassandra Promise from her sister, lifted her glass.

"Wait!" Tory held up a hand. She looked a little guilty or maybe a little humbled by the mention of the Promise. "Before we do that, let me say to Alex," she looked directly at Alex then, "that Ben is—" Tory sighed, unable to hide from anyone in the room the way she felt about Ben—the mere mention of his name had proven telling "—is far more than meets the eye. Just so you don't think you're imagining things," she added for Alex's benefit.

A smile slid across Alex's face. "I *knew* it."

"To the Promise," Kayla repeated, drawing all eyes to her. "And to the Cassandras!" She looked from one familiar face to the next, pausing a moment on the newest member of the group. Elle might not have attended Athena Academy with them, but she was a part of them now, just as Diana was. "The old and the new."

Sounds of agreement underscored one last clinking of glasses.

Not one of those present would ever forget what the Cassandra Promise stood for. They would always be there for each other, wherever life took them. Just a phone call away.

* * * * *

Don't miss the next
ATHENA FORCE *adventure,*
DECEIVED, by Carla Cassidy,
available in January 2005
at your favorite retail outlet.

Books by Debra Webb

Silhouette Bombshell

Justice #22

Harlequin Intrigue

*A Colby Agency Case
†The Specialists
‡Colby Agency: Internal Affairs

ATHENA FORCE

The Athena Academy adventure continues....

Three secret sisters
Three super talents
One unthinkable legacy...

The ties that bind may be the ties that kill as these extraordinary women race against time to beat the genetic time bomb that is their birthright....

Don't miss the latest three stories in the Athena Force continuity

DECEIVED by Carla Cassidy, January 2005

CONTACT by Evelyn Vaughn, February 2005

PAYBACK by Harper Allen, March 2005

And coming in April–June 2005, the final showdown for Athena Academy's best and brightest!

Available at your favorite retail outlet.

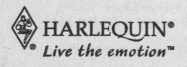

LUNA™

A sweeping fantasy set in an ancient Greco-Roman
civilization. A goddess has been born—the daughter
of Epona's beloved Incarnate Priestess and the
centaur High Shaman. Elphame is unique. Her story
of self-discovery is an epic adventure that will lead to
her destiny and an unexpected love.

On sale December 2004.
Visit your local bookseller.

Like a phantom in the night
comes an exciting promotion from

HARLEQUIN®

INTRIGUE®

ECLIPSE

GOTHIC ROMANCE

Look for a provocative
gothic-themed thriller each month
by your favorite Intrigue authors!
Once you surrender to the classic
blend of chilling suspense and
electrifying romance in these
gripping page-turners, there will
be no turning back....

Available wherever Harlequin books are sold.

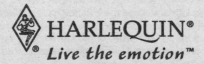

HARLEQUIN®
Live the emotion™

www.eHarlequin.com

HIE3

Silhouette

BOMBSHELL™

COMING NEXT MONTH

#25 STELLA, GET YOUR MAN—Nancy Bartholomew

Former cop and new P.I. Stella Valocchi knew there was something suspicious about the mysterious woman with a sob story who had hired Stella and her incorrigible partner, Jake, to find her brother. Suddenly Stella and Jake were under attack, dodging strangers with big guns and more muscle than brains. But it would take more than threats and a few bruises to stop Stella Valocchi!

#26 DECEIVED—Carla Cassidy
Athena Force

Someone was lying to retrieval specialist Lynn White, but was it her godfather, his intriguing head of security or the woman claiming to be her sister? Lynn's formerly top secret career was unraveling thread by suspicious thread—and with the FBI on her trail, she was running out of time to find her betrayer and prove herself innocent in a scam of earth-shattering proportions....

#27 ALWAYS LOOK TWICE—Sheri WhiteFeather

A slasher was on the loose, and it was up to police psychic Olivia Whirlwind to catch him. Plagued by visions of the slasher's latest kill, beautiful, tough-as-nails Olivia tried to stay professional—until she had a premonition that the man she loved would be the next victim. Now the situation was personal, and Olivia had to take matters into her own hands...and mind!

#28 THE HUNTRESS—Crystal Green

Heiress Camille Howard's life changed forever when she visited a small town suffering from vampire attacks and her boyfriend was kidnapped by the evil beings. One year later, Camille returned to find her long-lost love—and to hunt down every vampire in her path. But would she find the sweet man she remembered, or would her dreams be shattered by the reality of the monster he'd become?